# DRAGON'S FIRE

## MATT BANNISTER WESTERN 10

## KEN PRATT

Published in the United States by Wolfpack Publishing, Las Vegas

CKN Christian Publishing
An Imprint of Wolfpack Publishing
6032 Wheat Penny Avenue
Las Vegas, NV 89122

christiankindlenews.com

Paperback ISBN: 978-1-64734-348-4
eBook ISBN: 978-1-64734-347-7
Library of Congress Control Number: 2021933972

# DRAGON'S FIRE

# Dedication

*For my beautiful daughter, Katie Dawn.*

*"Do you not know? Have you not heard? The Lord is the everlasting God, the Creator of the ends of the earth.*

*He will not grow tired or weary, and his understanding no one can fathom.*

*He gives strength to the weary and increases the power of the weak.*

*Even youths grow tired and weary, and young men stumble and fall.*

*But those who hope in the Lord will renew their strength. They will soar on wings like eagles; they will run and not grow weary; they will walk and not be faint."*

*Isaiah 40:28-31*

# Acknowledgments

*For my family.*

*This story and the others I've written never would have been without your support, interest and encouragement. To my wife, Cathy, thank you for all the drives down the coastline talking about this story. It amazes me how I can get so frustrated in a tangled web of details and you can make those same complicated details sound so simple. To my son, Keith, your devoted interest, care and feedback are absolutely invaluable. I want to thank you for that! I want to thank my daughters and sons-in-law and grandchildren as well for always being supportive and believing in me.*

*I love you all.*

*I want to thank Mike Bray, Lauren Bridges and the rest of the staff at CKN Christian Publishing for their hard work to make this book possible. You're the best at what you do, and I have so much respect and appreciation for all of you. Thank you.*

# 1

Matt Bannister sat at the table in his office with his three deputies having a cup of coffee to start the day. His long dark hair was in a ponytail and his beard was neatly trimmed. He was a handsome man in his mid-thirties and had a rare grin as he listened to his deputy Phillip Forrester speak with frustration about his fiancé.

"I didn't hold the door open for her when I took her to Regory's Restaurant last night for dinner. I opened the door and went inside without thinking about it and she got upset. She would not talk to me during dinner. She ordered a small salad, barely ate any of it, and when we left, she blew up on me." He mimicked her voice, irately, "*Why didn't you hold the door open for me? I'm your fiancé and you won't even hold the door open for me? A gentleman holds the door open.*" He sighed with a roll of his eyes. "And then she said, *'I'm hungry.'*"

Matt laughed. "Well, a gentleman would have

held the door open for her. Shame on you, Phillip."

Phillip's eyes widened as the frustration burst out, "I didn't mean to hurt her feelings. Holding the door open for her did not even cross my mind. I always hold the door open for her but now she thinks the romance is over because last night I didn't!"

Matt took an exaggerated breath. "It sounds like you better take her to the Monarch Restaurant and buy her some salmon or whatever is most expensive tonight."

"And..." Nate Robertson added quickly, "don't forget to hold the door open for her." He laughed at his friend.

Phillip gasped. "Seriously, is this how it works? I neglect to hold one door and she doubts the sincerity of our relationship? Laugh if you want, but seriously, is this normal behavior? She was yelling at me on the street and refused to accept my apology. For crying out loud, I didn't think it would start a fight. And then she got mad at me because she was hungry!"

Truet said through a grin, "You should've fed her."

"I paid for dinner."

Nate, the big blonde-haired young man with a clean-shaven square face and short haircut, kicked his friend under the table. "Maybe you should turn the tables on her and tell her you're mad because she walked away from dinner hungry. And then add, a true lady wouldn't do that."

Phillip wasn't surprised his friend found it amusing but the tension in his relationship was troubling. He ignored Nate's comment. "Does Christine ever act like that, Matt?"

Matt shook his head. "No. Phillip, you always have to treat your lady like a queen. Go buy her something special from the bakery and go apologize to her. I suggest you get moving; the earlier, the better."

"Now?"

Truet Davis laughed. "Yes, now. And if I can give you some advice, sweep her off her feet when you kiss her. Hold her tight and let her know you love her."

The cowbell on the office door rung as an older man in his forties stepped into the office. He was followed by a young man that appeared to be in his late teens. "Marshal, I've been robbed. Someone stole the money and gold out of my safe and I don't know how they did it!" he shouted irritably.

"Excuse me, why don't you start with your name?" Matt asked while standing.

"I'm Lonnie Engberg. I am the owner of Engberg and Penn Assayers down the road a few blocks. And this is my apprentice, Mikey Gould. We are the only two that have a key to the office door and know the safe's combination but someone took everything! And I don't know how they did it. The office was locked when I left Saturday and it was locked this morning too."

"I stopped by your office some time back and introduced myself to Isaac Penn. I don't believe either of you were there. Doesn't Isaac have a key too?" Matt asked while shaking their hands.

Lonnie shook his head. "Isaac retired back in September and moved to Arizona for the warmer

3

weather. But it's nice to meet you finally."

"Likewise. So how much did they take?"

"About twelve thousand dollars' worth in gold, both in bars and a bag of dust I hadn't melted down yet. Plus, two thousand in coin and paper money. It's everything I have! I need whoever did it found." The desperation on his round face revealed the panic that was racing through him. It was infuriating to have his livelihood stolen and left begging the bank for a loan to keep his hard-earned business floating until he could pay the loan back.

"Did they kick the door open or jimmy it?"

Lonnie shook his head. "Neither! The door was locked and it can only be unlocked with a key. I have two locks on my door to keep it from being kicked in. Both were locked this morning when I opened and my safe was empty. Nothing else was touched."

Matt asked the young man named Mikey, "You have a key too?"

Mikey Gould nodded innocently. "Yeah, but I didn't do it. I swear I didn't." He was a respectable-looking young man with a friendly and youthful face.

Lonnie added, "Mikey didn't do it. He's as honest as anyone I've ever known. I need you to find the thief and get my money back."

Matt grimaced empathetically at Lonnie's crises. "Unfortunately, your business is not in my jurisdiction. Anything outside of Branson is my jurisdiction. Inside town is Sheriff Wright's. I'm afraid you'll have to talk to him. If he needs help, tell him to let me know. I'm sorry, I can't help you without his permission."

Lonnie's head sank like an anchor with a heavy sigh. "The Sheriff isn't going to care about my business. I'm independent and work with the placer miners and small mines. The Sheriff is bought by the Slaters and they would like to see me run of town."

Matt shrugged sympathetically. "As the Branson Sheriff, he is obligated to investigate and try to solve any crimes committed, whether you work for the Slaters or not. As I said, I can't help you unless he asks for me too."

"I'll try. Thank you, Marshal."

"Good luck. Nice meeting you both."

Matt turned towards Phillip, who still sat at the table. "You haven't left yet? Go get your fiancé something sweet. Get out of here."

Wu-Pen Tseng sat in his living quarters with a quill, writing on a tablet. He had far too much on his mind to pay attention to the beautiful Chinese woman who washed his feet and expertly clipped and filed his toenails. Her name was Ling Tseng. She was not Wu-Pen's wife; she was his servant, consort and property. Ling was responsible for the cleaning, cooking and feeding of Wu-Pen and his two guards, Bing Jue and Uang Yang. They all lived in separate rooms on the second floor of the building connected to the temple. By appearances, they looked like two different buildings but they were the same. On the ground floor next to the temple was a general market for Chinese goods of various kinds and essential living wares Above it, on the second floor, was where Wu-Pen had his office, separate living quarters, and a connecting room where Ling lived. On the other side of the hallway were four doors; two were rooms where Uang and

Bing lived, one was where the high temple priest lived, and the fourth was a storeroom. At the end of the hall overlooking Flower Lane was Wu-Pen's office where all the business regarding the Chinese Benevolence Society took place.

Others worked for Wu-Pen but they lived elsewhere and helped control the things that happened in the growing Chinatown. Tunnels were being dug to make moving around easier after dark. It was against the law for any Chinese to be out in public after sunset. With tunnels, basements and businesses underground the Chinese could prosper at night without the threat of harassment or arrest by the Americans. The basements and tunnel walls were being lined with stone and mortar to make them a permanent access way to the more hidden away activities in Chinatown. He had high hopes for the future and a vision that could make Branson a city of wealth and prosperity for Americans and Chinese alike if they could learn to work together. He wanted to add the Chinese Benevolence Society into the Branson Business Association and become a legitimate title among the American businessmen. William R. Slater and his pompous son, Josh, had shunned him away like a mangy feral cat. William had stated the Chinese were a temporary people needed until the railroad was completed, then they'd be run out of town. Those words did not sit well with Wu-Pen. If an honest tactic did not work, one must try another tactic of lesser means to get what he wanted.

The Chinese Benevolence Society helped the Chinese people secure employment and housing. It took care of the sick, the needy and made all the arrangements to and from the Chinese Six Companies in San Francisco and China as well. In short, whatever was needed, the Chinese Benevolence Society was there to help. Still, it cost money to function and every citizen of Chinatown paid their share for the services, protection, opportunity to earn, and blessing to be included in Chinatown. Every Chinese owned business paid a business tax and the more money they earned, the more Wu-Pen received for his leadership. The benefits were simple, if they paid their tax, they were left alone to labor. The Chinese were protected from abuse, harassment and robbery by Wu-Pen and his carefully chosen men. There had already been a few so-called accidents, disappearances, and mysterious deaths of Americans that had settled scores of abuse and murder of the Chinese people. Laborers hired by American companies and Chinese miners also had to pay a tax based on their earnings whether they lived in Chinatown or not.

However, if one chose not to pay their taxes and dues, the consequences were not good as some placer miners living on the mountain discovered. All Chinese who came to Branson paid Wu-Pen or faced the consequences. He could be a genuinely nice man and treat everyone well but when money owed was not paid, he could become brutally cold and ruthless. He ruled Chinatown with a smile and a clenched fist.

Like many young Chinese women, Ling was kidnapped and put on a ship bound for San Francisco to be sold into prostitution. She was spotted by Wu-Pen, who was taken by her beauty and bought her. Unlike his other purchases, she was kept in his home to serve him. It had been ten years and Ling could not complain. She was alive, well taken care of, and treated with respect, perhaps even love by Wu-Pen. She was twenty-five years old and could write to her family in China and send them money every month which Wu-Pen gave her in his generosity. Her life was one of ease and beautiful things. Her fate could have been very different, though, if Wu-Pen had not saved her from the cages and brutality that robbed many young Chinese girls of their lives. Her loyalty was to him alone and she wanted him to succeed in his endeavors. It pleased her that he valued her opinion and was willing to listen to her like a husband would his wife.

Ling dried his feet and pulled his cotton socks on. "All finished," she spoke in Chinese. Unlike Wu-Pen, she did not speak any English.

He stood and smiled at the beautiful lady. "Go tell Bing and Uang; we'll leave as soon as I am dressed." She immediately left him to do so. He gazed out his back window at a pile of lumber and a growing pile of stones to be used in the tunnels. The soil extracted from the tunnels was used on the road to keep the ruts and holes filled. In case any Americans asked what the stones were being used for, he had some men building a stone walkway along the front of all the buildings to keep the mud out of the homes and businesses that made up Flower Lane.

Wu-Pen walked to Main Street with Bing and Uang, in a heavy downpour of rain. All three wore long pipal overcoats made from woven rice grass that hung past their knees. They wore wide-brimmed hats with a pointed top and downturned brim that dripped the rain onto the strange-looking pull-over coats. Wu-Pen smiled at the few people who were walking in the heavy rain. The Americans either laughed at their peculiar appearance or hurried by with disdain. Chinatown's acceptance in Branson wasn't going as well as Wu-Pen wanted it to. Most Americans had never spoken to a single Chinese man, yet the disgust upon the white faces was disheartening. Wu-Pen knew their attire was strange and unique to the Americans but, the truth was, he would bet money that his long grass-covered pipal coat kept him dryer and warmer than any slicker bought at the store.

He paused at the door of the W.R. Slater Mining Company office on Main Street. It was a two-story clapboard building with a large false front declaring the business name in bright silver paint. He told his two companions to smile as he entered the building. A woman in her thirties attended a front desk.

"Yes?" she asked curtly.

Wu-Pen removed his hat to reveal his long queue and round friendly face. "Hello, Miss. My name is

Wu-Pen Tseng and I would like to speak with Mister Slater, please."

The woman raised her eyebrows skeptically. "You're getting water all over our floor." She did not sound one bit friendly.

"My apologies," he answered. All three men stepped back outside where Wu-Pen and Bing Jue removed their hats and pipal coats. Uang remained outside to hold them.

Wu-Pen smiled at the lady as he stepped back inside. "If I may, I will happily clean up our mess if you hand me a towel or a mop. Perhaps while you ask Mister Slater if I can have a minute of his time?"

She walked to a closet and pulled out a mop and handed it to him. "What do you want to see Mister Slater for? If you're looking for work, we can do that here."

"No. It's of a personal nature. If you could just let him know Wu-Pen is here and I will remain here until he agrees to see me, I'd appreciate it. I'll only take a moment of his time."

"William Slater or Josh? They are both quite busy today. I doubt they have time for you but I will ask if they can take a moment to see you."

Wu-Pen forced a tight-lipped smile. "Very good. William Slater, please. Let him know I will wait right here until he comes out to tell me to leave."

The lady walked down a hallway to a door, knocked quietly and went inside an office. William Slater walked out with a scowl on his face. He stopped short of Wu-Pen.

"What?" he demanded.

11

Wu-Pen grinned happily. "Ahh, Mister Slater. I wanted to request you to reconsider our Chinese Benevolence Society joining the Branson Business Association. I believe our association can benefit the community in multiple ways. Let me share with you how…"

William shook his head with a sneer on his thin lips and held up a hand to stop him from speaking. "I already told you we don't want you Chinese here, period. You are only here until the railroad comes and then you're gone either willingly or by force. Our businesses are not interested in anything you and your people can provide. So, quit asking; the answer is no. Now, I have a business to run. Goodbye."

Wu-Pen raised his eyebrows questionably. A ball of hostility grew in his chest aching to burst out in a flurry of violence that would humble the old man so low that he'd bow down to every Chinese man he ever saw again. Wu-Pen forced the notion away and raised a hand to shake instead. "Very well. Thank you for speaking with me."

William glanced at the extended hand, turned around and walked back to his office.

Insulted and angry, Wu- Pen made eye contact with the unkind lady behind the front desk. "Miss, as you can see, my friend mopped up the water we brought in. Sorry to bother you. Have a good day."

Outside, Wu-Pen put on his pipal coat and hat. He spoke to Uang, "Today is the day of final preparation. Tell Ling and the others that the dragon awakens at this time tomorrow. I gave William Slater a chance to avoid the consequences and I am insulted in return. Tomorrow, we will earn our respect with dragon's fire. Send word to the others. Go, for much must be prepared." He watched Uang run across Main Street back towards Chinatown.

Wu-Pen turned back to look at the mining company's office and spat on the door.

3

Billy Jo Fasana knocked quickly and stepped into
the house uninvited. She stopped in the family
room with her mouth opened in surprise. "The
bandages are off. Oh, my goodness, you look great,"
she said enthusiastically to Wes Wasson.

Wes had been scalped two weeks before, and the
doctor had sutured his scalp back on within hours
of it being removed. His greatest fear was it would
not adhere to his skull and flesh. To his great relief, it had. There was a new scar along his short
brown hairline, but his hair hid the remainder of
the scarring. He had been injured by a Shoshone
Indian named Chusi Yellowbear. Wes had picked
the fight but it had not gone the way he planned. It
was a humiliating experience to be outwitted and
tortured by a man he thought he would do away
with easily. His nose had been broken and slit
back from his upper lip to the bone with a knife.
The doctor had fixed his nose and it turned out

better than Wes was expecting. His thick mustache and goatee covered any scarring under his nose. With all of the bandages removed, he was pleased to recognize his handsome square-shaped face, small eyes and concave nose. He was stabbed in the leg and had both of his shoulders dislocated. Those injuries had healed well. The only wound not healed completely was his foot which had two arrows penetrate it when he stepped into a pit trap. Though his heel was healing, where the arrow pierced through his foot was still hard to put any weight on. He used crutches to move around but it was only temporary. He was lucky enough to survive and have a place to recover at his sister and brother-in-law's house.

Wes's face lit up like a lantern when Billy Jo entered the house. "Yeah, I do! I am almost ready to start whooping it up and go dancing. I figure another week or two and I will be on my feet again. And then, I plan on renting your house. I'll do whatever work it needs to have done and make it a home for you and your boys when you're ready to share it with me."

She sat beside him with a flirtatious smile. She had met Wes two weeks prior and his constant praise and flirtatious nature drew her to him like a honeybee to a flower bed. She enjoyed the lighthearted, playful conversations and his affections for her. He brought a bit of excitement into her life. "Wes, you are so full of yourself. What makes you think I want to leave Joe? Especially for someone like you?"

He grinned slowly. "Because, Sweetheart, a princess should be treated like a princess and not a maid."

Her lively blue eyes gazed into his with playful adoration. "You don't even know me."

His jaw dropped in exaggerated shock. "I know you a little bit more every time you come over. And you would not be here if you didn't want to be. So, yeah, I think you'll see the light eventually." He finished with a wink. Wes was an older man at forty-seven and had never been married nor wanted to be until he met the younger, Billy Jo Fasana. There was something about the blonde-haired, thick boned lady that he found irresistible. Wes loved how her big blue eyes twinkled and how her hair fell loose over her face and shoulders. She didn't care what anyone thought about her wearing men's jeans or a flannel shirt. She brushed her hair in the morning and let it do whatever it was going to do for the rest of the day. He found her fun to be around and enjoyed her humor. It amazed him that such a diamond to humankind could get caught up with a rattlesnake like Joe Thorn. Wes longed to make it right and become the jeweler that finally set the diamond firmly in a wedding ring.

A layer of seriousness came upon her. "Joe won't let me go that easily. My boys are his children."

Wes wrinkled his nose unconcerned. "To Joe, you're there to cook, clean, keep him warm at night and take care of the kids. That's straight from his mouth when I went out with him that one night. That's all you're worth to him and you don't want that. You don't want your boys growing up hearing that kind of trash talk either or they'll treat their women like that too. I'm not the best man in the world but I think you are beautiful, amazing and would be so much happier with me. And I think you know it too."

There was an unreasonable fear that overcame her anytime she spoke negatively about Joe. She always feared he'd overhear her speaking or find out about it and burst into the room. Anxiety enclosed her arms around her chest and made her uneasy. There was a lot of truth in what Wes said about her boys and her, though. Joe didn't have a relationship with any of them other than treating them like burdens most of the time. "No, I don't know that," she said weakly.

"Well, I know you're probably afraid of change but the only thing that scares me is not having you."

She laughed uneasily and slapped his leg playfully. "Wes, you are impossible! What if I don't want you? Did you ever think of that?"

He raised his eyebrows. "No. I can't say I have thought of that. I have my hopes set on you and you don't want to break my heart, do you? Come on now."

"Wes, stop it. It's fun to play around but I know you're not serious." Her brow furrowed as she stared at him quizzically. "Are you?"

He took a deep breath. "Billy Jo, I wouldn't tell you what a poor husband and father Joe is if I didn't mean it. He is not good for you. He's hit you before, right?"

KEN PRATT

She was uncomfortable. "Only when I deserved it," she said softly.

"You don't ever deserve it. How long have you been with him?"

"Ten years, off and on. We're not married."

"For ten years, he's probably been telling you that it's your fault he hits you. It is not. You are a beautiful woman and if I did not mean what I'm saying, I wouldn't be saying it. I am sincere. I want to rent your house and make it ready for you and your boys so when you do decide to come home, it'll be ready for you." He paused and added, "I want to make you happy for the rest of your life. That's all I want to do."

A lady can live her whole life and never hear such beautiful words. For a man to lift her higher than himself was a strange sensation that she had never experienced before. She enjoyed being with Wes but now the fun and flirtatious playing had come to a seriousness where it could be life changing. Like being caught in a dust storm, she was disoriented and taken off guard. She felt a strange excitement, yet a part of her feared the consequences of being caught talking to another man. "Wes..."

"Shhh," he said and touched her conflicted chin softly. He moved forward and kissed her gently. It was a soft, momentary kiss. He pulled back a fraction and she remained still. He kissed her again and it became more passionate as she surrendered to him and put her arms around him to hold him close.

She suddenly pulled away from him and stood

up frantically. "I need to go!"

"Billy Jo, don't run off."

Her face reddened and her voice broke with emotion, "I need to go. Joe's going to expect dinner when he gets home. I'll talk to you later."

Wes was perplexed. He feared he had pressed her too hard to decide between Joe and himself. "Are you going to come back?"

"I will. I'll talk to you later."

Wes watched her leave and wondered if he had made a big mistake by trying to kiss her. Their friendship had grown and he could not resist kissing her any longer. He was hooked on her. She just needed to realize her worth as a woman. She deserved far more than Joe Thorn could ever give her.

The heavy rain continued to fall and Billy Jo wrapped her coat tightly around herself while she walked quickly towards home. She hoped the warming temperatures and rain would melt the snow because, like everyone, she was anxious for Spring. Her heart beat quicker than usual and the anxiety was growing stronger the closer to Slater's Mile she walked. Joe Thorn was the only man she had ever kissed and the sensation of touching another man's lips scared her but, at the same time, there was an underlying excitement that brought a smile to her face. It couldn't be helped. She was falling for another man and he made her feel alive for the first time in years. The emotions inspired her to write poetry about dancing through fields of tulips and the freshness of a cool summer breeze on a burning hot day. There was no greater feeling than being excited about life and Wes was the reason for it.

Billy Jo never had a mother; she had been raised by a hardworking single father. She had met Joe Thorn when she was sixteen when she was sitting on her front porch. She was bored and a handsome older man swaggered over and began talking to her in a way that no one else had before. In hindsight, he knew what to say to a self-conscious teen girl who hadn't gained much male attention. It didn't take an hour and she was infatuated with the charismatic man named Joe Thorn who worked nights at a saloon at the time. Joe didn't come by to meet her father until Billy Jo swore she was in love. The first kiss, the first time being held, the first time she was seduced, all happened before Joe was introduced to Luther and asked his permission to court her. Luther Fasana forbid it but what he didn't know was that Billy Jo was rebelliously giving herself completely to Joe Thorn while Luther was at work. It came as a shock to them both when she was pregnant at sixteen. Joe asked her to marry him and she moved in with him, against her father's better judgment. Joe had never married her. They just lived together for going on ten years.

She always wanted a wedding ring but more than being a wife, she wanted what she never had, a happy family. Her first two pregnancies ended in miscarriages and then she gave birth to Wyatt. They had two sons together and still, Joe had no interest in marrying her. Billy Jo always wanted a daughter and dreamed if she ever had one, the baby's father would be as excited as she would be to welcome a new baby girl into the world. Joe never would be excited though. He barely spoke to the boys now and despised the idea of having any more children.

She walked quickly to Slater's Mile and stopped at a cabin not far from hers and knocked on the door.

An attractive young lady in her mid-twenties with long dark brown curly hair that hung loosely past her shoulders and stunning brown eyes, opened the door. She smiled. "Billy Jo, come in. The rain is pouring, isn't it?" Lucille Barton asked, closing the door behind her.

"Oh yeah. I'd rather have the mud than the ice, though. Hopefully, it will melt all the snow. Well, how were my boys?" she asked as her two sons came to her and hugged her legs.

"Fine. Wyatt burnt his hand on the stove, but not too bad. I grabbed some ice from outside and put on it. Other than that, it's been an uneventful day. How was your father? Is he feeling better?"

"Yes, he is doing well today," Billy Jo said. She had to fabricate a reason for Lucille to watch her two boys so she could walk into town. A sick parent was always a good excuse. "I'll check on him in a couple of days if you wouldn't mind watching the boys again for me."

"No problem." Lucille took notice of Billy Jo's joyful countenance. "You look incredibly happy. Is there a reason for that?" Lucille asked curiously.

Billy Jo chuckled. "Just walking in the rain. I love to see the rain coming back and not snow. It means Spring is just around the corner."

"I'm looking forward to warmer days myself."

"Come on, boys, we have to get home and make your Pa's dinner." She looked at Lucille with a liveliness in her eyes that wasn't there earlier in the day. "Thank you, Lucille."

"My pleasure. Oh, before you go, the boys made you something. Lawrence and the boys went out and got me a bucket of clay off the hill the other day and, today, the boys and I made plates with their handprints pressed into them. I need to dry plates in the fire and I hope they won't break. Then we'll paint them, won't we boys?" Lucille asked.

"Yep," Billy Jo's oldest boy, Wyatt, said. He had just turned eight.

Billy Jo watched her oldest son with pride, loving the idea of having their handprints to decorate her barren walls. "I can't wait to see them. Thanks again, Lucille."

# 4

Curiosity had gotten the better of Matt and he walked down Main Street to the Engberg & Penn Assayers Office. He stood outside looking at the door; there were two locks on the door, about six inches above and below the doorknob. There was no evidence of a pry bar or shim of any kind being used against the door jamb. He knelt to look at the wet threshold carefully. The rain had washed grains of metal filings away from the bottom edge of the doorjamb.

The door opened and Lonnie Engberg asked, "Marshal Bannister, it's nice to see you here. I hope you know what you're looking for. I couldn't see anything."

"I'm looking for anything that explains how someone got into your office," he replied thoughtfully.

Lonnie scoffed with frustration. "I hope you don't accuse me of trying to collect insurance money or blaming Mikey as the Sheriff did."

Matt glanced up at Lonnie curiously from under the brim of his hat. "Is that what Tim did?"

Lonnie said, "I told you he wouldn't bother to come here and look for himself. He just assumed I was making a report to validate a false insurance claim. And then he questioned Mikey like he was a criminal. And I assure you, if Mikey says he did not do it, then he didn't do it."

Matt shook his head slowly. "I like to be able to believe people before I find a reason not to, especially when you have metal shavings down here. Not many, though. It was cleaned up, except for what was brushed against the door jamb."

"What do you mean?"

Matt rubbed his finger along the door jamb and showed the fine powder of a metal key being filed down. "See? Someone filed a key to fit your locks. Are the locks different or the same key?"

"The same key opens both locks."

"I'd say someone who knows about locks made their own key right here on your doorstep and let themselves in. They cleaned the filings for the most part. You can see where it has been wiped down with a rag or something and pushed against the doorjamb. Whether it was done Saturday night or last night, I don't know, but that's how they got in. It looks to me like your suspect knows how to make a key. I don't know too many thieves who clean up after themselves or have the patience to make a key but there is one somewhere. Can I look at your safe?"

"Please. Come in."

Inside, Matt followed Lonnie into a small closet in the back of the office where the safe was. It was a heavy-duty steel Diebold Bahman safe with a combination lock. There was no hint of any attempted forced entry scratched on the green paint or any other noticeable marks. Matt turned the combination lock and stood with a shrug. "I don't know anything about locks or key making. I do know thieves can be quite gifted in the means of getting what they want. Have you noticed anyone watching you or lingering in here longer than necessary?"

Lonnie shook his head. "No. As you can see, the safe is in the back room and no one is allowed behind the counter at any time. People come in here and wait while I process their gold. Once they have their money, they're gone to the saloon or wherever they go."

"You buy gold from your customers right then and there, correct?"

"Sure, if the customer wants to sell it. More than half of the men that come in here are so fired up for Rose Street that they sell what they have for half price. Others want their gold made into ingots. Those folks pay me in gold. But for the sellers, I have to have money in the safe to run my business."

"How many people come in here on average?"

Lonnie rolled his eyes. "I buy gold and sell my services to all the placer miners all around here and there's a lot of them. It surprises me that there aren't more assayer offices in town because it's a gold mine. I suppose that's why I was robbed."

Matt looked carefully around the room for mirrors, window glare, or anything that might reflect where the safe was, but there was nothing except the technical chemist tools, chemicals, scales and instruments used to assay the gold and other minerals. "I'll ask around to see how difficult it is to forge keys and break into a safe like yours. In the meantime, I'd change your locks to two different locks and change the safe combination as well, if you can. Keep your eye out for any of your regular customers who have suddenly struck it rich."

"I thank you for coming by. Now we know how they got in anyway."

Matt frowned in reply to Lonnie's statement. "People talk, so keep your eyes and ears open. You might see one of your customers walking around in a new suit."

Lonnie grinned skeptically. "The average miner that brings their gold in here wouldn't waste good money on a suit when he could spend it on Rose Street. I hope you can find the thief and get my money back."

"I'll work on it. Are you going to be able to keep your business running?"

Lonnie nodded. "Yeah, I can get by with the help of the bank for now."

"Lonnie, I'll be honest with you, most of my experience is tracking down men, not solving robberies. I'll do my best but I won't promise you anything."

"I trust you'll do your best, Marshal. And that's all I can ask for. Thank you."

# 5

Joe Thorn came through the door to the aroma of a hearty stew brewing on the stove. He was soaking wet, cold and covered with dust from the silver mine. He was in a bad mood and wanted to be left alone as he closed the door and hung his coat on a nail and moved near the cookstove to warm himself.

"How was your day?" Billy Jo asked without interest as she stirred the pot of stew.

He shook his head slightly. "Wet. I don't mind the cold but I hate being wet. Do you have some warm water so I can wash up?"

"Oh, jeez. I didn't even think about that."

There wasn't a miner in the world who didn't want to wash up after working all day. It was in the mid-forties and pouring rain outside and he had walked a mile in wet clothes to get home. A warm bath waiting for him would be nice. However, it was infuriating that there wasn't so much as a pail of hot water and a washrag waiting for him. His voice was harsh, "It's pouring down rain and you didn't think about warming up some water? Do you remember to use the outhouse when you have to pee? For crying out loud, Billy Jo, is it too much to ask for some warm water to clean up with when I get off work?" He grabbed a metal pail off the floor and put on the coat that Billy Jo had used earlier that day and went outside to fill the bucket with water. He came back inside and plopped the pail on the cookstove carelessly with a darting glare at her. He stepped away and removed the coat and felt the inside of it. "Why is your coat wet?"

"Papa, I made a plate with Lucille today. I put my handprint on it," eight-year-old, Wyatt said excitedly. Wyatt and his younger brother, Brice, who was four, both had their mother's big blue eyes and had light brown hair cut short. "I made it for you and Mama." Wyatt had learned getting his father's attention off his mother when his voice turned hard sometimes avoided a fight. He was excited to have made a unique piece of art and wanted to share the excitement with his father.

Joe glanced down at his son. "Great. Now leave me alone." He turned to Billy Jo. "Why is your coat wet? Did you go somewhere and leave the boys with Lucille?"

Wyatt's youthful face frowned noticeably as he sat down on the ripped davenport with his arms crossed and his bottom lip extended outward emotionally.

Billy Jo felt the chill run up her spine. Lies were

the kindling that caused her anxiety to rise. It might not have been noticeable to anyone else but it took some effort to act calm and unconcerned, even while her hands began to tremble. "Yeah. I went to town to see my Pa. He's been sick and I just wanted to make sure he was okay."

"Sick?" Joe asked doubtfully. "That old man's never been sick a day in his life. How would you know he was sick anyway?"

"Georgina told me yesterday when she stopped by." It was a lie and she said a silent prayer that Joe wouldn't ask Wyatt if Georgina came by. Billy Jo would be in trouble if she were caught lying. She should have said she went to town to get some meat from the butcher on her father's account or something less dramatic than her father being sick. She bit her lip anxiously, waiting to see if Joe would question her story.

Georgina Dalton was Billy Jo's cousin and, although they had a close relationship, Georgina lived in Branson's upper society and had never come to Slater's Mile alone. Georgina was married to the silver mine's Superintendent, Ron Dalton, and Joe knew Ron had worked the day before. It sounded downright suspicious. "Why would she come out here alone in her fancy boots and dresses? I suppose she drove her own carriage too, right?" Joe asked doubting her story.

Billy Jo turned to look at him with annoyance. "To let me know he's sick. He *is* my father, after all. And no, William drove her." It was another piece of kindling added to the fire bed of lies.

Joe tilted his head and turned to look at Wyatt questionably. "Wyatt," he raised his voice with a show of authority. "Did Georgina come over here yesterday?"

Still hurt from being ignored, Wyatt glared at his father with anger showing in his eyes. He nodded. He had learned it was best to agree with his mother when Joe asked him a question with that tone.

"Speak when I talk to you!" Joe demanded loudly.

"Yes!" Wyatt exclaimed with his eyes glaring at his father.

Billy Jo sighed with relief.

Joe sat down with his wet clothes and untied his boots. "How is the old man? Are we going to inherit his half of the granite quarry soon? I look forward to that day more than you know."

"He'll be fine," Billy Jo said coldly. She was repulsed that Joe would look forward to her father's death. She despised the man who sat in front of her sometimes.

"Too bad. I sure hope you don't expect me to cry when your Pa passes away. When that day comes, I'll be as happy as a lark. I'll never have to work again once we inherit his business and house."

"I already have a house," she said spitefully.

"Yeah, I know. We'll rent it to Ritchie. Once we're half owners of the granite quarry, my friends and I can all live in town and work at the quarry."

"You'll have to talk to Robert about that. He runs the company now, not my Pa."

Joe snickered. "I'll just slap Robert around a bit and he'll do as I say. So does your Pa have Consumption or something?"

"No. He's just not feeling well. I think he'll be fine. He feels better today than he did yesterday."

"Hmm. Too bad." He peered at his brooding son. "Isn't that right, Wyatt? Don't you want your Granddad to die so you can have that bow of his, you like so much?"

Wyatt grimaced. "No. I love Granddad but I don't love you."

Joe's eyes narrowed on his son. "I suppose you think that hurts my feelings, right? Well, Wyatt, it doesn't. I couldn't care less but you will do what I tell you to do."

"I didn't say I wouldn't," Wyatt said under his breath with his arms still crossed.

"What?" Joe asked sharply.

Wyatt glared at him harshly. "I said, I know!"

Joe's eyes widened. He didn't have the patience or energy to waste on a disrespectful child. He was already irritated about not having hot water to wash with and it didn't take much more than a pouting child to anger him. "You better lose the glare before I slap the snot out of you! You hear?"

Billy Jo stepped in between them. "Why are you raising your voice at him? He wanted to tell you about what he made today, and you ignored him. He hasn't done anything and you threatening to slap him for wanting to please you?"

Joe grimaced. "Go cook your food and shut up. I won't have my son glaring at me like he's a big boy when he's still wetting his pants."

"I do not!" Wyatt exclaimed defensively.

Joe rubbed his eyes like he was crying. "Oh, hubba, hubba, hubba. Darn near! You're such a piss ant," he said with disgust. "What...are you going to start crying now? I should make you fight the Hotchkiss boy around the corner and toughen you up a bit. A Thorn hurts. Remember that. If you're going to use my name, you better be tough enough to keep the namesake. A Thorn hurts anyone who gets in their way, boy. And it's about damn time you start getting away from Mama and into the world of men."

Billy Jo was repulsed. "You're not going to make my son fight anyone. He's eight years old!"

"I already told you to go cook dinner," he said threateningly. "I won't tell you again."

Billy Jo sat down on the davenport beside Wyatt and put her arm around him. "Dinner's done. You can change your clothes and eat dinner at any time. But I will not allow you to scare your own son because you're in a bad mood."

"How am I scaring him?"

"That Hotchkiss boy is fifteen years old! Of course, he can whip an eight-year-old. I am sickened that you would even say something so stupid!"

"I don't care if the little weasel wins; I just want him to get back up and be a man. If he's going to glare at me like a big boy, he better be able to back it up!"

"He's eight years old!" she shouted.

Joe leaned forward with a wild glare. "I don't care! If he's big enough to look at me like I'm a piece of crap, then he can learn the hard way to be respectful."

"That doesn't make any sense. You're like a child yourself," she said with disgust and walked past him towards the kitchen to check the water Joe set on the stove. If he went into the bedroom and washed, it would give them all a few minutes to cool down.

Joe grabbed his muddy boot and threw it at her. It hit her in the back. She gasped as she arched her back painfully. "You son of a..."

He was immediately behind her and reached around her neck and cupped her chin, closing her mouth with his hand and pulled her against him tightly. "Don't move!" He looked at Wyatt with his hardened eyes. "Get in the bedroom with your brother."

"Pa, please don't hurt Mama. I'll be good, I promise," Wyatt pleaded.

"Get!" Joe yelled and watched Wyatt run behind Brice into the bedroom and slam the door behind him.

They could hear Wyatt and Brice crying in the bedroom.

"What did you say to me?" he asked with a sneer. Billy Jo was already beginning to weep. It was the fear and expectation of what was to come ahead.

## 6

Lucille Barton had set the four small plates with handprints and names of the children skillfully etched into the clay near the cookstove to dry overnight. Tomorrow, she would place the plates in the cookstove and build a fire over them and let the clay harden in the coals for the next twenty-four hours. She hoped that would harden the clay into earthenware decorative plates. She had placed two holes on the top of each plate where she planned to tie coiled strands of yarn of multiple colors to create a loop so the little hands could be hung up on the wall. She didn't have a lot to work with, but it would be nice, nonetheless.

Lucille's father, Enoch Pennington, had been a master craftsman from Germany and relocated to Pennsylvania, where he married Greta Hatch. Enoch and Greta had four children and raised them, but when their youngest son was fourteen years old, Greta conceived again. Nine months later Greta gave birth to Lucille. The older four children grew up and moved out to start lives of their own while Lucille was just a child. She grew up as an only child in a loving home and was well educated and the joy in her parent's eyes. Her parents owned a pottery shop and worked together to create earthen and stoneware and far more decorative pieces of art as well. Commercial dining sets and cookware could be bought in any store but a large earthenware vase with a beautiful glaze and raised roses on the sides was easily found in the Pennington's Pottery Shop. Lucille grew up working with clay and learning how to form a desired shape on the throwing wheel and how to use the tools of the trade to turn a lump of clay into a work of art. She learned about glazes, mixing colors, textures and heat temperatures used in the kiln. Lucille was especially gifted at drawing and using the fine tip of a brush or a knife to etch designs on a piece to make it a more refined art. She learned the trade and loved working with her parents in the family business, so much so, that her father had planned on handing the pottery shop over to her when he retired. Lucille's life was like a dream, she loved her home, her career and she was in love with a wonderful young man named Lawrence Barton. She planned on marrying Lawrence and together they would raise their family working in the pottery shop just as her parents had done.

Unfortunately, life had other plans and Enoch died unexpectedly of a heart attack when Lucille was eighteen years old. Though they were all devastated, none of Enoch and Greta's children were as broken as Lucille. She had been very close to her father and all those dreams of Enoch walking her down the aisle when she married Lawrence were suddenly gone. Heartbroken, devastated and mourning a great loss, it was the hardest time in Lucille's life to get through. She knew a big part of her life would be missing but she also knew her mother and her could keep the pottery shop open and earn a living as they always had before. Her mother was a good woman, a loving and a wise person, but she wasn't a strong lady. Lucille's four older siblings came home for the funeral and raided the shop's inventory taking what they wanted and giving other pieces away to old friends and guests that came by to pay their respects. Lucille confronted them about it causing some bitter feelings but her mother allowed them to empty the shop of merchandise. With nothing left to sell, her siblings surrounded their mother like a flock of vultures and talked her into selling the pottery shop to a baker who happened to be her oldest brother's best friend. Lucille would have argued, but the negotiations and sales contract were finalized while she was spending the day with Lawrence. Now, without a business or means of supporting themselves, Lucille's older siblings urged their mother to sell her home and move to New York with Lucille's older sister where they thought she would be happier and well taken care of.

Lucille was treated like a child and given no voice in any of the decisions being made. She was being forced to move to New York and leave everything she knew behind including her beloved Lawrence. While they packed up the house for the dreaded move, Lawrence asked Lucille to marry him. She accepted and they married right away in the local courthouse so her mother could be there before she moved. The resentments between her siblings and her were growing and although Lucille's siblings were in town, none of them bothered to attend.

The newlyweds lived with Lawrence's parents and younger siblings on their forty-acre farm. A year later, Lawrence's parents sold their farm and moved to Utah and bought a much larger farm. Lawrence worked with his father and brothers to make the farm successful but, as the years went by, the farm prospered but very little went into Lawrence's savings. They still lived in his parent's home even though they had two sons of their own.

Tensions were building on the farm and the young couple decided it was time to move out on their own. They saved enough money to purchase a team of mules and a wagon to move off the family farm. They heard the winters weren't so harsh and the land was cheap and plentiful in Oregon. The soil of the Willamette Valley was so fertile it was almost magical, they heard. Oregon sounded like it was a farmer's paradise and the tensions on the farm in Utah were making life miserable for them. With the decision made, they packed their wagon and followed the road west. However, a lack of proper planning had left them out of supplies and out of money by the time they found Branson. It was fall and with winter coming, they needed to find somewhere to live to keep their boys warm and safe. They heard the silver mine was hiring and provided housing as well. It did not take Lawrence an hour before he applied for a job and was hired immediately. He left the main office with a key to a cabin at Slater's Mile and could not be more thankful. However, they still had no money to buy food and other necessities, so Lawrence sold their two mules and the wagon to the livery stable for half of what it was worth. It was a tough decision to make knowing they'd be stranded in Branson but Lawrence had a wife and two boys to think about. Selling them would pay for his clothes and boots needed for the rough work ahead and enough food and supplies to get them by until his first payday.

It had been over three months and they were still struggling to save any money. Lawrence made two dollars a day but the company took the rent for the cabin out of his paychecks. It left them enough to buy food and a cord of wood every few weeks for the cookstove. They were learning that other people in their community stole wood for their cookstoves and a cord of wood disappeared faster than a bag of coal, which most people used at Slater's Mile. Everything they ate had to be bought, along with any other supplies. With two little growing boys, there was no way of getting ahead financially. When they started to save money, someone came into their cabin when they were away and stole their savings out of a jar. It was an eye-opening revelation that they lived among thieves in what was supposed to be a close-knit community. In truth, Lawrence hated his job and they both hated living in the small cabin. They prayed that the Lord would lead them out of the mine and into a real home and a safer job for him but they remained, with no changes in sight.

Lawrence yawned as he came out of the bedroom after washing up from work. He carried a bucket of warm soapy water with a washrag in it to the front door and emptied the water outside. He said, "I can't wait to take a real bath sometime. If I didn't think it would be stolen, I'd say let's buy a bathtub."

They had a round tin tub big enough to bathe the boys and for Lucille could sit in with her legs hanging out and wash with a sponge every few days. Although Lawrence wasn't considered a big man, it was too uncomfortable for him to squeeze into the tub. He had to be content with washing with a rag and sponge or go into town and pay to bathe in a bathhouse, which he had never done.

Lucille answered empathetically, "I know. They're only seven dollars at the hardware store for a five-foot bathtub, I think."

Lawrence shook his head as he sat down at the small round dining table that had come with the furnished cabin. "No. We'll have better things to spend our money on eventually. I can tough it out a while longer. It would be nice to sit in a real bathtub again, though."

"Billy Jo has one and its six feet long, I think. I'm sure she'd let us borrow it."

Lawrence was in his mid to late twenties with a handsome, clean-shaven face and short brown hair. He was one of those young men with a face and countenance that when someone saw him, they just knew he was a nice man. "I don't want to ask Joe Thorn for anything. I put up with him and the rest of those fella's every day as it is. He might want to watch you bathe in return for the favor of letting me use his tub. Those fella's I work with have no moral anchor in anything except hell, which we're tunneling towards."

She put her hand gently on his on the center of the table. "I wish you could get away from there. I know you don't like to miss work but maybe you could take tomorrow off and go speak to Billy Jo's father. She said he would probably hire you if you went and talked to him."

He sighed tiredly. "I can't afford to take time off and if the fella's around here found out I did that, I'd be harassed, if not fired for taking the day off to look for another job. And then we'd be living in a tent somewhere if we had a tent to live in. Maybe this weekend we can talk Billy Jo into introducing me to her father or maybe Matt if we can find him. I don't see the mine slowing down anytime soon."

"I can ask her."

Lawrence spoke softly so his boys wouldn't hear his disheartened tone, "I'd like to take the day off and go do that but it's not worth being fired. There are no secrets around here, everyone knows everyone's business and I can't take that chance. But I do hate my job. I go to work as the sun comes up and I'm in a dark hole most of the day. The sun's going down by the time I

40

come home most of the time. I feel like all I know anymore is darkness and heathens. I miss the sunlight and smiling people. I know we have not gone to church in a while but we need to go back. I'm feeling overwhelmed by darkness."

Lucille frowned caringly. "I would like to go to church too but I'm not walking the boys two miles in the snow or in pouring down rain to go to church for an hour and a half and then having to walk them back two miles in the weather back home. Their boots won't keep their feet warm or dry enough. Mine either, I have holes in my boot soles and socks." She shrugged. "We'll go back to church as soon as it warms up and stops raining. Don't get too discouraged, Lawrence, this is all just temporary."

Discouragement, like a field fire, consumes the soul, steals ambition and the joy out of living. Lawrence remembered back to the day they moved into the cabin and met Richie Thorn. Richie's final words after their introductions were 'Welcome to Slater Slums of Shacks and Rats. Once you're in, you can never get out'. For three months, he had labored and Ritchie's words were becoming prophetic. He spoke to his beautiful wife with the same quiet soft voice, "That's what I said three months ago and we're still not getting ahead. Do you know how many times I have been told to watch out for the mule that I lead in and out of the mine all day? Watch out for loose rocks, cracking beams and other hazards to keep my mule safe. I've been told the mule's more important than my wife. Do you know why they tell me that? Joe told me today why they worry so much about that mule. Do you know why?"

Lucille shook her head.

"Because the mule cost money. I am replaceable but they would have to buy a new mule and train it if anything tragic happened. If that doesn't tell you how valued I am, then another way to put it is the jackass is worth more than me. I think about that when I have to pick up the hot nuggets it leaves behind, so the bosses won't step on them. I'd love to get a job above ground, Lucy, but where? As soon as I lose or quit my job here, we have to move. You have one day to get out of the company housing or the company men will toss us out. We have nowhere else to go and no money. Where does it all go? I don't know. It is very much like Richie said, once you're in, you're in for good and there's no way out."

Lucille prayed silently for a safer position for Lawrence with better pay. He worked so hard to provide all they needed to survive. Her concern was not his pay so much as his spirit staying optimistic and full of life. She squeezed his hand with an understanding smile. "If you must know, we're saving about five dollars a month and there's close to twelve dollars in our money box. So, we are doing fine right now. Billy Jo has a house she might rent to us if I offered her some money upfront if you wanted to take tomorrow off and look for work above ground. Lawrence, honestly, we'll be okay. Jesus will take care of us; you know that as well as I do. And to me, you're the most important Jackass in the world." Her smile turned into a laugh as she slapped his hand playfully.

He slowly grinned. "Thanks. I appreciate that." He watched at her beautiful smile affectionately. "Do you think she would rent her house to us?"

Lucille shrugged. "I don't see why not. Shall we ask her? It is not too late yet. We can just say we want to be in town instead of living out here."

"I don't want Joe knowing I want to quit," Lawrence stated.

"He doesn't need to know. And if he asks, we'll just tell him you've become so attached to jackasses that you want to ride one to work."

"Oh, stop it," he said with a slight grin. "All right, let's get the boys dressed and we'll walk over and ask her."

Outside, the rain had ceased, leaving a muddy road of melting snow adding to the day's heavy rains. They walked up the road passing other cabins and stopped short of Billy Jo's cabin. They could hear Joe Thorn's angry voice rising in volume and Billy Jo's whimpering cries that sounded frightened from on the street. The unmistakable sound of a sharp slap across the face was followed by a loud cry, followed by more angry shouting, curses, yelling and more hits, and screaming.

Five-year-old Michael asked uncomfortably, "Why is she crying?"

"Let's go back," Lucille said uneasily.

Lawrence stared at the cottage with a strange ugly hollowness forming within him. "Yeah."

Next door, Ritchie Thorn stood on his porch leaning against the door jamb. He shook his head. "I wouldn't go knocking on his door if I were you, Lawrence. He might start beating on you."

Lawrence acknowledged Ritchie. "I wasn't. But you could, he is your brother. You know it isn't right."

Ritchie shrugged his shoulders. "It's not my fight. It's none of my business. I like Billy Jo but she needs to learn her place. She has been a bit mouthy for the past two weeks or so. What are you all doing out in the rain anyway?"

"We came over to see them. I think we'll head back home and talk to them later."

"Good idea, Lawrence," Ritchie said as he went back to listening to his brother's fight.

As they walked back towards their cabin quietly, Lucille stopped and turned to look into his eyes unexpectedly. "I'm thankful for you. Thank you for loving me the way you do. I cannot imagine living life like Billy Jo. I feel so bad for her."

Lawrence smiled slowly and wrapped his arms around her in a warm hug. "Sweetheart, it's my honor to be married to you. Now, let's get these boys home and read them a book before bed. They shouldn't be hearing that kind of stuff and I don't want them going to sleep thinking about what they heard."

## 7

Billy Jo lay awake a good portion of the night weeping softly so as not to wake Joe. Her thigh was bruised and would be black and blue in the morning. Her ribs hurt with any adjustment to get comfortable in bed, but he could breathe without wincing in pain. The only evidence anyone would notice was a cut inside of her fattened lip. Her face wasn't bruised this time and she was thankful for that. She had been in love with Joe for a long time and always hoped each time he hit her, it would be the last, but it never was. It was a routine of abuse followed by remorse and promises that were never kept. She had left him several times but he could be very sincere and charming and that was what she always fell for. That one fantasy that the thoughtful, loving and remorseful Joe Thorn would last. Now that she had moved back out to Slater's Mile, it was turning bad again.

Her two boys needed a father to teach them how

to be good men and her thoughts turned to what Wes Wasson had told her. The worst thing Billy Jo could imagine was one of her sons becoming like Joe. He wasn't a good man and he wasn't a good father. He was a despicable man and becoming more of a threat of harming Wyatt when they argued. She had a decision to make between living the same routine with Joe or taking the first step to a better life. She lay awake collecting the courage to take that step and leave Joe. Her boys needed a father but they needed a father who could teach them how to be a real man. From her own father's example, she knew a real man kept his word, was honest and treated people right. A real man walked with integrity. Wes Wasson could teach her boys how to be good men. He wanted to raise them as his own and Billy Jo was ready to give him the chance to do so. The happy home and loving family she fantasized about with Joe was never going to happen. It could happen with Wes though. He would marry her and treat her right. They might even have a daughter and she was confident that Wes would beam with the glory and wonder of bringing a new life into the world. He would be such a proud father for her boys and any children they had together. There was the possibility that she could finally have the happy marriage and loving home that she always dreamed of. The hope of that possibility gave her courage to take a stand.

"You got my breakfast ready yet?" Joe hollered as he tied his boots. He hated putting wet boots on in the morning with dry socks. After fighting with Billy Jo, he forgot to put his boots near the cookstove to dry overnight. The semi-dry mud flaked off onto the floor, leaving a trail of dirt as he stepped towards the bedroom. He had not bothered to apologize for laying his hands on her the night before. He had not apologized in a long time.

"Almost," she answered softly. She was making bacon, eggs and putting it between two slices of buttered bread. She glanced back to make sure he wasn't in the room and then snorted in through her nose and sucked the mucus into her mouth. She let a thick wad of mucus fall onto the egg and covered it with a slice of bread.

Joe answered as he walked out of the bedroom pulling on another flannel shirt. "Good. Your dinner was barely edible. I don't know how many times I've told you I can't stand gobs of fat in my stew. I don't understand why you don't get good meat for stew; it's your Pa's account. You ought to be getting good thick steak, not that bagged pork fat you like."

"The fat keeps you strong."

"No, the fat makes me want to puke! The next time you go to town to get meat, get some steak and have the butcher cut the fat off before you bring it home. You are disgusting, Billy Jo! No wonder you are fat and getting fatter by the day. I should've known you'd end up looking like your Pa. Big and fat."

She handed him his breakfast sandwich with a coy smile. "Enjoy your breakfast." He'd never know she spat in it with the egg there. "Your lunch is packed. You can leave now."

He glanced at her irritably as he took a big bite of his breakfast. "I am leaving. I want the bathtub full of hot water when I get home. I need a bath and so do you. You stink."

She watched him devour the sandwich with a sense of satisfaction. She couldn't get away with hitting him over the head with a frying pan but she could spit in his sandwich and if he knew what she had done, she could watch him puke before he beat her again. She despised him more every time she looked at him. The future was being wasted with him, and life would never get better if she didn't change the path she was on. She touched the welt and cut inside her lip with her tongue to remind herself to be courageous. Even though her heart beat faster and pulsated in her ears, through a dry throat, she blurted out, "Joe, I'm taking the boys and moving back into my house."

He swallowed the last bite of his sandwich. "No, you're not. I'm not letting you take my kids." He raised his voice, "Who's going to make my meals, Billie Jo? Huh? You're here to cook! I work my hands to the bone to support you and the boys and you think you are going to leave me? I'll tell you right now, you're not, or I'll come into town and drag you back here by your hair! Do you hear me?" His eyes burned into her without an ounce of mercy. It was too early to put up with her nonsense.

Billy Jo could feel her spirit bowing down in fear. She licked the cut on her lip and continued, "I'm not going to let you hurt my boys or me anymore. We're leaving."

48

He stepped quickly to her and grabbed her chin with a hard squeeze. "No, you won't or I'll hurt you and the boys! Do you hear me?"

Her eyes watered but she could not talk with her cheeks being squeezed.

He glared into her eyes and spoke lowly. "You'll be here when I get home and that bath better be hot. If you are not here, I'll be coming to get you. And I won't be nice." He pushed her back and let her go. "I have to get to work." He grabbed his coat, hat and lunch pail.

She opened and closed her mouth a few times. "I don't love you anymore, Joe. The boys don't love you either. How can we? All you do is treat us like burdens and slaves. I won't be here when you get home and I'm not coming back, ever. None of us love you anymore. It's over," she repeated.

He smiled coldly. "No, it's not. We've been here before and you'll come crawling back when you miss me. We already know that, so you might as well stay here and be done with the emotional babble."

Tears fell slowly from her eyes. "I can't do it anymore. The boys and I are leaving and we're not ever coming back. I'm not your woman anymore, Joe. Once you leave, it's the last time you'll see me in this cabin."

He stood at the opened door and stared at her warningly.

"Joe, let's go!" his brother, Ritchie, yelled from the road.

He pointed at her threateningly. "Don't you leave."

Her heart was broken and it showed on her expression, as she explained, "I hoped we could be a family. I tried to be a good wife for ten years and you are never satisfied. I've realized you will never be satisfied with me. And I have fallen out of love with you. You hit me for the last time. I don't have any more to say than that. I deserve better."

For the first time, he could see she was serious, and it angered him. He could not control himself as he shouted bitterly, "You deserve better? You're too fat and stupid for anyone else to want you. But if you want to go, fine. Get the hell out of here then!" he yelled. "Take those screaming brats with you and get out!"

She whimpered while trying to hold back her tears, "I am."

He stepped quickly to the small table and grabbed a coffee cup and threw it against the wall shattering it on impact. He glared at her, breathing heavily. "Fine, go! I hate you too! I hate all of you!" he shouted. He heard his son Wyatt begin to sniffle. He turned towards the bedroom and saw Wyatt's lips trembling with his growing tears. Joe groaned in anger and walked outside slamming the door behind him.

Billy Jo exhaled and dropped to her knees in relief. She held out her arms for her son. Wyatt ran forward and wrapped his arms around her in a tight hug. He began sobbing in her arms.

## 8

Joe Thorn was irritated with Billy Jo. He didn't like smacking her around but the woman was as bright as a frog and more annoying than a centipede trapped in his jeans. How he had gotten caught up with her was easy to explain, she was a cute blonde teenager in a world of men, and Joe caught her attention before anyone else did. He probably wouldn't have kept her around so long but she could cook better than most and cleaned well enough too. It was much nicer to come home to a tasty warm dinner than to have to cook for himself and cheaper than eating at the saloon. Most of the time, they got along okay, but recently there was a bit of a disconnect, a bit of distance that he couldn't identify. She seemed to have a wandering gaze in her eyes and a slight smile on her lips while deep in her thoughts. He would ask what she was thinking, and she always replied with "nothing." There was a part of him that certainly believed that. Most amphibians didn't spend much time pondering how someone invented the wheel. Billy Jo didn't seem to, either.

To make his irritating morning much worse, while Joe was checking in with the timekeeper this morning, his foreman, Jim Longo, accused him of high grading silver ore from the mine. It was an allegation of stealing pieces of ore rich with silver deposits and taking them home to sell to the assayer in town for a profit. It came as an unexpected surprise and the accusation was made in front of the other employees, which was humiliating. Joe had denied it as anyone else would but Jim Longo was married to Billy Jo's cousin, Karen. Unfortunately for Joe, she told Karen about his box of silver ore under their bed and Karen told Jim. Though Joe tried to deny the allegation, Jim made it clear that Joe had one chance to save his job and that was to admit to stealing the ore and bring it back. If he still denied it, Jim threatened go over to Joe's company housing and look for himself immediately. Joe was forced to admit to high grading the ore and was used as an example and final warning to the other mine employees. Joe was humiliated and angry.

How stupid did Billy Jo have to be to tell Karen that he was stealing pieces of ore rich in silver? Karen was his supervisor's wife! Even the subject of Jim Longo was a frustrating one. Jim Longo came to the mine five years before as a greenhorn mucker like all newbies generally start out. Joe remembered Jim's first day on the job and thought he was a fish out of water in the mining business then. Five years later, there was nothing Jim Longo could tell Joe that he didn't already know about mining. But Joe could still teach him a lot. A year before when the dayshift Supervisor job opened, there were quite a few men with years of experience and knowledge who applied for the position, Joe included. When it came to seniority on the job, one of the longtime employees like Joe should have gotten the job, but seniority didn't matter. Ron Dalton promoted his brother-in-law to the mine supervisor's position. It was a slap in the face to Joe and every other experienced man that had labored in the ground for a whole lot longer than Jim.

The politics within the Slater Mining Company were enough to make a pig puke. The only promotions that opened went to either family members or good friends of the administration's personnel. A hard-working man with more knowledge and experience in the industry's dangers was passed over again and again. Simultaneously, a family member or a close associate's son was promoted to a safer and better-paying position. It was a constant irritant that festered in Joe like an abscessed tooth. He would've liked nothing more than to have buried his fist into Jim's mouth while he humiliated him about the ore. It wasn't like the company was going to miss it but that extra bit of income made a significant difference to Joe. To Joe and other employees, it only seemed fair that they should be able to take a little of what they labored for home with them.

Candlelight flickered off the rough-hewn walls of the exploratory winze they were cutting downwards in an incline. They had mined five hundred feet down and the heavy rain and melting snow raised the water level and filled the last hundred feet of the winze with water and still rising when they reached the mine that morning. Hoses for the Cornish pump up on the surface were run down and after some time, the winze was drained.

Joe was a double jacker along with his partners, Walter Kendricks and Bobby Alper. Joe and Walter took turns swinging their hammer and hitting the drill steel about twenty times a minute to drill a blasting hole into the granite. After five minutes of consistent hammering, they would trade-off to let the other man swing his eight-pound hammer twenty times a minute for the next five minutes while the other man rests. After each hit, Bobby turned the drill steel so it wouldn't become lodged in the rock. They labored to drill nine holes in the face of the hard granite from the top of the face to the bottom around eighteen inches to two feet deep. The powder man, who set the explosives in the individual holes was dependent on the placement by the drill setters. Ideally, every drill hole was set two feet apart and at equal depths for consistent blasts that would remove the material that had been drilled. Joe and his two-man crew were exploring for veins of silver ore in a deeper southward angle. They had found a small vein back up the winze, thirty yards or so, that had hints of gold ore. Ron Dalton gave the orders to keep cutting down to the seven-hundred-foot level to see what could be found deeper. Another crew of four men followed the quartz vein discovered and had cut a drift for sixty feet so far that was proving to be higher yields of gold-bearing material the further they went. Other crews were cutting winzes in different directions, and one crew was cutting a shaft straight down intending to reach a thousand feet to see what could be found at deeper depths.

Not all the mining was exploratory. Most of the other employees were pulling silver ore from good-sized veins and stopes from the mountain the mine was located on. It was good solid work for the men like Joe but danger of multiple kinds lurked like a black pit viper hidden by the dark ready to strike at any given moment. There had been many injuries over the years and plenty of deaths as well. If there was anything that Joe could honestly say good about Ron Dalton and Jim Longo, it was they cared about the men's safety while at the same time pushing production, producing results to keep the stamp mill going.

Three shifts worked around the clock at the silver mine. Day and evening shifts worked production pulling out waste rock and mineral-bearing ore. In contrast, the graveyard shift was the shoring crew who made the back and ribs safe, leveled floors for expanding rails and setting timbers where the new blasting was cut away or wherever else help may be asked for. A good number of Chinese worked the graveyard shift scraping and leveling floors for the ore cart rails. Now that the water level was rising, it would become a new responsibility to pump out the water starting tonight so the day crew could get right to work drilling and blasting.

Joe urinated on the wall and spat on the floor. "Why do I keep her around anyway? I could find a better-looking woman in a day. They're all over Rose Street." He could hear the pounding hammers of the other crew drilling in the new drift up the winze.

Bobby Alper answered, "Because you don't want Syphilis creeping around in your house. Billy Jo's worth keeping, heck at least she doesn't have anything like that."

Walter Kendrick was a large man in his late thirties with shaggy, ear-length yellow hair and a shaggy yellow beard. Walter lived with his wife and four children in one of the cabins at Slater's Mile. He shook his head. "Joe, I don't know why it is you always have an issue with your lady. I know Billy Jo and she's a nice young lady."

Joe picked up his hammer and looked at Walter. "You're not married to her."

"Nor are you. But you should be. Those boys of yours deserve to have their family secured."

"Secured?" Joe grimaced in the candlelight. "What in the... What does that even mean, Walter?"

Walter set his hammerhead on the ground and leaned against the handle. "Marriage, Joe. You should marry that girl. She loves you. What more do you want?"

Joe spat the dust out of his mouth. "I want her to do what I want her to do. The only times we fight are when she does something stupid or says something stupid. She drives me crazy sometimes.

I get irritated when she and the boys won't shut up! I'm down here all day and go home and all I hear is chaos. We need a mansion is what we need, so that I can get away from them for a while. I don't want to hear the boys crying, fighting, whining like little girls over nothing at all. For crying out loud, I get so sick and tired of not being able to relax and not being left alone! And that wench went and told her cousin Karen that I stoled a pile of ore! That's Jim Longo's wife and I'm sure he'll tell Ron and everyone else too. I could've lost my job today because of her!" he said, raising his voice. "I swear she's as bright as a maggot!"

Walter spoke evenly. "You know better than to steal. If you're caught high grading, you can get fired. That's always been a rule anywhere you go. I suppose you could be mad at Billy Jo for telling Jim's wife but you decided to take it."

"Yeah, I know!" Joe exclaimed angrily. "I'm not bringing it all back. I deserve some of the benefits of my work. Don't you boys get tired of working your butts off and buying scraps of food for your table while watching the Slater's ride around in their fancy coach and clean suits? Augustus French was blown to hell by that charge that didn't go off because no one relayed the message that there was still a live charge in the rock! Whose fault was that? Not the company's the law says. His death didn't cost the Slater's a penny; it just shattered more ore to process. You could say they made money off his death because it was ore and not waste rock that exploded. They didn't say one word about that even though Augustus lost his life. Thank goodness he didn't have a family. What about Mark Simpson? A hundred-pound piece of the back just broke loose and crushed his head. He had a family and what did his family get? They got kicked out of their cabin two days later! That's what we are to them, just muscle, nothing more. Why shouldn't we take a little bit of the goods in our pockets and earn a touch more than we make? We deserve it. Billy Jo almost cost me my job and I'm beginning to think she planned it. She says she's leaving me. Why not get me fired too? Women are conniving and scheming that way. If she's there when I get home, I might toss her out in the rain and make her leave for what she did to me today."

Walter spoke softly, "First of all, what happened to Augustus and Mark is tragic but we know the risks of working here. My wife kisses me every morning, knowing I may not come home again. That's just the life we live as miners; we know the risks. What I'll never understand is why you're still here. I mean, Billy Jo has a nice house in town, and her father owns the granite quarry, which is a lot safer than here. I don't know why you don't get out of here and go to work there? Move out of Slater's Mile and live like decent people. You two might get along better."

Joe chuckled scornfully. "I'll never bow down to Luther Fasana and ask him for a job. I'll own half of that company when he dies anyway. I don't need to do a thing to get it other than just wait."

Bobby answered, "You might need to marry Billy Jo. She'll be the owner, not you."

"What's Billy Jo's is mine. We don't need a judge, minister or lawyer handing us a piece of paper to say that. I'll just take it as payment for putting up with her."

A flickering light appeared in the winze drawing closer and soon, the powder man who was in charge of the dynamite and blasting came into view. His name was Danny Rosso. "Boy's, I don't hear a lot of hammering going on down here. It sounds like you're talking more than working."

Walter grinned with a nod of his head. "That's about it. Joe is having woman problems."

Danny peered at Joe, annoyed. "Well, get it figured out. I need drill holes. I already did two blasts today; I was hoping you boys were about ready for me."

"No. We were flooded this morning. It put us a bit behind," Joe answered bitterly.

"And talking?" Danny asked curtly.

"Yeah, and some talking too. So what?"

Danny was irritated. "Joe, we all heard that you're high grading the company, and that's fine with me, but when you're slowing down my job, it makes me look bad. You had two holes to drill today to finish from yesterday and it's almost lunchtime and they aren't done."

"We were flooded and I don't know why they didn't pump the water out last night, but there was plenty here this morning. That's not our fault. We'll get the holes drilled after lunch. You can do your part soon enough."

Danny raised his voice slightly, "Those fella's over there are drilling their last hole. I was planning on blasting them both one after the other so you all can get back down here around the same time after the muckers get it hauled out. Jim's going to pissed off if I have to blow one and then wait an hour before I can even start setting up to blast yours. That's two hours of downtime. I wanted to blast them both during your lunch."

Bobby put a three-foot-long drill steel in a hole centered in the face about a foot deep. "We'll get it going right now."

"Now, what the hell does he want?" Joe asked bitterly as the sound of an ore cart backing down the rails towards them. He shouted, "We haven't blasted anything! What are you doing down here, Mucker?" he asked irritably.

"I was promoted up to a trammer, Joe. You know that." Lawrence Barton said. Muckers loaded the waste rock or ore into the ore carts for removal. Trammers lead the mules in and out of the mine to deliver the load to the proper destination, whether it was to the ore room at the top end of the stamp mill or the waste rock pile that was dumped out of the way on the side of the mountain.

Danny grimaced. "Why aren't you helping muck the ore in drift eight?"

Lawrence Barton held the reins of a mule, walking it backwards down the dark winze with a small lantern on the cart. "I'm going that way but Jim Longo asked me to bring down some water for you, fella's," he said as he let go of the reins and grabbed three one-gallon jugs of water and set them down on the floor. He had brought seven gallons of water down, one for each man working in the winze.

"Thanks' Lawrence," Bobby said.

"You're welcome."

"Hey, has your wife said anything about Billy Jo lately?" Joe asked curiously.

Lawrence hesitated. "No, just that her dad was sick."

Joe scoffed. "Get out of here, Mucker. You're no help at all."

Lawrence walked back to grab the reins and had begun walking up the winze when he was blown backward by the powerful percussion of an explosion that threw him through the air and onto the ground. Stunned by the initial blast, he laid on his back with his ears ringing loudly. He could still make out a loud thundering sound and feel the ground shaking as a rock bounced off the floor and rolled between his legs. Lawrence glanced upwards and saw the top of the winze coming down in slow motion in his lamp's light. For a moment, he hesitated not quite grasping the horror of what was happening. Lawrence began to panic and turned to his stomach and crawled away as fast as he could. The ground vibrated as he tried to scramble back towards the end of the winze as the ceiling above him cracked loudly. Suddenly, he screamed in anguish from the crushing pain of the bones in his foot and lower calf being shattered and pinned to the ground by an unimaginable weight of rock that had fallen six and a half feet onto his leg with unmerciful force. Stones of smaller size fell around him and rolled against the ore cart. One rock of some size landed on the back of his head, nearly knocking him unconscious and, momentarily, silenced his screams. He covered his head with both arms in fear of being buried as smaller rocks pelted him and bounced off all around him for what seemed like an eternity. The initial percussion sent a gust of wind through the winze blowing out every candle's wick, leaving nothing but total blackness and a heavy fog of dust lingering in the air. Lawrence could see the lantern's faint light on the ore cart through the dust but, with a snap of the harness, the light disappeared as the ore cart rolled downhill on the rails towards the others.

The shockwave had knocked all four men off their feet and blew out their candles, leaving them in a cloud of pitch-black dust-filled space five hundred feet underground. The thunderous sound of falling rock and splintering timbers that shook the floor told them all they needed to know and it filled them all with dread. The winze had collapsed. There was no sound at all for a mere second and, then, they heard the anguished screams of Lawrence Barton in the pitch blackness.

"Is everyone okay?" Walter urgently asked. He coughed from the dust while getting back up on his feet.

"Yeah. I think we're in trouble," Danny Rosso said, sounding stunned.

"Joe? Bobby?" Walter asked in the darkness.

Bobby answered with a shaken voice. "Are we in

hell? Someone light a candle!" he screamed in sheer terror. Lawrence's screams of agony echoed loudly off the face and made it hard to hear anything else. "Stop screaming! Can someone shut the screaming up!" Bobby exclaimed. "Joe, where are you?" He could see nothing except blackness.

"Shh! What's that sound?" Joe asked, quickly trying to listen to a dull hollow sound over Lawrence's anguished cries.

"Watch out!" Joe shouted and jumped out of the way of the out of control heavy steel ore cart that came speeding down the rails towards them. It hit the end of the rails and flew wildly into the men, slamming against the rock wall with a distinctive grisly crunching sound. Walter, hit by the cart, fell down with a pain-filled cry. Bobby Alper, also injured, began groaning painfully. The small lantern on the cart flew towards the front and bounced off something soft and fell into the cart, shattering the glass that protected the wick and breaking the basin open. The kerosene ignited in the wick's flame and a fire burst upwards inside of the cart. In the flame's light, it was clear to see Danny Rosso had been hit by the cart and driven against the steel drill Bobby had placed in the wall. The drill's blunt end stuck out of his chest leaving him impaled on the steel. He had been crushed from the waist down by the ore cart. Danny stood in place, already dead.

Bobby held his left arm groaning; his arm was broken. Walter laid on the ground beside the cart with a sharp grimace with his hand on his hip. He asked Joe to help him to stand. Able to see in the firelight, Joe took hold of his hand and helped Walter to stand but Walter could not stand on his own. He rested his hands on the ore cart on the opposite end of the fire to support himself. "Good heaven's!" he said, looking at Danny.

"What the hell happened?" Joe asked either of his two friends over the screaming of Lawrence. Joe noticed Danny's body and stared in shock. He felt the pending doom that awaited them all.

# 9

Joe Thorn coughed from the dust in the air. He was shaken to the core by the horror of seeing his friend, Danny Rosso's, body crushed and impaled against the rock flickering in the orange light of the flames. He could hear Lawrence's cries for help but he remained frozen. A moment ago, he was arguing with Danny about drilling holes and now he was dead without any warning. Slowly, he became aware of Bobby's painful grunting and the soft praying for their safety and rescue by Walter. Realizing the kerosene fire that had burst up in flames was growing dimmer, he reached into his pocket and pulled out a candle and lit it in the dying flames.

"Lawrence!" Walter Kendricks yelled through a cough. "How bad are you hurt?"

"My Leg! It's caught under a rock. I can't move it!" he cried out desperately.

"My arm's broke," Bobby Alper volunteered.

"Someone light a candle!" His voice shook as the winze grew darker. He sat against the wall hunched over in a tight ball with widened eyes. His breathing was becoming rapid and shallow, he was beginning to hyperventilate.

"Joe, are you hurt?" Walter asked.

"No. Are you?" he asked still shaken by what had happened.

Walter forced a grin but the pain could be seen on his face. "Yeah, I think the cart broke my hip when it hit me." He put his attention on Bobby, who was unable to catch his breath. "It'll be okay, Bobby. Just take it easy."

"I...can't...breathe," Bobby struggled to say.

"Bobby, breathe. Take a deep breath," Joe said, lighting the extinguished candle set in a candle-holder hammered into a crack in the rock above them. He stumbled over a good-sized stone that had rolled forward and stopped in the middle of the floor.

Bobby shook his head as he held his chest with a horrified expression. "I...can't."

Joe knelt and grabbed Bobby's light cotton shirt. "Look here!" He pointed at his own eyes. "We're going to be okay, alright? Exhale and breathe in. Exhale and breathe in deeply. We're going to be fine. I promise. Richie and all those men out there are going to get us out of here. Okay? So, calm down, we're going to be okay." He patted his friend's cheek softly with his hand. "We'll get through this, Bobby. Deep breathe in and exhale."

Bobby pointed at the body of Danny Rosso, impaled on the drill steel.

Joe looked towards Danny and said, "I know. But we're alive. You're alive." The screams and wails of Lawrence were echoing and overwhelming in the winze. Joe yelled, "Lawrence, shut up for a minute! Shut up!" He turned back to Walter. "I can only do one thing at a time!"

Walter's hip was in agony. He squeezed his lips together tightly while taking a deep breath through his nose. "Go check on Lawrence. I'll talk with Bobby. Joe, we need to know if we're trapped in here or if we can get through that collapse."

Joe said to Bobby, "There's no reason to panic. We don't even know what the collapse looks like yet, Bobby. How about you give us a chance to look it over before you hyperventilate yourself to death, Okay?" He forced a smile and turned the candle he held towards the collapse and walked up the winze to help Lawrence and take the first look at the collapse.

Joe found Lawrence lying face down in the darkness with his lower right leg caught under a massive chunk of granite with a solid wall of fallen rock and timbers wedged tight and compacted on top of it. The back of Lawrence's head had a good-sized cut that saturated his hair in his blood. Blood mixed with water also trickled out from under the collapse in a broad stream. Most of it came from the mule that was crushed under the collapse but Joe wondered how much blood Lawrence was losing from his crushed foot. Joe hated to ignore Lawrence but he needed to know the extent of the collapse and raised the candle close to the wall of debris to get a closer look and to watch the flame for any sign of air flow. He was not comforted to find there was minimal air movement. It was not too surprising, there could be a hurricane at the mine portal, and they wouldn't feel a breeze as deep as they were. Just the same, though, he had hoped to see the flame flicker or blown out. Water dripped steadily from the ceiling and from cracks all along the wall. It reminded him of another concern as the water table had risen and would continue to collect at the bottom of the winze where they were trapped. The water level that morning had flooded the winze to right about where he now stood and the more it rained and the snow melted, the higher it would fill the winze with bitterly cold water.

Air quality was a concern but he guessed they had a couple of days' worth in their ninety feet of space. The flooding and the risk of hypothermia are what scared him the most. He had to remind himself that his brother and the others would be working to save them and it helped to calm his nerves. He was alive, the only one uninjured and had to remain composed and strong for the help and encouragement of the others. The reality was he was trapped in a thirty-yard section of flooding space with three injured men and one dead man too. He was startled when a hand grabbing his ankle.

"Joe, can you get that rock off my foot?" Lawrence asked with a desperate cry.

Joe shook his head. There was nothing he could do to help Lawrence with that much weight on his leg. "No. It's too big. I don't know how I can help you, Lawrence. And I don't know how much of that blood is yours or the mule's."

Lawrence rested his face on his arm and began to weep. "Lord, I don't want to die," he wept with a cracking voice.

Joe knelt where Lawrence could see him. Lawrence was lying flat on the wet ground and covered in the mule's blood. "I don't know what to do," Joe said helplessly. "I can't move the rock off you."

Walter held onto the cart and squinted to see what he could in the candlelight. "Any airflow, Joe?" he hollered.

Joe shook his head. "Not much, if any."

"How's Lawrence?" Walter hollered.

"Bad. His foot is caught under a huge piece of the back that came down. We couldn't budge it with a mule."

Walter grimaced. "Oh, Lord, help us out here." He stared at the water building up in the bottom edge of the winze already. "How bad is his leg?"

"Bad! It must be as flat as a hotcake. There is a lot of blood coming from under the rock. I'm pretty sure it's the mule's, it was crushed underneath all of this. But I don't know if Lawrence is losing any or not."

Walter stared down at the ore cart in thought for a moment and came to a decision while listening to Lawrence plead for Joe to do something. "Joe," Walter called out, "I'm not moving too good and Bobby's arm is broken. I can see his arm from here. They will be working to free us but I don't know how extensive that collapse is or how long it will take them. What I do know is we need to keep our heads and think. The first thing we need to do is get Lawrence free from the rock to make sure he doesn't bleed to death or die of hyperthermia." He pulled off his suspenders and unbuttoned them from his pants. "You're going to have to make a tourniquet with my suspenders. So, come grab a short drill to crank it down tight." When Joe walked back down to him, Walter said, "You're going to have to take his leg off."

"What?" Joe asked, horrified. A chill ran down his spine at the thought of causing Lawrence more pain than he was already in. His eyes widened and he shook his head. "I can't do that! He's alive and okay right where he is. Let's just wait for a rescue."

Walter explained calmly, "We might be down here for days, Joe. The water's going to rise and he'll be the first to die if we don't free him. It's best to do it now while we can."

One truth every miner knew was that ignorance kills in the mine and he knew it probably applied to the medical field too. Joe knew absolutely nothing about surgical procedures and even if he was a surgeon, they were deep in a mine and he had no means of amputating a leg. "How am I going to do that? Do you want me to take a hammer and chisel my way through his leg with a rock drill? The drills won't cut through flesh," Joe stated sharply.

"What?" Lawrence's voice shouted from the darkness.

Walter turned towards him and sighed sadly. He

shouted, "Your leg's no good, Lawrence. We have to cut it off."

Lawrence began to panic. "You can't do that. How will I support my wife and my boys?" he cried.

Bobby spoke through deep breaths, "How's the collapse? Can we get out?"

"No. But don't panic, they'll get us out," Joe responded.

Bobby shouted anxiously, "The water's going to rise a hundred feet or more overnight. It's not going to do us any good to survive if we're going to drown!"

"Stop it!" Joe demanded angrily. "We're not dead and we're not going to be. Sit there and breathe!" The pressure of being trapped with his own mortality in question and the more immediate concern of what to do about Lawrence's leg was becoming a heavy burden on his shoulders. Walter was right. The water coming in was ice cold and Lawrence would die if they didn't take his leg off.

Lawrence shouted, "I can stay here until they save us." He was terrified of losing his leg. "The doctor can fix my foot."

Walter bit his bottom lip. He spoke loudly, "We don't have a choice, son. There's not a doctor in the world that can put your leg back together from what Joe tells me. And we need to do it now before your body gets too cold laying in that water."

"With what?" Joe asked, raising his hands helplessly.

"Danny carries a knife for cutting fuses. I can grab that." Walter carefully slid his feet alongside

71

the ore cart until he could reach over to the body of Danny Rosso and took the six-inch blade knife from its sheath on his belt. "Here, Joe."

Joe Thorn was slow to step forward. He could remove a splinter out of his son's finger and pull his son's tooth but to cut off a man's leg wasn't something he felt comfortable with no matter what the circumstances were. The responsibility for changing a man's life forever wasn't one he wanted on his conscience. Joe spoke nervously, "They'll be coming pretty soon to dig us out of here. Maybe we can wait. I don't know if I can do that. What if I mess up and kill him?"

Walter narrowed his eyes irritably. "We already lost one man and if we wait, we'll lose another. That collapse lasted what...four or five seconds and it started up the winze from here. There could be forty, fifty feet of hard rock between them and us or a hundred feet. We don't know. That whole winze could be buried. We may not even get out of here alive but damn it, we're going to do our best to try. Now get over there and tie that tourniquet as close as you can to where you have to sever it off. Try to keep as much of the good leg as you can. If he gets gangrene, the doc has more leg to work with that way. Don't worry about messing up. I'll put it to you like this, the only thing that is going to save his life is you cutting off that leg."

"You're not going to help?" Joe asked Walter softly.

"I can't walk," he said, leaning on the ore cart. "Bobby, go with Joe and hold the candle for him. Grab a short drill for the tourniquet and then tie it off with your boot strings." The drills were solid iron bars between one and three feet long with a blunt head on one end where the hammers hit it and on the other end was a flattened broad dull edge that cut into the rock.

"Joe, cut a piece of the harness off the cart for Lawrence to bite down on." There were about four inches of it connected to the cart still. Joe quickly cut the leather harness off the cart.

Lawrence had tears flowing from his eyes, terrified of the pain ahead and being helpless to prevent it. He was prayed out loud while Joe manipulated the suspenders under his body. Joe forced the suspenders down his leg below his knee until he couldn't get it any further down his leg due to the tibia bone pinned against the ground. Joe tied the suspenders around his leg below the knee and used the steel bar to turn the tourniquet. Lawrence could feel the pressure constrict his calf muscles and the pain increased. Lawrence cried out as Joe tightened the tourniquet as much as he could.

Joe had Bobby hold one end of the drill while Joe tied it in place with his boot string around the thigh. Joe set the candle on a flat rock and lit another candle to see more clearly. Bobby held it over another stone to collect the wax on the opposite side of the leg. Joe cut Lawrence's pant leg to expose his flesh and picked up a candle to sanitize the knife blade. Joe took a deep breath and put the piece of leather in Lawrence's mouth. "Bite on this, my friend. I'm sorry but I have to do this."

Lawrence bit down on the leather strip hard as he could when he felt the knife blade cut into the skin and muscle of his calf. Joe cut as fast as he could to get through the muscle and tissue around the leg down to the bone, seeing by the flickering candlelight. Lawrence cried out loudly and shook his head and pounded on the ground to relieve the pain.

After about five minutes of cutting, Joe looked down the winze towards Walter and shouted, "I can't cut through the bone! Should we bust through it with a drill?"

"Hold on a minute," Walter answered. He maneuvered through an inch of water to the body of Danny and reached into his pockets. Walter found a wadded-up handkerchief and a jackknife in one pocket. He searched another pocket and found a small rolled-up length of firing cord. "Oh, Lord, please," he whispered with a worried breath. He slowly maneuvered himself around the cart a bit further to be able to reach into a pocket on the far side of Danny's body and pulled out a single blasting cap. "Thank you, Jesus."

He handed the blasting cap to Joe. "Place this under his bone. Make sure it's under the bone and not beside it. And then set a drill on top of it and give it a whack with your hammer. It should blow the bone apart and free him. Be sure to cover your face when you hit it."

Joe stared at him in disbelief.

Walter shrugged. "It's that or hammer the knife blade through the bone. This way it's quick and easy."

Joe didn't have the heart to hammer a knife blade through the bone and grabbed a three-foot-long drill and a hammer. He went back and apologized to Lawrence for what he was going to have to do. He put the drill steel on the ground at the edge of Lawrence's shinbone and began to hammer the drill under the bone to wedge it upwards just enough to safely set the blasting cap under the bone without it exploding and taking off Joe's fingers. Lawrence screamed in anguish and tried to lift his body to ease the drill from being hammered against his leg bone. It was excruciating and there was nothing he could do to make it stop.

Joe hit the drill with the hammer until the bone lifted just enough to set the blasting cap under the bone and then slowly, he pulled the drill back until the bone rested on the blasting cap. Joe stood up and placed the flattened edge of the drill on the exposed portion of the blasting cap. He told Bobby to walk away a safe distance and then turned his head and hit the drill with his hammer. The blasting cap exploded and blew bone fragments in all directions. Lawrence passed out from the pain. Joe relit one of the candles and inspected Lawrence's leg. His leg was blown free of the rock but the bone was fragmented and splintered.

"That worked. But now his bone's jagged as a saw blade," Joe shouted down the winze.

Walter spoke, "Use the knife and drill to try to even up the bone. Then use a full candle to cauterize the leg while he's out."

"How did you know he's out?"

"He's not screaming. Get it done now."

Joe used the knife blade to break off the splintered bone pieces as best he could. He used the candle flame to burn the nerve ends, vessels and muscle tissue. When he could hold the candle no longer, he collected the soft wax and rubbed it over the splinted bone to help seal it from the open air. They pulled Lawrence away from the debris and sat him next to the wall, where he remained unconscious.

Walter nodded approvingly. "Good job."

Joe was worried. "I hope he lives."

"Me too. I'm praying so. Now that Lawrence is free, the most important thing we need to do is keep any matches we have dry. How many candles do you have left? I have three."

"Two unused ones."

"Four," Bobby offered.

"We have two burning, so that makes eleven. Blow one of those out, so can we save it. Let's be sparing on our candles and keep our matches dry. All we can do now is relax as best we can and wait. And Lord willing, He'll help us to get out of here. Until then, we have good water, thanks to Lawrence. Help me move uphill where Lawrence is so we can keep him and ourselves warm."

Joe said, "Let me get Danny's body off that drill first." He pulled the cart back just enough to put his body in front of it and pulled Danny's body forward enough for the drill to come out of the wall. When it did, Danny's body fell face down into the water with the drill still sticking out of his chest. Joe stepped aside and let the cart roll forward again. He looked at Walter. "Now, he won't be watching us."

Walter said, "Let's just pray they can get us out of here soon."

Joe took a deep breath and exhaled. "For the first time in my life, I won't argue about that."

into the water which drilled in the top of
his bit. The droplet skated off the cut rock
toward ... to be lost as it ...
... happen ...

Wait ... Jim played ...
... ask you ...

Jim ... gone ... said ... shoving
... the floor of the ...

## 10

Ross Van Horn was forty-nine years old and had worked in the Nevada mines for most of his life before coming to Branson. He was a short and stocky man with broad shoulders and a stern scowl that was as hard as the rock they mined. He walked through the main adit carrying a broken sledge-hammer handle and eight-pound head that a new hire broke over a drill steel. The new hire claimed to have double jacking experience but his inexperience may have fractured a good drill man's forearm with the free-flying hammerhead. Ross was angry and wanted to talk to Jim Longo about firing the liar before he hurt someone else. Ross had sent the liar to go shovel mule dung throughout the mine. A man who cannot swing a hammer could not go wrong shoveling dung.

The ground shook with a jarring shock wave followed immediately by the unmistakable sound of a large amount of falling rock that vibrated the adit floor, which was the main access tunnel into the mine. Fear came in levels and the rumbling sound raised the hair on the back of his neck. Men he knew were in trouble and might not have survived the collapse. Through the sunlight coming in through the portal of the adit ahead, he saw a cloud of gray dust blow out of the south winze with what appeared to be an underlying brownish colored smoke lying closer to the ground. The idea of it was alarming but impossible in their mine. Ross's fear level rose dramatically higher when an acrid smell that irritated his eyes and throat filled the adit.

His eyes widened in horror and he dropped the hammer he was carrying. Black powder smoke from the dynamite they used was white. This smoke was brown, which meant it was a nitrous explosion and not black powder. If nitrous fumes, particularly nitrogen dioxide, overtook the adit, it would travel through the mine, making it far too dangerous for anyone to work in. Ross began running towards the portal yelling, "Blow the whistle, blow the whistle! Everyone out! Everyone get out of here! Henry, go tell them to blow the damn whistle and hold it down until the steams gone! Peter, get everyone out of mine, Go!" he coughed over the strong fumes. He held his breath and ran towards the portal to get out of the mine. Ross reached the portal just in time to grab a young man who was running back inside urgently. "Stay out here," he said with a cough and dragged the boy out into the fresh air.

Leon Jenson was a trammer who was dumping some ore when the explosion happened. He had stayed out until he heard someone say it was coming from the south winze. "My father's in there! I have to help him," he explained to Ross with panic in his eyes.

"Those fumes will kill you! We have to wait for it to dissipate," Ross said, catching his breath with a cough from the gas he had breathed in. The steam whistle blew loudly and kept sounding to let everyone know to evacuate the mine. The whistle mounted at the portal sounded four times per shift; to start work, lunch, end of lunch and when the shift was over. A long, non-stop whistle was an emergency call to evacuate the mine. Soon men came running out of the mine coughing from the nauseous fumes that filled the air.

"Ross, what about my Pa?" Leon pleaded, feeling the terror of possibly losing his father.

"Pray he's okay but I won't let you go in after him."

"You can't stop me!" Leon shouted and stepped around Ross; he was grabbed by Ross and thrown across the ground fiercely. "The hell I can't! Try to go in there again and I'll bust your head open and if you survive that, you'll be better off than going in there! Do you hear me?" he shouted.

Leon's glare softened into desperation as he could see the seriousness in Ross's eyes. "But my Pa's down there."

Ross shook his head. "Leon, go move your tag out of the mine. We'll get your father out when we can. We need to know who is out of there and who is missing." He yelled loudly above the commotion,

"Everyone, move your tags! We need to know who is still in the mine."

Jim Longo ran up the hill from the assay lab towards the portal. "Do you know what happened?" he questioned Ross anxiously.

Ross shook his head. "No. An explosion in the south winze and it wasn't dynamite, Jim. It had brown smoke and that's nitrogen dioxide in there. The explosion was a lot bigger than what we use. I don't know what it was. Nitroglycerine, maybe?"

"We don't use that," Jim responded, confused.

"I know! I can't explain it. Let's do a roll call and see who is missing. That winze is full of gas and it's just going to sit in there like a heavy fog for hours."

Jim widened his eyes in thought about what to do. He had no doubt Ross knew what he was talking about and trusted him even though there was no possible explanation of how the gas could be in their mine. Nitrogen dioxide was a lethal gas that was heavier than oxygen and would set in the winze like bricks of lead if they didn't get some air movement down there. "I have an idea. How far is it from here to the bottom of the winze? Two thousand feet or so?"

"From here? About that." Ross agreed.

"All right." Jim spotted the nearest employee to him and ordered, "Go to the storehouse and ask Vincent how many feet of air hose we have. I need two thousand feet of air hose to hook up to the compressor and I need it now! If he doesn't have that much, tell Vincent to find it! I don't care from where. Go!"

The stamp mill's loud rhythmic pounding became an annoyance as he tried to think and have a conversation. "I'm shutting the mill down. We might be stealing their air hoses."

"What's your idea?" Ross asked dryly.

"Wiring a hose to the bottom axels of an ore cart and sending it down the rails to pump air into winze to help dissipate the gas. It should move the gas out of there and supply those men with fresh air if they're alive. Get these men signed out, so we know who is left in there. I'll be back." He could still see men running out of the mine, coughing and exhaling to breathe in some fresh air.

Ron Dalton sat in his office reading ore reports from various drifts from the company assayer when he heard the stamp mill go quiet. He peered out his window and saw a crowd of men standing outside of the mine with a cloud of dust rising out of the portal.

A moment later, his office door opened and a young man said, "Mister Dalton, the mine collapsed!"

"Where?"

"I don't know."

"Is anyone hurt?"

"I don't know, Sir."

"I'll be right there."

The mine office was upriver from the stamp mill and the mine portal. Several buildings made up the mine site, including the large step-down stamp mill, the pumphouse, boiler house, storeroom, office, and various sheds. Ron put on his coat and hat and walked up the mine to find Jim Longo. He saw a few men hurriedly carrying air hoses from the storage sheds and the storeroom toward the portal where Jim Longo was attaching hoses. An ore cart had a hose wired securely to the bottom of it.

"What happened?" Ron asked.

"An explosion of some type. We don't know."

"Are any men missing?"

Jim answered, "Nine. Seven worked in the south winze and I sent a trammer with water down there before it blew. Danny Rosso must have been down there too. He's unaccounted for. We're going to run an air hose down the winze to help clear out the fumes. Ron, it was not a powder explosion; it was a nitrous explosion of some sort. We don't know what."

"Nitrous? Are you sure?"

"According to Ross, yes. Nitrous dioxide is creeping throughout the mine. We have several men who are having trouble breathing already. And there's probably carbon dioxide and carbon monoxide both laying low in the winze if it was nitrous, as well. We have to get some air flowing down there for an hour or two before we can do anything."

Ron asked, "How can I help?"

"Right now, I just want everyone having trouble breathing to get to the doctors right away. Jacob is getting a wagon hooked up and will drive them to town in a hurry."

"Very good. Do we have everything we need for a rescue?"

Jim exhaled. "I think so. In an hour or two, we'll be able to see what it looks like down there."

## 11

It had been a slow week without too much happening around the county. It allowed Matt some time to take care of the office's more administrative and financial responsibilities. It also allowed him to relax and spend more enjoyable time with his fiancé, Christine Knapp. He had investigations pending into the deaths of Leroy Haywood and Roger Lavigne. They were two very odd deaths that he suspected were done by someone of Chinese descent but he could not prove it was his prime suspect, Wu-Pen Tseng. Now there was a robbery of the assay office and again, he was perplexed how it had been done. Someone made a key to get in and had to have known the safe's combination or been a master thief or a locksmith to open it. In the back of his mind, Wu-Pen's name kept rising as his first suspect and yet, he couldn't catch Wu-Pen in so much as a lie. If Matt spoke Chinese, he could ask questions around Chinatown, but he did not.

There were only two people who spoke Chinese and English to his knowledge. Wu-Pen could, of course, and the only other person who did was his Uncle Luther's employee, Ah See. He decided to talk to Ah See and hear what he had to say about Wu-Pen. Matt put on his coat and hat to go to the granite quarry.

He moved towards the door just when Truet Davis stepped into the Marshal's Office. He was wet from the rain and said, "They brought a wagon load of miners to the doctor's office. Some of them are pretty sick, apparently. I talked to Bruce Ellison. He said there was an explosion at the mine and the fumes made them all sick. He's not as sick as some of the others. He said there are some miners buried in a cave in, including Joe Thorn and Bobby Alper. Bruce is pretty upset about it."

"Slow down. What happened?" Deputy Nate Robertson asked.

"That's bad," Phillip Forrester added sympathetically.

Matt Bannister frowned. "Truet, Nate, let's get our horses and ride out there. We better see if we can do anything to help. We'll stop by Slater's Mile and see if Billy Jo is okay. She's hooked up with Joe again."

The three of them rode two miles out of town to Slater's Mile to check on Matt's cousin, Billy Jo. They turned off the main road to the mine onto the access road leading into the company housing and met Lucille Barton walking out of Slater's Mile. She was visibly upset and had her two little boys with her along with and Billy Jo's two sons. Lucille's two boys were dressed warm but the heavy rain was already soaking through their clothes. Billy Jo's two sons were not dressed for the rain and wore flannel shirts that were far too big for them like coats. Lucille was hysterical, shaken to the core with fear at the news of her husband being trapped in the mine. All four of the children were already wet and cold. Her two boys were crying.

Matt stepped out of the saddle with concern. "Misses Barton, are you okay?"

She shook her head emotionally while holding her little boy, Ray, in her arms. Her voice was high pitched and desperate, "I was just told the mine caved in and Lawrence is missing. I have to get there and be with him."

"Oh, no," Matt said as a flood of empathy and concern came over him. The fear of losing her husband showed clearly in her anxious and lost expression. Matt removed his hat and put it on his saddle horn. "There's no better time to pray. The one thing I know is you never give up hope, okay? Until you hear, otherwise, you keep your hope alive. That's the best we can do, Misses Barton. Let's pray right now:"

"Father, we come before you and ask for your protection and mercy upon Lawrence and the other men trapped in the mine. We ask for your protective hand upon their lives and that you will spare them today. I ask that you comfort Lucille's heart and give her the strength and courage to get through this agonizing time of waiting to know about Lawrence. We also ask that you'll help the other men working to free them. We know you are in control and we will trust you with their lives. We put our hope in you, Lord, Amen."

"Thank you," she wept.

"You're very welcome. Is Billy Jo home?"

She shook her head. "I have her boys."

"Did she go to the mine?"

She shook her head, squeezing her lips together tightly weeping.

Matt asked Wyatt Fasana. "Where's your mother?"

Wyatt shrugged with his bottom lip quivering. "In town. She said Grandad was sick again."

Lucille spoke, "Her father's been sick for a while now. I thought he was getting better. I have to go be with Lawrence, Matt."

Matt's heart was breaking for her but he was also quite aware of the children being wet and shivering already. "Lucille," he called her by her first name. "It is far too wet and cold for these children to be in this weather for very long. The silver mine is no place where children should be."

"I can't wait here!" she exclaimed emotionally. "I want to know what happened to my husband! I don't know if he's dead or alive. I can't stay here and no one is here to watch them! I waited for Billy Jo, but she hasn't come back. I have to find my husband!" she exclaimed pointedly and then began crying uncontrollably.

Matt put a hand on the outside of her shoulder to get her attention. "I can understand that. Can I get your permission to take the children to my sister-in-law and let her keep them warm and fed? She'll take good care of them while you wait at the mine. Can I do that? You could be waiting for hours and this is no weather or experience you want these children at, I promise."

She stared into his eyes as if debating if she could trust him or not. "How will I find them?" she asked in a broken voice.

"I'll bring them back when you go home. I'm coming out to the silver mine after I take Billy Jo's boys to my sisters-in-law's house. I hope you'll let me take your boys there, too. Your children will be fine. Trust me."

She continued to stare at him hesitantly even though she could see he was quite sincere. She finally relented and nodded her head.

Matt spoke at his cousin's two sons, "Wyatt, you and Brice get on Nate's horse." He bent over and spoke with Lucille's oldest boy Michael and the toddler, Ray, to explain to them where he was taking them for a little while. Matt was a stranger and they had never been away from their mother before. They were crying and little Ray was screaming when Matt held him in his arm and got in the saddle before helping Michael up behind him. Crying women and children were a soft spot in Matt's heart and he did not want to traumatize the boys, so he spoke softly and handed the reins to Ray and took turns letting the boys control the reins while they rode into town. It calmed them both and made the ride fun for them. He and Nate took the four boys to Albert and Mellissa Bannister's house, where Matt explained to Mellissa what had happened. Mellissa warmly welcomed the children into her home with a loving hug for each of them. Her eyes were filled with sympathetic tears as she held little Ray Barton in her arms when Matt and Nate left. Truet had given Lucille a ride to the mine.

Matt and Nate rode to Luther Fasana's house but the door was locked and no one was home. They rode out to the granite quarry and found Luther in the office with his red tick hound lying lazily beside his feet. The dog got up and jumped up on Matt to be petted.

Matt bent over to pet the dog that used to belong to his friend Chusi Yellowbear. "Uncle Luther, we stopped by your house. Are you feeling better?" Matt asked after a quick hello.

Luther was perplexed. "I didn't know I wasn't feeling good. What makes you think that?"

"That's what Billy Jo told her neighbor when she left her boys there. It seems like you've been sick a lot lately."

"No, I'm fine. Why would she say that? I haven't seen her in at least two weeks," he said through a yawn.

Matt shrugged his shoulders. "I don't know. The mine collapsed and I heard Joe is inside somewhere. I don't know where she is but I figured she'd want to know that her boys are at Albert and Mellissa's."

Luther bit his bottom lip and clicked his tongue against his cheek. "I dislike Joe Thorn a great deal. But I hope he is okay. It's never good to wish harm on someone, no matter how much I may dislike him. I'll get my grandsons right now and take them to my place. I haven't seen Billy Jo. I see she's using my accounts at the stores and butcher but she hasn't talked to me. So, if you find her, let her know I'm feeling fine and thank her for the concern. Maybe she ought to come to see me some time. I guess she'll have to sooner or later to get the boys."

Matt chuckled lightly. "If I see her, I'll let her know."

"And if they need any help out there, tell Ron we'll do whatever we can."

"Will do."

## 12

Billy Jo sat on the davenport next to Wes Wasson, holding his hand. In truth, he had taken hold of her hand and she allowed him to keep holding it. She had shared with him that she was moving back into her house and no longer in a relationship with Joe. She had shown him the bruising on her ribs and the cut inside of her lip and Wes held her comfortingly and that bit of comfort was something she longed for. She felt safe in his presence. The sensation of feeling secure in a cold and hard world was one she hadn't known since she was growing up. She felt secure then and now she felt it with Wes. The kiss the day before had broken a barrier of fear that she was now free from and kissed Wes again with brighter eyes and full expectation of a brighter future.

His smile couldn't be contained with the excitement of winning the heart of the lady he couldn't get his mind off.  He had not expected to fall so hard for a young lady but here he was letting go of her hand and putting an arm around her shoulders to hold her closer. "If I could, I'd rent a wagon and go with you to get your things, the boys and move you back home. Unfortunately, I'm not able to yet."

She leaned against his shoulder and slapped his leg casually. "No worries. I'll go back and get the boys and a bag of clothes and bring them home. All our furnishings are at my place anyway. My Pa will go back with me if I forget anything. Joe will hit on me if I'm alone but he won't do anything with my pa or cousins around."

"I just want you to be safe. I don't want to see you all busted up the next time I see you," Wes said softly.

"No, I'll be fine. He won't get home for hours, so I have plenty of time. Me and the boys will stay at my Pa's tonight until I can get some wood delivered and some food in the house. And when you're ready, you can move in," she said with a grin.

"Are you sure you want me to move in? It's going to be a while before I can work like I used to be able to."

His sincerity touched her heart. "I'll take care of you until you heal."

"What about money? I have a little left but I intended to get to work when I talked about renting your house. I'm healing but my foot is healing slow. And so are my shoulders, to be honest. I couldn't throw grain bags for long, right now."

Billy Jo's blue eyes gazed upon him, adoringly. "My Pa owns the granite quarry; all I have to do is use his accounts and he pays for everything for the boys and me. He despises Joe but I think he'll like you a lot better."

"I hope so. I look forward to meeting him. Do you think I could find some work at the quarry?"

"Absolutely. I can get you hired on there."

Wes laughed. "You sound so sure of that."

"I am. I'll be moving into my house tomorrow or the next day, depending on when the wood is delivered. You can move in anytime you want to afterward."

Wes hesitated. He wasn't used to someone taking care of him nor wanting to become a burden. "I'll wait until I can put weight on my foot and go to work. I am looking forward to it but until then you can come over here without worrying about Joe finding out. We can make it official-like."

"What?"

"Huh?"

"Make what official like?" she asked with a knowing smile.

He grinned slowly. "Us."

She turned into him to kiss him. Their lips touched and opened into a passionate kiss. She pulled away just a bit to say, "Who knew we'd find each other two weeks ago?"

He chuckled. "I did."

She kissed him and closed her eyes as his arms went around her. She didn't stop kissing him when she heard the front door open, she knew Florence Ellison was supposed to be coming home from her neighbor's soon.

"Billy Jo?" Bruce Ellison asked with surprise.

"Uncle Wes?"

Billy Jo sat back in a hurry wiping her lips with her sleeve. She stared at Bruce with horrified eyes.

"You caught us," Wes said with an easy grin. "What are you doing home?"

Bruce was stunned. "There was a cave-in. Joe's still in the mine. We don't know if he's dead or alive."

Her jaw slowly opened with shock. "There was a cave-in?"

"Yeah. Everyone in the south winze is still there. Joe, Bobby and Walter Kendrick and four others in the drift. Danny Rosso and Lawrence are missing too. About ten of us inhaled some bad fumes and came to town to see the doctor. I'll be okay but some of the other guys who couldn't hold their breath long enough to get out are in bad shape. It was a nitrogen dioxide from something in the air. I don't know what they found. I would go back to help but I'm just not feeling well." He paused and then asked, "What are you two doing? How do you even know each other?"

Wes smiled. "We met at her place. We kind of hit it off if you know what I mean." He laughed.

"What about Joe?"

"We didn't hit it off so well," Wes answered with a wry smile.

"No, I was asking Billy Jo."

She answered awkwardly, "I'm leaving him. But I do want to go out to the mine and make sure he's okay." She stood up. "You said, Lawrence, not Lawrence Barton, right?"

"Yes, Lawrence Barton. He was down there

too, I guess."

"Oh, my gosh!" she exclaimed and walked over to grab her coat and put it on. "Lucille is watching the boys. I have to go, Wes. Sorry. I'll be back tomorrow." She asked Bruce, "Are you going back out there?"

He shook his head. "No. I'm going to lay down. The doctor told me to get some rest."

Matt Bannister and Nate Robertson rode back towards the mine when they approached a blonde-haired woman wearing blue jeans and a long flannel shirt showing under a soaking wet wool coat. She glanced back at the riders as they came close to her side.

"Matt," she said, surprised. "I heard the mine caved in. Can you give me a ride out there?"

Matt narrowed his eyes irritably. She repeatedly lied about her father to leave her children with a neighbor and his curious nature wanted to know why. Secrecy usually yielded no good and when it came to Billy Jo and her choices, he expected the worst. "I can. From what I understand he's trapped in the mine. But first, do you know where your children are?" he asked suddenly with annoyance.

"Of course, I do!" she answered sharply. "Lucille has them. Why do you always speak to me like I'm a child? Do you think you can ever talk nicely to me?"

Matt ignored her statement. "Lawrence Barton is still in the mine too, so I took the Barton children and your boys to Albert and Mellissa's to keep them warm and dry. Your father is going to pick them up now and taking them back to his place. That's where you will find them."

"Oh. Well, thank you. I never expected something like this to happen when I left them this morning." She reached her hand up to be helped behind the saddle.

Matt took her hand to help her and said, "Lucille told me you said your Pa was sick a lot lately. Oddly, he didn't know that. He wanted me to tell you he's feeling fine and thanks for the concern."

Being caught in a lie angered her. She pulled her hand out of his and crossed her arms defensively while her cheeks reddened and her eyes grew hard. "I'm not your wife, Matt. Where I go is my business!" she snapped bitterly.

Matt was taken off guard by her reaction. He noticed her lip was swollen. "Billy Jo, you're plenty old enough to do what you want. I see your lips fattened again."

"If it is any of your business, I'm leaving Joe and moving back into my house," she answered irately.

"Good. I hope you stay away from him this time," he said. "Now how about you climb on; I'll give you a ride to your place so you can change into some dry clothes and then we'll ride out to the mine. Lord willing, Joe and the others will be okay." He lowered a hand to help her swing up behind the saddle.

She remained crossed armed and glaring at him coldly. "You don't like him anyway, so what's it matter to you?"

Matt grinned and shook his head. "I don't have to like Joe to hope he's okay. Can we start over, Billy Jo, or shall I leave?" His voice hardened, just a touch.

Her eyes filled with moisture. "I just found out Joe could be dead and you harassed me about where my boys were. How do you expect me to be? Joyful?"

"Oh, I see," he said with a degree of sarcasm. "First of all, I did not harass you, I told you where your boys are. You are mad because I caught you lying about your Pa. And I haven't even asked you why yet."

"Maybe it's because I need to get a break from my kids occasionally. Did you ever think of that? Maybe I shouldn't have told Lucille that, but I did. Okay? It is nice to get away from them sometimes and their fighting. Why couldn't you just tell me where my boys were rather than questioning me? I don't want to be interrogated like one of your criminals! It seems like every time I see you, you're interrogating or yelling at me about going back to Joe or something. Why is it we seem to get on each other's nerves the more we try to talk?"

Matt paused to take a moment to think her words over. "You're right. I was rude to you when I rode up. I apologize..."

"Oh yeah, I'd say so! It's not anything I'm not used to though. You're always rude to me."

"No, I'm not either. But we can argue about that later. How about we just get you home and then out to the mine?" He reached a hand towards her to help her up behind him. "Get on."

"Thank you," she said with a bitter look in her eyes as she swung up behind the saddle. "I hope Joe's okay. I don't know what I'd do without him."

Matt turned his head back towards her. "I thought you just said you were leaving him?"

"I was until I heard what happened," she answered honestly.

## 13

Three hours had passed from when Matt had taken the children into town and when he rode onto the mine property with Billy Jo. Mine employees stood around the mine's portal anxiously waiting and taking turns to help where they could. Loose rock was hauled out, but the compressed rock and splintered timbers that made up the collapse's bulk were much more complicated to extract. A large section of the ceiling and right-side wall had collapsed. Locating any survivors was every man's goal but the rescuers' safety was just as important. They first needed to brace the fractured ceiling and walls of the winze with new timbers and caps. Shoring was required to protect the rescuers from any fractured material that could potentially collapse. It took time but for the safety of the men working, it needed to be done. How far along the winze the debris fell, there was no way of knowing until they reached the end of the collapsed material. The work was strenuous with a lot of tension was in the air. There was plenty of smaller free rock that could be picked up and hauled out but the majority of the collapse were large pieces that needed to be drilled and blown into smaller pieces to move. It was a very slow process of drilling a hole or as many as needed to be able to remove it. The powder man measured just enough black powder to break the rock and not cause a larger problem with more falling in. An air hose on the ground pumped in clean air but they had to evacuate the winze to allow the Nitrogen Dioxide to dissipate after every blast. When the air was good enough to go back in, an ore cart was rolled down the rails, filled quickly and pulled out as fast as they could rush the mules and dumped outside of the mine. As soon as one ore cart left the winze, an empty one was entering it. Once a few feet were cleared, timbers needed to be measured, cut and set in place with a cap and wedges hammered in place to make the space as safe as they could before the work could continue. Every man volunteered to become a mucker, trammer or a drill man, a carpenter, or anything else they could do to help reach their fellow miners.

Richie Thorn worked as hard as he could to reach his brother, as did others related to the trapped men. Branson was a small community and many family members worked together at the mine. It would be quicker to use one of the new compressed air-powered drills. But with the questionable integrity of the rock around them, it was safer to drill holes for the explosives by hand. It gave less vibration, dust, fewer fumes and noise. Being able to hear the slightest sound of shifting rock, cracking, or any sound out of the ordinary was vitally important as it could save the rescuer's lives. It was a slow process and was going to take some time.

Downhill in front of the stamp mill beside the river, Wu-Pen Tseng and about twenty-five Chinese men had set up a vast tent made of multiple canvas tarps sewn together over the top of a same-sized canvas tarp floor. They staked the sides down tight and put up a canvas lean-to about ten feet long on the front of the tent held up by poles buried six inches in the ground. It was quick, efficient and they put a small potbellied stove inside with a metal stove pipe running out the top of the canvas wall. The tent was about forty feet long and twenty feet wide to keep the miners' families warm and dry. On the tent's left side was another covered lean-to where a series of campfires were used for cooking by the Chinese. Under the lean-to in front of the large tent was a series of tables that served hot and cold Chinese food, coffee and tea. The tent was furnished with small folding stools made of wood, bolts and canvas seats where the miners or families could sit and eat on plates Wu-Pen provided.

Matt walked over to the tent and admired the line of campfires set up with men in strange-looking grass pipal raincoats cooking over the fires. The aroma of the cooking food was inviting. Matt went inside the tent and was not surprised to see so many women with their families praying or impatiently waiting for anyone to give them some hope that their loved ones were alive and well.

Wu-Pen smiled when he saw Matt and approached him quickly. "Marshal Bannister, are you hungry? We have lots of food. How about a hot cup of coffee or tea?"

"Coffee would be nice."

Truet stepped to Matt's side. "There's not much we can do here. The community is pulling together pretty well. The Reverend's here and the Sheriff was here. Wu-Pen has this all set up and a lot of people are praying for survivors. Your friend, Lucille's been pretty upset. Billy Jo is sitting with her and a group of ladies."

Wu-Pen brought Matt a cup of coffee. "Here you are. If you get hungry, please feel free to help yourself. No cost. It's our way to give to this community in a time of need. Plates are over there. If you need a blanket or anything else, please ask."

Matt furrowed his brow curiously. "You did all this, this fast?"

Wu-Pen smiled proudly. "Yes. Chinese food does not take long to make. All our people helped and brought what we had to offer. I do not feel like it's too much. I have men of experience to help move the rock but the Americans are not welcoming them. They are here if allowed to help. We will be here until those men are found in this tragedy."

Matt put out his hand to shake. "Thank you."

Wu-Pen shook his hand. "Our pleasure."

Truet stated, "The food's good."

"I'm not hungry right now. I am impressed,

102

though," Matt said, looking around and smelling the aroma of the food. He took a drink of the coffee. "It's been four or five hours since the accident and they have this all organized and set up already?"

Truet widened his eyes in emphasis. "Yeah!"

"Wow. Have the Slater's been out here yet?" Matt asked.

Truet shook his head. "Not to my knowledge. I've walked around a few times but honestly, there isn't much we can do except be here."

Matt sighed. "I feel helpless just standing here, myself, but that's what we'll do just in case things heat up later. If nothing else, we'll give our support to the families and miners. That's where our responsibilities are today."

Matt carried his coffee cup outside and leaned a corner of the stamp mill to watch the men uphill at the mine. He prayed quietly as the rain continued to fall. He wished he could go into the mine and labor to help but all he could do was wait like the wives, sons and daughters inside of the tent. The irony was interesting, those agonizing families who had probably never spoken to a Chinese person were being kept warm, dry and fed by the least appreciated people in Branson.

A group of men walked downhill from the portal to get something to eat and drink. A shorter broad-chested man with a round face left the group and neared Matt. "Marshal Bannister, you might remember me. I introduced myself when you first started here in town. I'm the day shift assistant supervisor, Ross Van Horn." He coughed into his hand a few times.

"Sure, I remember. How are you doing, Mister Van Horn?" Matt asked while shaking the man's other hand.

Ross answered, "Not well at all. I got a few breaths of that bad air and it's got me shorter on breath. I'm heading out to see the doctor after all. The big boss man told me to get, so I am going. Whatever caused that explosion was a dandy."

"Explosion?" Matt asked, surprised. "I thought it was a cave-in."

Ross shook his head. "No. There was an explosion unlike anything we use and it was a big one."

Matt narrowed his brow. "What does that mean?"

"We use black powder dynamite. You know, it smells like sulfur. This explosion filled the mine with Nitrogen Dioxide. It's a far more acrid smell and had brown smoke. Nothing we use does that."

"I don't understand."

Ross took a deep breath to expand his lungs and coughed. "The Slater's are cheap as hell. We use black powder dynamite and it's the only explosive we use. Nitrous gas, like Nitrous Dioxide, comes from dynamite made of nitroglycerin. It's more powerful, and trust me, that shock wave was big even from five hundred feet below us. Whatever exploded was nitrous based. I can't explain what it was or where it comes from. But I felt the shock wave, saw the smoke and breathed in the fumes. I know what it was."

Matt frowned curiously. "You don't know how it could've happened? Could there have been a mix up with the shipping?"

Ross shook his head slowly. "Not a chance. We buy straight from a black powder company. Nitroglycerine would run them out of business. Besides, we only blast at the end of the winze where they're mining, not the road's junction. It appears to have exploded where a drift leaves the winze like a fork in the road. There is no explanation why anything would explode there. None at all. We clear the men out before any dynamite is even taken down there anyway. If there was an accidental explosion, no one would be down there except the powder man. He is missing too, by the way. So even if it was an accident on his part, it still doesn't explain the Nitrous Dioxide." He intentionally lowered his voice, "I'll be honest with you, Marshal, we sent ten or so men to the doctor for breathing the fumes; I'm going myself as I said. We don't want to tell the families this but it will be a miracle if any of those men are alive. If those fumes made so many men sick far from the blast point, just think what it did to anyone who survived being that close to the source. Those men up there are working hard to save their friends and brothers but the odds are against finding anyone alive. If the falling rock didn't kill them, the gases will, and if the gases don't, the flooding will if we don't get to them fast enough. Carbon monoxide, carbon dioxide and nitrous dioxide, all three will be down there. It's been almost five hours and it's a losing battle. When those men are found, this place is going to be nothing but wailing families. And we'll probably never know how it happened because there won't be much of a trace."

"No natural possibilities like pockets of gas or anything like that they might've run into accidentally?" Matt asked.

Ross shook his head. "No. It's unexplainable. Once the way is clear and the men are out, Lord willing alive, we can look and maybe figure it out but until then, I know what I saw and it wasn't normal. I have to go, Marshal."

"There's a lot of unexplainable things going on around here, lately," Matt replied quietly.

"Oh yeah? Well, this is another. Take care, Marshal."

## 14

Lawrence was awakened abruptly by the fire consuming his leg. He screamed and flailed his arms to quench the excruciating flames but there was no fire, there was no light. His hand hit a steel bar on his thigh and he hurriedly tried to untie the knot that held it in place. Disorientated by the pitch-black darkness and the sound of trickling water and constant dripping. He didn't know where he was or how he got there, all he knew was he was on fire without a flame in an abyss of darkness and alone. It terrified him.

"Lawrence, we're right here," Walter said sitting beside him. "It's okay. Joe light a candle."

"I can't see! My leg's on fire. Put it out! I can't see my leg!" Lawrence began to scream. "Get the fire off my leg!"

Joe lit a match then lit a candle in a holder that he had pounded into the wall above where they all were sitting. With the cold water coming in and no way of staying dry, they all sat together against the wall close to solid timbering that held the ceiling securely. In the faint light, Joe watched Lawrence's terrified expression become one of shock when he gazed at his lower leg.

"My leg...where's my leg? Oh, Jesus, Lord, please no." He covered his face with his hands and began weeping.

Walter put a large arm around Lawrence's shoulders and pulled him close. "You'll be all right, Lawrence. You know God never lets us go through something without a plan of his own. Although this looks bad right now, once we're out of here, you'll be all right somehow. The Lord promises that. Right?" Walter was in similar circumstances as Lawrence. With a broken hip that may never heal, he knew his working career could be over as well. He held tightly onto his faith and trusted the Lord to take care of him and his family. Walter wanted to remind Lawrence to do the same.

Lawrence glared at Walter. He shouted, "How can this be all right? I don't have my foot!" He pointed towards his feet. "Look! How is it going to be okay?" His pants were cut above the knee and his leg was blown off a few inches below it. Splinters of bone protruded out of his freshly cut flesh. He moved his left foot and tried to move the right foot but nothing happened. He covered his face and wept.

Walter exhaled sympathetically. "We didn't have a choice, Lawrence. Your foot was crushed flat and we couldn't leave you on the ground to die. I know it looks bad but you're a Christian man and I'll remind you that Jesus isn't going to abandon you and your family because you lost part of your leg."

Horrified didn't quite define the terror of seeing his foot missing and a jagged bone sticking out of his leg. His leg burned like hell and the pain was constant but he felt numb to the people around him. Walter's words about the Lord seemed ill-timed and angered him. "The Lord isn't going to replace my foot!" he replied bitterly to Walter.

"No, he isn't. Lawrence, all I'm saying is don't limit the Almighty by your circumstances. He is far greater than you or I will ever know while on this earth. So do not lose hope for the future because you lost part of your leg. The Lord's provided for us pretty well so far and I believe we're going to get out of here."

"Provided?" Joe Thorn asked scornfully. "Are you kidding? We're five hundred feet underground with one-man dead. You have a broken hip, Lawrence lost a leg and Bobby's got a broken arm. We're all soaking wet and hoping they can save us before we all die of hypothermia. I wouldn't say we're blessed, Walter."

Walter took a drink from a jug of water. "We have fresh water, the air's not bad, we found everything we needed to help Lawrence, and despite our wounds, we're still alive and in good shape, really. I call that a blessing. And I don't think Jesus would have brought us this far for nothing. I believe we'll be saved. We'll be okay."

Joe wiped a few small rocks away and laid

down on his side on the rough wet floor to ease the soreness of sitting on the hard ground. The wet ground didn't matter as he was already wet. Keeping the matches dry was their highest priority and Joe kept his matches shoved down into the upper part of his work boot. "What do you think, Lawrence?" he asked.

Lawrence drank some water with Walter's help. "I think my leg is killing me."

"Are you losing your faith?" Joe asked.

Lawrence rubbed the large painful bump on the back of his head and noticed the sticky matted hair from a cut. His breathing was heightened with his attempt to deal with the throbbing pain. "No. You've always teased me about being a Christian but the truth is that even if I were killed today, I would've gone to Heaven. And if that's the worst that can happen to me, then fine, it isn't that bad at all. That's my faith and I will stand on that. What's yours?"

Joe took a deep breath and exhaled as he turned to his back on the uncomfortable cold ground and looked up toward the flickering candlelight on the winze ceiling. "I don't know."

Lawrence grimaced with a wave of discomfort. "Joe, I really don't feel like talking but if we don't get out of here, you need to know this. If this is our last day on earth, that means you will be facing the Lord very soon. The Bible says, *'It is appointed once for man to die, and then the judgment.'* You can laugh at Christians like me if you want to, but the fact remains, judgment comes after death and the results are dependent on your faith and acceptance of Jesus. No one else can help you, forgive you or accept you into Heaven. It's just that simple. Accept Jesus as your savior and live for him and you'll be securely in God's hands."

Joe looked at the exhausted and agony-filled expression on Lawrence's face and said nothing more.

Bobby Alper stood up to ease his aching backside. His broken arm was swollen and discolored and supported in a sling made of his two boot strings. "I grew up going to church but haven't gone in years. I'll tell you guys what, earlier when the blast happened, and Lawrence was screaming in the darkness. It scared the hell out of me because that was probably about as close to hell as I ever want to be. I read what Jesus said about hell and I want no part of it. If we survive this, I swear I'm going back to church and becoming a Christian again. All I've been doing is sitting here, praying and begging God for one last chance." He gasped emotionally and covered his face with his good hand to wipe his tears.

Walter found it painful to stand but it was equally painful to sit on the hard rock without the mobility to adjust his weight like the others could. His discomfort was revealed in his voice, "Bobby if you ask Jesus to forgive your sins, he will welcome you right back into his family like the story of the Prodigal Son. He has not forgotten you and loves you just as much as he ever has. Heed that call, Bobby, and come home where you belong. Jesus is saying, 'come home, brother, our Father is going to celebrate today because of you.'"

Bobby wiped his tears off his face. He turned towards the wall and bowed his head. "Jesus, forgive me for my sins. I pray that you'll accept me back into your Kingdom today. I swear, I'll serve you right this time if you'll give me the chance to." He began weeping quietly into his hand.

Lawrence leaned his head back against the wall and watched him. "Welcome home, Bobby."

"Am I the only one that didn't grow up in a Christian home?" Joe asked.

"It appears so," Walter answered trying to lean more towards his good hip.

"What about Danny? Did he go to heaven?" Joe asked, sounding bitter.

Lawrence's eyes widened. The blast and what happened after was a bit of a blur to him. "Is Danny dead?"

Walter took a breath. "He is. The ore cart slammed him against the rock face." There was no need to go into the details. Joe had asked him a tough question. "Joe, I don't know what Danny's relationship with Jesus was like. What I can tell you is that Jesus is the perfect judge and his justice is right and true. I hope Danny is in heaven."

"What makes you and Lawrence so high and mighty that you'd go heaven but just hope Danny did?" Joe snapped quickly.

Walter grunted as he tried to lift himself to readjust the weight on his hip. He answered simply, "Just Jesus. It's all about Jesus and relying upon him not just for salvation but also for everything in our lives. Jesus makes all the difference between heaven and hell. That's all the reason I can give you, because above all else, what else matters? If you went to hell today and you thought back on your life, what would matter more than your sudden knowledge of Jesus? Nothing matters more. We all have regrets but that would be the biggest regret you would live with for all eternity. You should have listened and accepted Jesus. It doesn't get any deeper or more important than that."

"Regrets," Joe said slowly. "Are any of you thinking about what you regret? I mean, if we don't get out of here."

Bobby answered, "Not being faithful to the Lord. I knew better. I just got caught up in the drinking and womanizing and such. Never again, though!"

Walter sat thoughtfully as he held Lawrence under his arm to keep him warm. They were all cold but Lawrence was the smallest of the men and was having a harder time staying warm. "I regret missing the years of my children's youth. I worked all the time and missed them growing up. That's a regret I have."

Joe spoke, sounding slightly bitter, "Lawrence, I know you don't have any regrets. You're the perfect husband, perfect father, and a good guy, geez, you're like the perfect man."

"I regret coming to work today," he responded.

Joe laughed as did the others.

"No, seriously. Lucille asked me to take today off and talk to the granite quarry about a job. I wanted to get out of the mine. We were going to ask Billy Jo if we could rent her house. I regret not taking today off. I'd still have a leg and wouldn't be here."

Joe shook his head slowly. "Bad timing all the way around. Even if you had skipped work and they hired you, you'd still be out of luck. Billy Jo told me she was moving back into her house today. You just don't have good luck at all," Joe said with a slight chuckle. "Seriously, do you have any regrets, Lawrence?"

"Not taking today off. I regret not going to seminary to be a reverend. I got married and worked all our marriage life on my Pa's farm. I wish I had studied to be in the ministry."

Walter offered, "Maybe now you can."

Lawrence exhaled tiredly. "There's no seminary around here. I wanted to learn Greek and all about Hebrew history and customs. Things like that." He hesitated. "What about you, Joe, any regrets?"

Joe gave a quiet, dull chuckle. He felt the strange warmth of moisture fill his eyes and sniffled. "Too many to name. Dang, it seems like my whole life is a regret now that I lay here thinking back. I have a lot of regrets."

"Do you want to name a few?" Walter invited.

Joe scoffed. "Where to start?"

Lawrence shifted uncomfortably on the rock floor. The slight movement brought a wave of pain from his leg. "Maybe with Billy Jo and your boys?"

Joe peered at Lawrence with downturned lips. "Yeah. I haven't been the best husband and father to them, have I?"

"You're not a husband," Bobby stated.

"True. I suppose I should have married Billy Jo.

114

I've been with plenty of women but I've never been with one longer than her. I wish I would have treated her better and the boys. Walter, when you said you regret not spending time with your children, it punched me in the gut. I'm guilty of that too. Most of the time, I don't want to put up with them when I'm tired, impatient or just want to be left alone. I was never too excited when Billy Jo said she was pregnant, to begin with, but I love the boys. And now, lying here, I hope I get the chance to hold them one more time and tell them that I love them. They probably haven't heard that in years, if ever."

"Joe, you have to let your kids know you love them," Walter volunteered.

Joe spoke quietly, "My boy, Wyatt, told me that he hated me last night. I don't think it was a momentary thing either. I think he hates me. Brice probably does too. At least that what's Billy Jo told me this morning. She said none of them love me anymore and that's why she was taking the boys and leaving." He shook his head slowly as the moisture grew thicker in his eyes. "But the biggest regret, right now, is I got angry and told Billy Jo I hated them too this morning, and Wyatt was standing in the bedroom door. You should've seen his face. Yeah, that's a regret."

"Oh Joe…" Lawrence said empathetically. "He's such a good kid."

"I wish I would've married their mother and raised them in a marriage like yours, Lawrence. I watch you and Lucille take your boys for walks and play with them. I see the way you all laugh and enjoy each other. Billy Jo and I don't have that. The reason I've always made fun of you is because of the way you are. You're happy no matter what, your wife's happy, your children are happy. I look in my boys' eyes and all I see is anger. Believe it or not, I try to be a good father, but I'm not. I don't even know where I went wrong."

Lawrence spoke, "We came by your place last night and heard you and Billy Jo fighting. What you two do is your business but it doesn't help to scream at their mother and hit her. We could hear that from the street."

The slab of granite that crushed Lawrence's foot couldn't have been a heavier weight than the guilt that weighed on Joe's chest. He sighed and spoke softly, "I suppose not. That is another regret. Like I said, I have many. Normally, I'd keep working, drinking and moving forward day by day without thinking about it at all. But now that we're here, those regrets are all I can think about. Do you ever feel like your life is nothing more than mistakes you can't fix? Even though I wish I could. I wish I were more like you, Lawrence. I hope I get a chance to tell Billy Jo and my boys that I'm sorry." His eyes burned with moisture. He stood and asked, "I wonder how high the water's getting?" He lit another candle and walked away towards the end of the winze.

"I think he's crying," Bobby whispered.

Soon Joe came walking back up towards them. "The tail end is full of water. You can't see the cart anymore. I figure we've been in here about what five-six-seven hours? I figure they have about a day to get us out of here until we're swimming and sucking in air bubbles if we can find one in the darkness." He sat down on the wet ground. "I haven't heard them getting closer to us at all, have any of you?"

"They are working as hard as we would be, I'm sure of it," Walter said confidently. "Until then, I suggest we extinguish the candle for an hour or two to save it. We may have a long wait ahead."

DRAGON'S FIRE

## 15

Matt stayed out of everyone's way and did what he could to help, including carrying water, coffee, tea, and meals to the portal to feed the hungry men. He still didn't feel like he was helping near enough. Matt was out of his element though and he knew it. Miners were a tough and courageous breed of men who risked their lives everyday deep within the earth doing physical labor that Matt doubted he could do all day long. His aunt, Mary, owned a silver tea set that she kept in a glass door hutch to be seen but not particularly used. Matt never considered how many men risked their lives or died to pull that silver out of a mine. Silver was desirable; whether it was a silver dollar or silver-plated revolver, the precious metal had value and appealed to most everyone. Dentists used silver to fill cavities daily and many men like Matt wanted a silver wedding band. However, very few considered the dangers to the men who pulled the silver out of the ground. Matt had always respected the miners' toughness in town but he had failed to appreciate them and the way they were earning his respect now for their dedication and no-nonsense determination to reach their friends.

Wu-Pen had asked Matt to talk to Jim Longo to see if he could use the Chinese men's help that worked for the mine. So far, they had been unwelcomed to help.

Jim Longo's face was covered with patches of mud from working inside of the mine. He sighed with exhaustion. "We're going to be working all night, so yeah, we can use the Chinese help to muck out the waste rock and help carry wood and build shoring. After I eat, I'll take some of them up there and give my men a break and a few hours to rest. These guys have been working nonstop since this morning. How is the Chinaman food, is it any good?" Jim asked quickly, looking at the large pots and bowls of unfamiliar dishes.

"The food is surprisingly good. Grab a plate and I'll let Wu-Pen know so he can get his men ready to work. They've been standing around waiting for hours."

A mine employee stood near Jim listening to him talk to Matt. The man was rough looking, with ear-length uncombed brown hair, green eyes and a beard. He approached the table to look at the food with disdain. He turned towards Jim. "What is this crap? I can't believe you're eating this moss and cat meat. You're not really going to let the coolies help us up there, are you?"

"Yeah, we can use their help and you can take a break, Mark," Jim replied simply. "They can do the mucking, as I said."

"I'm not working with them! You can take all these Chinese back to town where they belong. Take the damn slop, they call food with them!" Mark shouted. He stepped around to the backside of a table that held a large pot of hot soup that Bing Jue was serving. The miner flung the pot of soup off the table, spilling it out on the ground. Bing stepped back quickly and glared at Mark fiercely.

"What are you sneering at? Go home!" Mark shouted at Bing and pointed towards town.

"Mark!" Jim shouted, "knock it off! They are here helping us. Get back up to the mine or go home!"

Mark ignored Jim and with a resentful sneer, he threw a hard-right fist towards Bing's face.

Bing's right hand moved with blinding speed to stop the roundhouse swing with his open palm catching the inside of Mark's elbow, stopping the momentum in mid-swing. Bing Jue then swung his opened flat palm towards the side of Mark's head, connecting with the temple with the soft, padded side of his flattened hand. The blow was solid and flowed as naturally as the water around a rock. Mark collapsed to the ground, unconscious.

"Mark!" Jim set his plate on the table and stepped quickly to his side, where he knelt. He glanced up at Bing. "What did you do to him?"

Wu-Pen walked to the table quickly. He spoke in Chinese and Bing answered. "Ah, yes," Wu-Pen explained, "he will be okay. Bing did not hurt him.

He is merely incomba…incompa…"

"Incapacitated?" Matt asked, knowing Wu-Pen was searching the word.

"Yes. He is incapacitated for a few moments. He might have a headache for a while."

Jim asked Bing Jue. "Why would you do that?"

Wu-Pen widened his eyes questionably. "A better question is, why would your friend want to hit Bing when he is only trying to help? Truly, Bing means no harm but a fight he did not want to do. There is enough to frighten the ladies inside the tent without a fight. Yes?"

Jim nodded. "I suppose I have to agree. Let your friend know I apologize for Mark. He is normally not like this. It's just a stressful night."

Wu-Pen smiled. "I understand and there are no hard feelings."

Matt observed Bing's humored smirk while he watched Jim and a few other men help Mark to stand upright. Mark was uneasy on his feet and shaking his head slightly to regain his focus. One quick blow with the fleshy side of a hand had knocked Mark unconscious without any effort at all. Matt watched Bing knowing he never wanted to fistfight him or Uang Yang.

"Matt," Lucille Barton said, touching his sleeve to get his attention. "Can I talk to you for a minute?" She had a scarf over her hair and around her neck to stay warm when she came outside the tent. The worry that haunted her soul was revealed on her face.

"Absolutely."

"My children are with your sister-in-law and brother, right? I've been so absent-minded since hearing about Lawrence that I need to know. Are my children okay? Billy Jo said her father was picking her boys up. I'm wondering if I should have my boys with me because they've never been left with strangers. Ever." Her eyes were reddened from crying.

Matt smiled comfortingly. "Your boys are fine. My brother Albert is a very nice man and probably on the floor playing with them as we speak. Mellissa too. They love children and nothing's going to happen to your boys. I explained to Mellissa what happened out here and she's expecting to put them up for the night if that is what you're worried about. Did you want to go home? If so, I can go get your boys and bring them to you."

She shook her head quickly. "I can't leave, Matt. I need to stay here and be with Lawrence when he comes out of the mine."

"I can understand that."

An anxiousness appeared on her brow. Strangers watching her boys for the night just didn't feel right. "I don't know your brother and his wife, so this is odd…Is there any chance you could bring them to me?"

"Lucille, I don't think this is the best place for children. What I can do is reassure you they are fine. Mellissa will take good care of them."

"They've never been away from me," she said with a high-pitched voice. "I need my boys, but I can't go home. What if they bring Lawrence out and he's dying and I only have a minute to tell him I love him? What if my boys miss the chance to say goodbye to their father?" she sniffled as tears fell from her eyes. "What if I don't get the chance to see him because I'm not here?"

Matt frowned. It didn't matter what he thought was best, the boys were her children and he had no right to refuse her. "If you want them here with you, I'll go get them."

"Thank you," she said, biting her lip. "I would appreciate it. If I can't have my husband, then I need my children." Her frown deepened as her lip trembled emotionally.

Matt put his hands on the outside of her shoulders. "All right. Give me a few minutes and Truet and I will get your boys. But I do want you to know that you're not alone out here."

She closed her eyes momentarily and then looked at Matt with a disheartened expression. "That is nice to say to people, Matt, but it's not true. Aside from Lawrence, I have no one else. Billy Jo is the only person I talk to and she only uses me to watch her boys. All I have is Lawrence. And if he's gone..." She shrugged with a widening of her eyes. "Then, I don't know what I'll do."

"You trust the Lord, Lucille, that's what you do," Matt said as he watched Ritchie Thorn take a plate of food into the tent. He appeared to be exhausted and heavily burdened. Matt continued, "No matter what happens, the Lord is holding you in the palm of his hand. You may think you have no one here but the Lord does. Okay?"

She nodded silently with a downturned face and wiped her nose.

Billy Jo let out a loud, deep wail that sent a chill down Matt's spine. A loud chorus of wailing and crying erupted from inside of the tent. Lucille's eyes widened in terror. "Oh no..." she turned and went back inside. Matt followed.

Billy Jo was holding Ritchie Thorn, who was quite emotional himself. Other families were hugging each other and wailing. Names of loved ones were being called out by grieving spouses and older children and mothers. It was a loud, chaotic scene that forced Matt's stomach to drop into a hollow pit.

Billy Jo left Ritchie's arms to step towards Lucille, speaking as she came forward, "They're dead. They're all dead." Billy Jo sobbed and wrapped her arms around her.

Lucille stood frozen with her mouth open. She shook her head refusing to believe it. "No...Lawrence can't be..."

"He is," Billy Jo wailed. "No one survived!"

Matt questioned her, "How do you know they're all dead? Jim said they wouldn't be found until tomorrow morning, at least." His words went unheard. "Billy Jo, who told you they were dead?"

"I did," Ritchie said with watery eyes. There was none of his usual animosity or arrogance that usually flowed out of him.

"How do you know that if they haven't reached the miners yet? I just talked to Jim five minutes ago and he said they wouldn't reach them for hours."

"I know," Richie said and sniffled. "Both crews were working down there near the explosion. Very close to it and nitrous dioxide filled the mine. There is no way anyone survived. If the rock didn't kill them, the gases did," his voice broke as he finished.

Lucille's bottom lip began to quiver. "There's no chance they survived?" her voice was high pitched.

Ritchie wiped his eyes. "No."

Lucille closed her eyes and began to whimper as the news took hold on Billy Jo.

"But you don't know for sure?" Matt asked Ritchie.

Ritchie spoke with a heavy heart, "Joe's one of the toughest men I know but he's gone. I love my brother, Matt, but no one can survive those gases and the winze was full of them. They're going to pull bodies out of there, not live men."

Matt exhaled heavily, knowing Richie was probably right. "Ritchie, you know far more about that stuff than I do. So, I won't pretend to know as much but all these people are here hoping for good news, no matter how unlikely. I've seen slim odds come out well before and I thanked the Lord every time. You may very well may be right but I'm going to hope they are all alive somehow. I trust a very big and powerful God who can work the most impossible of miracles if he chooses to." He paused to look at Ritchie and then Billy Jo and Lucille. "What I'm saying is if God wanted to spare anyone of those men or all of them, He can. And I won't assume anything until we know for sure. The Lord may not save any of them but he could and that's enough to keep hoping for. Don't give up on hope. It's the last great thing you have. You pray and you hope they are alive. You do not give up on them until you know they're gone for a fact. God still does miracles even today."

Billy Jo stepped quickly over to Matt and wrapped her arms around him and fought from crying. "I love you, Matt."

"I love you too."

Lucille stared at Matt with tears flowing from her eyes. "You're right. This is no place for my boys. They need to get a quiet and warm night's sleep. Your sister-in-law won't mind?"

"Not at all. Mellissa will love them like her own."

"Thank you."

Ritchie shook his head. "You all can hope all you want. No one is coming out alive."

Matt responded gently, "Ritchie, you can be hopeless if you want but give these folks some room to have some hope. It's the only thing they have right now to hang on to."

Ritchie replied bitterly, "It's false hope! You must have something to hope for that is based on reality. And the reality is no one can survive that gas, not even my brother."

Matt asked, "Why are you still here working then? You can't bring them back to life if you find them, so what's the hurry? Why not send everyone home and dig them out in a day or two? Is there a reason why you all are working so hard to reach them tonight?"

Richie's head lowered. "Because if anyone is

alive, we want to get to them out of there."

"Every family here tonight hopes you do get their loved one out of there alive. I don't find that kind of hope too much to ask for. Do you?"

Ritchie shook his head with shame-filled, downturned lips. "No, I guess I don't. I'll get back to work."

## 16

It had been a long night and Wu-Pen was tired like everyone else that stayed and served the rescuers and families. He took a minute to step back and look at the endurance of the Chinese who had worked all night and still smiled as they served the Americans. The day before, the Chinese were treated as misfits, with loathing and as unwanted pagans, now they were being appreciated. Wu-Pen had sat with and comforted wives, mothers and the children of the trapped miners while providing anything they needed, including blankets, pillows, food and drinks. He kept the rescuers fed, filled with coffee and went out of his way to meet any request he could. He had sent people back to Chinatown to get more supplies to keep cooking and serving for as long as it took until the search and rescue attempt was over. He even had their Chinese doctor available to mend wounds and two miners had allowed him to treat and suture cuts received in the mine. Wu-Pen smiled proudly as he watched his servers, the dishwashers carrying stacks of plates and silverware to the river, the cooks chopping vegetables and making noodles, even Bing Jue and Uang Yang were smiling and friendly as they stood near Wu-Pen serving coffee and tea or a bowl of warm soup. The preparations and organization of the camp set up had been a huge success.

Wu-Pen was losing money by providing for the rescue but he also listened to the families while staying warm, dry and fed. They were thankful to him and his people. He listened to the miners talk about the collapse and the bitter spirit they held against the Slaters for not bothering to show up. They all knew if it wasn't for the Chinese, the grief-stricken wives and children would not be taken care of. The mine employees held a high regard for Wu-Pen and his people for volunteering to help and committing to stay for the length of the attempted rescue. Wu-Pen had made a lot of friends and the hostility that had shown itself earlier was turning to smiles and handshakes. Translating a quick conversation between a miner and a Chinese cook that ended in laughter and a healthy hand shake pleased Wu-Pen's heart. The respect and acceptance would carry forward and, soon, the Chinese would be an accepted part of the community.

The sun was rising on a new morning and a group of three men came walking towards work. They were part of the day shift crew for the stamp mill. Like the two shifts previously, they would stay out of the mine and loiter around in the stamp mill cleaning or changing out any parts that needed to be changed during a shutdown.

Wu-Pen recognized one of the men walking towards him as Oscar Belding. Oscar was the third and final man still alive that had killed two Chinese men by throwing them over the edge of the granite quarry pit. Wu-Pen had waited for two long months for this day to come and he moved nearer to the table where Bing Jue served coffee. He whispered in Chinese and then grinned widely as he greeted the three American men. "Good morning, gentlemen, could I interest you in some fresh coffee or tea? Breakfast, perhaps?"

Oscar Belding answered, "Yeah, I'll have some coffee."

Wu-Pen spoke in Chinese to Bing and he poured the coffee into ceramic cups and handed them to Wu-Pen who handed them to the men one by one. He handed Oscar his cup and said, "Have a wonderful day."

Oscar took his coffee cup and walked away without saying a word with the others to check in with the timekeeper. Wu-Pen watched Oscar and he asked Bing in Chinese, "Did you give it to him and only him?"

"Yes, only him."

Wu-Pen smiled. "Good. Take the bottle and some dirty dishes to the river and wash the plates and destroy the bottle where it will never be found."

Bing nodded and carried a small clear vial with a cork plug hidden in his palm and a few dirty plates to the river to wash them. He pulled the cork out of the bottle and rinsed it in the current of the river before tossing the vial into the strongest part of the rising river to be taken downstream, where it would sink to the bottom eventually. He came back to the drink table and nodded to Wu-Pen to indicate it was done.

Wu-pen smiled approvingly and then greeted other men to offer them coffee.

Matt had walked around inside of the stamp mill curiously. He had not been inside of one before and the massive machinery and mechanics fascinated him. He had gotten a tour by one the graveyard shift employees but he had gone to check out for the day with the timekeeper. Matt found a quiet place to sit and closed his eyes for a few minutes. He was tired and having little to do to keep him busy was allowing sleepiness to overcome him. The families in the tent were exhausted and had cried themselves into a quiet stupor or closed their eyes for a few minutes here and there. Most could not sleep knowing their husbands were unaccounted for and they refused to miss a moment where any information could tell them their loved ones were alive. Matt might have closed his eyes for five minutes when he was startled by someone yelling, "Sleeping on the job, Marshal?" It was one of the day crew employees shouting as he walked by with a hearty laugh.

"Almost," Matt responded quietly.

Oscar Belding stopped in front of him. "Matt, you might as well go home and get some rest.

There's nothing for you to do here. There's nothing for us to do here either but if we want to be paid, we gotta be here."

Matt stood up. "I want to be here for the families. At least they'll know I care, anyway."

"That's more than the Slater's have done. I know Billy Jo is your cousin. I hope Joe Thorn is okay. But from what I heard, that's doubtful. Joe's not a close friend of mine but I hope the best for all those men." He furrowed his brow slightly and widened his eyes for a second.

Matt answered, "I hope so too. I think I'll go get me some coffee and try to wake up a bit."

"The coffee's good. I haven't had any Chinese food yet but I heard it wasn't bad. I'll grab some at lunchtime if they're still here."

"I liked it. My fiancé has been wanting to go to Chinatown and try their food. I'll have to take her there now."

Oscar offered a smile. "I heard you're engaged to Christine. Congratulations. You know every man that's gone to the dance hall knows her name. I don't know if there's a more beautiful lady in the world. You're a lucky man."

"Thank you. We have not planned a date yet but we are thinking late May or early June. I look forward to it, though."

Oscar laughed. "I bet! Have a good day, Matt. I..." he paused and smiled awkwardly. His shoulders swayed as he nearly lost his balance and shook his head with a bewildered look on his face.

"Are you all right?" Matt asked.

"Yeah, I'm fine. Just a little nauseous there for a second. It's probably from having a little too much to drink last night with the boys at the mile. You know, as a memorial for our brothers buried up there. I might have overdone it a bit. I didn't eat dinner last night and I didn't want to get up this morning either."

Matt walked out of the stamp mill and got a cup of coffee from the drink table. He took a sip and yawned.

"Marshal, you look tired, my friend," Wu-Pen said with a kind smile.

"I am. You look a bit tired yourself."

"Yes. It's been a long night but we help keep the men strong with all they need to work through the night. My men have been helping and I believe we are making friends here. What do you think?"

Matt had to admit what Wu-Pen and his fellow Chinese were doing for the people was quite admirable. "I know they are thankful for you and your people. It was truly kind of you."

Wu-Pen grinned. "It is our privilege and duty to help our fellow man in a time of need." He nodded to a young Chinese man as he carried an armload of used coffee cups out of the stamp mill to be washed in the river. Another young man followed with an armload of plates and forks and spoons. "It takes much work and these men, you see, will not be given anything except food and drinks for their service. I am proud to be here with them."

Matt put his hand appreciatively on Wu-Pen's shoulder. "Thank them all for me. From all of us, actually. If you'll excuse me, I need to check on my cousin." He walked into the tent and found Billy Jo sitting on the canvas-covered ground patting the floor beside her. He sat down and put an arm around her and she rested her head on his shoulder. "How are you holding up?" he asked.

She shook her head slowly. "I just hope Joe's okay. I don't know why I love him but I do."

"Were you really leaving him?"

She said, "I was leaving him for good this time."

"And now? If he is alive and well, what then?"

She sighed tiredly. "I don't know. You know you love someone but you don't realize how much until something like this happens and you may not get to see them again. I might give Joe another chance. I don't know. No, I would. I will. He has to be alive, right?" she asked, turning her head to look at him.

Matt yawned. "If anyone can survive it, I'm sure it's Joe."

"You make him sound like a cockroach or something."

Matt chuckled. "No. Just a man with a big will to survive. You know, I wonder if being trapped in there has a way of changing people? I think it would."

"Joe's always been...well, Joe. I don't think he'll change from that. I'll miss him, though, if he doesn't come out of that portal. My boys will too. Can I ask you something?" she asked.

"Of course."

She turned her head to look at him. "Why don't you like me?"

The question baffled him. "Why would you ask that? I do like you."

"You don't act like it. Ever since you came home from Wyoming, all you've done is get mad at me and try to correct me. Before you left, when I was little, you were my favorite cousin and then you disappeared. I was so excited to hear you had come back and I hoped we'd be close but we're not. The only two cousins I have that have anything to do with me are Georgina and Karen. It gets lonely."

Matt pulled her a touch closer. "I want better for you than Joe Thorn. I'm sorry to say so as he's in the mine but the truth is the truth. He's not a good man and that's the only thing I've raised my voice to you about. It's frustrating to love someone and have them keep going back to a man that treats them like rubbish. Look, your lip's been split and I bet you have bruises too. It has nothing to do with liking you or loving you because I do. It has everything to do with expecting more from you because I do love you. We're family, Billy Jo, but you keep running back to the same dog that keeps biting you. After a while, people wash their hands and wait for you to decide to leave that dog alone. Sorry if I made you feel like I didn't like you. The opposite is true; I love you. I just want what's best for you and your boys."

"Do you think I should leave him if he comes out alive?"

"I think he's had every chance but it looks to me like he's doing what he's always done. That's not much of a change."

Billy Jo smirked, thinking of Wes Wasson while

she rested her head tiredly against Matt's shoulder. "Do you think I'd find someone to love me again?"

Matt chuckled lightly. "Someday, you're going to be a half owner of the granite quarry. You'll be one of the most sought-after ladies in the county."

She grinned and slapped his hand that set on his leg. "No, I won't."

"Yes, you will. That's why you must be wiser and not fooled by men being nice. Every man is nice at first. A good way to judge character is to remember, what comes out of the mouth is what's in the heart. You can always tell a good man from a bad man by what they say and how they say it over a period of time. You have to be wiser than before, Billy Jo, because eventually, you're going to have a lot to lose, if not your health, life or your boys'."

She yawned. "I think I might fall asleep."

Matt smiled and let her rest her eyes while she leaned on his shoulder. Thirty minutes later, Billy Jo slept peacefully when the same stamp mill employee that had startled Matt earlier frantically stepped into the tent.

"Marshal! I think Oscar's having a heart attack! He needs help!"

Billy Jo was jerked awake by the man's urgent voice and Matt left her to follow the employee into the stamp mill.

Wu-Pen sputtered, "I'll get our doctor!" He began yelling in Chinese with urgency in his tone.

Matt was led to Oscar, who was on the stamp mill floor, grabbing his chest, sweat covered, in pain, and struggling to breathe. Matt had no idea how to help him but he knew he had to do something. He shouted to the men gathering around in a circle, "Get a wagon and hurry!" His thought was to get Oscar to Doctor Ryland as fast as he could. He prayed as he watched Oscar's face turning a deeper shade of blue. A helpless sensation consumed him as he knew there was nothing he could do for Oscar.

An old Chinese man ran forward ahead of Wu-Pen carrying a wooden case and put his hand on Oscars' face to feel his skin, his neck to feel his pulse and then his chest. He opened his box and pulled out a bottle of white powder and was about to pour it in Oscar's mouth when Oscar's head dropped to the floor and his body went limp. The Chinese man stared at the body and felt for a pulse again. He bowed his head disheartened. Wu-Pen asked a question in Chinese urgently and the doctor answered solemnly.

Wu-Pen sighed sadly. "He is too late. I am sorry."

The doctor, an old Chinese man, stood up after closing his box. He made eye contact with Matt and bowed slightly. His face revealed his grief of not being able to help Oscar. The old man and Wu-Pen walked away quietly. Unseen to anyone was the pleased smile inside of Wu-Pen. He walked to the drink table and said in Chinese to his two guards, "The third man, Oscar, is dead. Chee Yik, Kot-Kho-Not and Ah See are avenged. The first and second phases of the dragon's fire are complete. Now we finish the third. Serve well." He smiled at Billy Jo, "Ahh, the Marshal's cousin. How can we serve you this morning? You must be hungry."

## 17

The pitch blackness in the winze was overbearing but they needed to burn their candles sparingly because there was no way of knowing how long they would be trapped there. In the lack of any light source, the darkness was perfect blackness and a man could not see the hand in front of his face. The sensation was frightening and most uncomfortable as well. It is no wonder scary stories are more threatening in the dark and children fear extraordinarily little in the daylight. The men knew where they were and they knew what they would see when a candle was lit but still to have good eyes and not be able to see anything except blackness was a bit frightening.

"Who has the watch? Can you stop your watch? The ticking is driving me crazy!" Bobby Alper shouted. The steady sound of dripping water from multiple directions was the only sound except for the rhythmic ticking of someone's watch, which was becoming too much for Bobby. It sounded like a countdown to his demise and he had enough. He couldn't take the sound of the ticking any longer.

Walter Hendrick stirred uncomfortably. "That's my watch. I'll see if I can't stop it."

"What time is it?" Joe asked tiredly.

"I can't see."

Bobby shouted, "Well, light a candle! We can light a candle for a few minutes. What are they doing up there anyway? Do they even know we're trapped down here?"

"Settle down, Bobby. They'll get us out of here as soon as they can."

"How can you be so calm, Walter? The water's rising, we're freezing and we may never get out of here!"

Walter lit a match and squinting to adjust to the sudden light. He smiled at Bobby. "And just like that, God created light, Bobby. Even in here. Faith brings peace and that peace is the light in a dark world." He winked at Bobby with a slight smile. "We'll be okay. We have all we need. Look, even the match is burning right, so we have good air still."

Bobby noticed the slumped over body of Lawrence Barton. "Is Lawrence still alive?"

Joe answered, "Yeah, he's just out. Hey, move that candle down to make sure that tourniquet is holding tight." They looked and saw very little blood leaking out of the severed leg. The foot-long drill tied in place by bootstrings was still holding the tourniquet tight.

Walter brought the light near his pocket watch.

"It's seven-thirty in the morning. We have been here for just over twenty-four hours now and trapped in here for about twenty. You fellas do know our families will be waiting for us when we are saved, right? I promise they are going to forget all about any arguments you might've had and give you all the biggest hugs and kisses you'll ever have. I know my wife and children will. I look forward to that."

Bobby took a big breath, relieved to see his hand in front of his face again. He had his broken arm in a sling made from both of his bootlaces, holding each side of his broken bone. It was uncomfortable and throbbing but it was better than letting his arm dangle lifelessly. He had his good arm close to his side, trying to stay warm. All four men sat together to share body heat. The temperature was not necessarily cold but the water coming in through the rock that saturated their clothes was. "I just want out of here."

Joe's teeth chattered. "Yeah, we're all going to have our women hugging on us, except for Bobby. He's going to be staring at Ritchie, wanting a hug." He laughed. Bobby shared a cabin next to Joe's with Ritchie Thorn.

Bobby wanted to elbow Joe but he was too cold to move his good arm and the jarring of his body would become an echo of throbbing hell from his broken arm. He settled with a shivering, "Shut up."

"You're the only one without a woman," Joe chuckled teasingly.

"You're one to talk. Billy Jo may not be waiting for you, either. Remember she was leaving you?"

"True," Joe said solemnly. "Maybe we should blow that candle out and save it." He sounded heartbroken.

Bobby argued, "No, give me a chance to enjoy the light. I swear I am quitting as soon as I'm out of here. I don't ever want to do this again. I'll go work for Billy Jo's father or at the livery stable shoveling horse crap if I have to but I am done mining. I am done!"

"Shhh!" Joe shouted. "Do you hear that?" He smiled. "I hear them getting closer. Do you hear that?" He turned towards the pile of rock and cupped his hands to his mouth and screamed, "Hey! Hey! Can you hear me?"

"We're in here!" Bobby shouted with renewed excitement and energy.

"Joe," Walter motioned, "Grab that hammer and start beating on that rock!"

Ron Dalton stepped into the large tent that had been set up for the miners and the family members and, not surprisingly, found many worried wives, older sons and daughters, and a few little ones as well. Ron saw his wife's cousins, Matt and Billy Jo, sitting on two small folding chairs beside a curly dark-haired lady quietly waiting.

Ron spoke loudly, "May I have your attention, please. My name is Ron Dalton. I am the Mine Superintendent here. I can proudly say I know all the men inside the mine personally and they are good men. We have worked all night, pulling out debris and are getting closer to reaching where the men were working. We had two crews working down there, one in the winze and one in a drift. We haven't reached them quite yet but we do know there are survivors. We have no information on who or what shape they're in but they are making contact by hammering on the rock. Lord willing, all the men survived, and we estimate getting them out of there by noon. I know the men working to rescue them are rejuvenated and working with a determination to get the job done and return your loved ones to you as soon as we can."

"Praise God!" Henrietta Hendricks cried out, holding her fourteen-year-old daughter. Her older son and daughter, both in the late teens, began weeping with relief.

"But you don't know who?" Ellen Rosso asked from the canvas floor where she sat with her two teenage daughters about the same age as Henrietta's youngest.

Ron shook his head. "Not yet, no. We do know, well, it sounds like it's coming from straight down the winze."

"Mister Dalton, I'm Lloyd Jenson's wife, Wilma. I know Lloyd's working in the drift. Have you heard anything from the drift?"

Ron spoke as clearly as he could. "At this time, we are not sure where the hammering is coming from. It could be from the drift but it sounds like it's coming from the winze. All I do know is we do have some survivors, at least one anyway, and Lord willing, every one of them will walk out of there."

A dark-haired lady of about thirty years of age raised her hand questionably. Her exhaustion and concern showed clearly on her ashen face. "My name's Betty Zuwalski. Eunice is my husband. As you can see, we have three children, John's eight, Roger is seven and Sarah is three. We live in the Slater Mile. Mister Dalton, no one has dared to mention it, but what if my husband is dead? How am I going to live? Where am I going to go and how could I afford to go anywhere? We don't have any money. If my husband is dead, I still have children to feed and keep housed. Is the company going to help with that?"

Ron had hoped no questions like that would be asked. "Misses Zuwalski, I know your husband and he's a very good man. I'm praying that Eunice and all of them come walking out of there alive and well. But if not, company policy pays the funeral expenses of those men who are killed on the mine property."

Betty answered sharply, "I don't care about his funeral. I care about being able to house and feed my family! He works for you and he works hard. I'm asking about your loyalty to him. Are you going to give us enough money to live on?"

Lucille Barton spoke softly, "I'm in the same place Betty is. Your employees have families who depend on our husbands. If our husbands are killed, there is a life insurance policy on them that will give us enough money to make a new start, right?"

Ron hesitated. Knowing the dangers of the mining industry, he had taken a life insurance policy idea to the main office for situations like this one but William Slater rejected it because the cost was too expensive. Ron tried to prepare for families in this same situation by using some foresight but, once again, he was the one taking the brunt of the heat that came from the Slater's business decisions. "As for an insurance policy, no. I hoped to bring life insurance to our employees for the security of the families but it was…unfortunately not possible due to the dangers and risks of our industry."

Henrietta Hendricks asked heatedly, "So, what are we going to do if Walter is dead? Or Eunice or anyone? What are we supposed to do? Is the company going to compensate us for our husbands' lives? Walter has worked here for years and never shirked on a day's work. Does that mean nothing to you? If our husbands are dead, what do we get?"

Betty added bitterly, "We get kicked out of our company homes onto the muddy streets without a dime, right?"

"Oh, but the Slater's are warm and dry, aren't they?" someone hissed angrily.

"Ladies," Ron raised his voice to be heard. "Please. If your husbands are, Lord forbid, deceased, I will do whatever I can to make sure you and your children are cared for. However, I am not the owner of this company and do not make the policies. I can only recommend and do my best to encourage what's right. My job is to run the mine, not the company policies. Okay? Those are questions for the people above me. And you'll find them in town in the main office. Out here, we mine and right now, we're trying to save our fellow miners. I understand your concern and I hope someone from the main office will come up here and answer those questions for you. I don't have those answers. Now, if you'll excuse me, I need to get back to work. I just wanted to let you know we do have survivors because I know the rumor was there was not going to be any. Well, there is. We just have to get them out."

"We heard Oscar Belding died this morning. What about his family?" Betty asked bitterly.

Ron nodded his head slowly. "Yes, Oscar Belding died this morning from an apparent heart attack. It's very tragic. He was a very nice man. Again, I have nothing to do with deciding policy procedures. That's above me."

"Has William Slater even been out here since the cave in?" someone asked.

"No, but they are aware of it. And wish us the best at getting everyone out alive. And that's our hope."

Danny Rosso's seventeen-year-old son, Micah, who also worked for the mine, said with disgust, "Well, you'd expect them to come out here to tell us that themselves, wouldn't you?"

Ron agreed. "I would, Micah. I can't tell you what the company's going to do if your loved ones are deceased. As I said, that's not my decision. If it were, you'd be taken care of, because I think it's only right. And I'll stand up for you if it comes to that. I promise you, I will. Right now, I'm hoping for the best. I must get back to work." He left the tent as quickly as he had come inside.

## 18

The rescuers worked their way to the drift and discovered there were no survivors. Ron Dalton came to the tent and informed the families that Eunice Zuwalski, Jason Collins, Fred Longley, and Lloyd Jenson had been found deceased. The worst fears of every mining family had become a reality and the sudden cries of the deceased's parents, wives, children, and siblings were heartbreaking. Although Ron had tried to be gentle, the news hit like a cold blade of steel piercing the heart. Betty Zuwalski wrapped her arms around her three young children and began to wail uncontrollably. Lloyd Johnson's wife, Wilma, nearly passed out from exhaustion as the news hit her and her four older sons like a baseball bat to the gut. Jason Collins was a twenty-two-year-old young man whose father and two older brothers worked for the mine and were working to rescue him. His father and two brothers came to the tent and took Jason's mother home where they could mourn in private. Fred Longley's family wailed loudly upon hearing the news. The cries were deep and sorrowful. The four families were quickly held and comforted by the others who were still waiting to hear the fate of their loved ones. Lucille and Billy Jo both wept as they held the other women and offered their love to them even though they knew their men could be dead too.

Matt left out of the tent and walked to the river's edge and closed his eyes as a pair of tears rolled down his cheeks. He had invested the past night encouraging those same families to keep hoping and not to give up on their faith. To see the families he gotten to know through the night collapse into sorrowful cries broke his heart. He knew prayers are sometimes not answered the way he would've liked but for those families, he truly hoped and prayed for those men's safety. Instead of a day of praise, it was a day of devastation.

Matt heard some commotion up at the portal and soon the news came they were pulling a second wagon up the portal. One wagon collected the dead bodies and the other was for the survivors from the winze. The word of survivors spread fast and the waiting families refused to remain in the tent and walked hurriedly up to the portal. Matt watched some men walk Betty Zuwalski and her children out of the tent and across the bridge towards her home. The families who had lost their loved ones were leaving the mine with the help and comfort of close friends and relatives. Matt watched them all walk away and decided he would go to each of their homes in the coming days to offer his condolences and see what he could do to help them. He wanted them to know he cared.

Another wagon was brought up to the mine's portal for the injured but they had not brought anyone out of the mine. Blankets and coats were taken in as was a call for two stretchers. Twenty minutes later, Bobby Alper was the first man helped out of the portal by two miners. He was covered with a wool blanket and walking stiffly, but the grin on his face to see his parents and siblings quickly became tears of thankfulness and tight hugs. His broken arm didn't seem to be bothered by his family's hugging. He wept while holding his mother in a tight one-armed hug for a long moment before he hugged his father and siblings again.

A moment later, Joe Thorn came out of the portal with a wool blanket wrapped over his wet clothes. He shaded his eyes from the daylight while searching the crowd of faces for Billy Jo. He grinned with relief and stepped quickly towards her. She ran towards him and met him with an emotional embrace. He closed his moist eyes and held her tight. "I thought I'd never see you again. Billy Jo, I'm so sorry." His body jerked as he fought with all his might not to start crying.

She wept on his shoulder. "Thank God you are alive. I was so scared." She didn't seem to mind his wet clothes.

"Me too, Baby, me too!" He kissed her and then smiled down at her. "You've never been a more beautiful sight! Billy Jo, I swear, I'll never mistreat you again if you'll come home with me. I don't want to lose you and the boys."

She kissed him excitedly.

Two men carried Walter Hendricks out of the portal on a stretcher towards a wagon. He smiled at his family and shouted, "My hips broken, but I'm fine! Praise the Lord!" His wife, Henrietta and their children ran towards the wagon to hug him and thanked the Lord fervently.

Lucille touched Joe's sleeve. "Have you seen Lawrence? Was he with you? He's missing." Her voice revealed the panic within her.

Joe released his embrace with Billy Jo and stared at Lucille empathetically. He spoke gently, "They should be bringing him out anytime. They're bringing him out on a stretcher."

"What do you mean?" she asked urgently.

Just then, two other men carried Lawrence's limp body out of the mine on a stretcher and carefully set it in the wagon next to Walter. She gasped and her bottom lip began to tremble uncontrollably as a look of horror came over her face.

Joe spoke softly, "He's alive, Lucille." His eyes filled with thick tears and his voice broke emotionally as he said, "We had to cut his leg off or he wouldn't have survived." Joe's face contorted and trembled as he fought to stop himself from crying.

Lucille began to bawl and ran quickly towards the wagon and leaned over the back of the wagon to reach for his hand. She could see where part of his leg was missing under the blanket that covered him. She was horrified to see the dried mix of blood and mud on his unconscious face. "Lawrence, I'm here. You are safe now. Don't you dare die on me! Do you hear me, Lawrence?" she cried loudly.

His eyes opened tiredly at the sound of her voice. He saw her at the end of the wagon by his legs stretching to hold his hand. He smiled. "I love you." His eyes closed again, but his smile remained.

"Don't you die on me!" she screamed emotionally.

Walter, who was lying beside Lawrence said, "He'll be okay, Lucille. He has been through a lot. His body's just needing to rest. Climb up here and ride to the doctor with us.

"What happened to his leg?" she asked, visibly upset.

"I'll explain on the way but you might as well come us. Henrietta, help her up here," he said to his wife. Henrietta was already in the wagon and helped Lucille climb into the wagon.

Billy Jo watched Lucille climb into the wagon and noticed how emotional Joe was when he watched her. She asked, "Are you okay?"

He looked at her and shook his head with more emotion showing than she'd ever seen him display. "No."

Seventeen-year-old Micah Rosso tapped him on the shoulder. "Joe, where's my Pa? Have you seen him?"

Joe turned his head to look at Micah and noticed the young man's mother and younger siblings waiting for Danny Rosso to come out of the mine. Joe had already notified Danny's two brothers inside the mine that Danny had been killed and was under six and a half feet of water at the very end of the winze. The winze would have to be pumped out before they could retrieve his body. The two Rosso brothers had taken it hard and had not yet come out to notify Danny's family. Joe didn't have the heart to tell young Micah.

"Joe?" Micah asked with great anxiety in his voice.

Joe could only stare at him through blurry moisture-filled eyes and a chest that would convulse into uncontrollable bawling if he said a word. He shook his head slightly and said softly, "Micah..."

"Micah!" Alan Rosso called as he came out of the portal with his two brothers, Wade and Tony. "Come here." Alan gathered the large Rosso family together away from everyone else and a few seconds later, Ellen, Danny's wife, and their children began wailing from the deepest depths of human sorrow.

Joe Thorn dropped to his knees and began to convulse in uncontrollable sobbing.

## 19

Christine Knapp reclined comfortably on Matt's davenport with a blanket covering her legs while reading a book. She knew Matt had been at the mine all night and would be sleeping and asked Truet for his house key to let herself in. Christine thought it would be nice to clean the house and make Matt a hot breakfast when he woke up. She did not want to wake him up, though, so she made herself comfortable and enjoyed the silence and a book she had brought from the dance hall. An unexpected knock on the door startled her out of the pages of the story. She put her book down and paused in front of the door with a touch of uncertainty. She knew it was most unlikely but she knew all too well that Matt had enemies and stood off to the side of the door like Matt always did. "Who is it?"

"Is this where Matt Bannister lives?" a lady's voice questioned.

"Yes," Christine answered awkwardly.

"Is he home? My name's Lucille Barton and Matt took my children to his brother's house yesterday and I'd like to get them and go home."

Christine opened the door and saw a soaking wet young lady about her age shaking in the rain with reddened eyes. "Come in. You look like you are freezing. Let me get you a blanket and a towel." she said as she closed the door behind Lucille.

Lucille shook her head. "No, thank you. I would just like to go get my children and go home." Droplets of water fell from her hair onto her face mixing with her tears before running down her cheeks.

Christine could see the lady was emotional and heavily burdened. "Matt's been out at the mine all night and is sleeping. I'd rather not wake him up. But I can take you to your children if you know which brother he took them too."

Lucille's bottom lip began to tremble. "I don't know." Sleeplessness and emotional exhaustion had taken their toll and she was fighting to control her emotions. Doctor Ryland had to remove a few more inches of Lawrence's leg to reach the solid bone not fractured by the blasting cap. The doctors were keeping him in their office for a few days before he could be sent home. The turmoil inside of Lucille was as ruthless as any she had ever known. She was overwhelmed and just wanted to get home with her two sons and get some sleep.

Christine asked, "Do the name's Lee and Regina or Albert and Mellissa sound familiar? We can go to both if necessary but we'll find your children."

"Mellissa sounds familiar. I think it was Albert

and Mellissa's. He just said they would take good care of them. I shouldn't have let him take them." She began to weep from exhaustion.

"Your children are fine. Let me put my boots on and I'll walk you there." She asked caringly, "You must've been at the mine?"

Lucille morosely nodded with her lips beginning to quiver. Her eyes were already covered with thick tears.

"Is your husband okay?" Christine asked softly.

"No." She began to whimper. Christine stepped forward and hugged the drenched young lady. Lucille put her arms around Christine and held her tight as she cried uncontrollably into her shoulder. In a city where she did not know anyone, it was comforting to have a caring hug when she needed someone to hold her the most, even if it was a stranger. After a few moments, Lucille got control of herself, broke away from the hug and wiped her eyes and nose. "I'm sorry."

The front of Christine's dress was damp from hugging Lucille. "No, don't be sorry. My name is Christine. I'm Matt's fiancé. What is your name again?"

"Lucille Barton. I've been up since yesterday morning and I just want to get my boys and go home." Her lips puckered and trembled with emotion.

"Let me get ready and we'll go find them. Can I ask, did your husband survive?"

Lucille nodded with exhaustion. "Thankfully but he lost his leg." Her face contorted miserably. "I don't know what we're going to do." She wept.

Christine wrapped the wool blanket from the davenport around Lucille to help keep her warm. Christine put on her coat and tied her hat under her chin for their walk in the rain. They walked seven blocks to Albert's large home and knocked on the door. Sixteen-year-old Joshua Bannister answered it. He was a solid built young man with broad shoulders and short dark hair with a hint of a mustache growing on his upper lip.

"Hi, Christine. Come in," he said, looking at Lucille curiously.

"Thank you, Joshua. Is your mother here?"

"Oh, yeah." He turned towards the back of the house. "Ma!"

"Momma!" Five-year-old Michael Barton yelled excitedly and ran out the large family room towards the back of the house into the parlor and hugged his mother tightly. She knelt and held him close. She fought from crying. "Where's Daddy?" he asked.

"Oh, hi!" Mellissa Bannister said with a friendly smile as she stepped out of the family room, carrying three-year-old Ray Barton in her arms. She watched Lucille hug Michael. The first thing she noticed was how wet, exhausted and miserable Lucille appeared as she fought to control her emotions.

Christine spoke, "Mellissa, this is Lucille Barton. Lucille, this is Mellissa Bannister."

Lucille stood, wiped her face, and looked at Mellissa's friendly face. She was a heavy-set woman who had shoulder-length brown hair that fell loosely, except for a decorative hair comb that held her bangs out of her lively brown eyes. "Thank you for watching my boys." She held out her hands to take hold of her son.

Mellissa handed Ray to her. "It was no problem at all. The boys have been wonderful."

Lucille hugged Ray and began to weep. Ray grimaced. "You're wet, Mama."

"Yes, she is," Mellissa agreed. "Come inside and warm up."

"No," Lucille said. "I don't want to get your floors muddy. And you have done enough, thank you. I just want to get home and…" she paused.

Mellissa watched her skeptically and then spoke to her son, "Joshua, why don't you take Michael into the family room for a minute so I can talk to his mother, please. Go play hide and seek or something."

Joshua agreed obediently. "Michael, go hide and I'll count to twenty. Go, buddy, go!"

When they were out of the room, Mellissa asked softly, "Lucille, how is your husband?"

Lucille struggled with trying to hold herself together.

Christine answered for her, "He survived but lost his leg. He'll be staying in the doctor's office for a while. They had to operate on him today, she was telling me on the way over here. And Lucille's been up since yesterday morning waiting to hear if her husband was alive or not."

"You haven't slept at all?" Mellissa asked her.

Lucille shook her head.

156

"And you live where? Do you live at the company housing?"

She nodded.

Mellissa sighed empathetically. "Sweetheart, Matt told me you didn't have any family around here, is that right?"

"Lawrence is all I have," she spoke softly with a broken voice.

"Lucille, I can't stop you, but I wish you wouldn't take those boys out in that rain. They are having a great time playing with me and the kids. My husband too. Why don't you take your boots off and let me find you some dry clothes and you can go upstairs and get some rest? We have an extra room for you and the boys for the night. I'll take care of the boys and get you something to eat too."

Lucille shook her head. "No, I need to go home with my boys."

"Why? Wouldn't you just be walking back into town tomorrow to see your husband anyway? All that walking back and forth in the rain and mud is just going to get you or your boys sick. It would be no problem if you stayed here tonight. You need to rest and I can take care of the children so you can get some sleep. I'll start a warm bath for you right now and then get you into some dry clothes for the night. I insist you stay. While you soak in the bath, I'll make you something to eat and then we'll get you into a nice, warm and soft bed."

"I don't know…"

Mellissa interrupted her, "Are you going to feel like making a fire and cooking dinner for the boys when you get home? Our house is already warm, dry and I have to make dinner anyway. Please, let me help you. And tomorrow, you will be right here where you can go see your husband for as long as you like. Your boys are no trouble at all."

"You wouldn't mind?"

Mellissa's sincerity was clearly visible. "Not at all. I am insisting you stay the night. So, get those muddy boots off and I'll get a bath going for you."

Lucille sighed. "Okay."

"Great." She glanced at Christine. "Kick your boots off and stay awhile, Christine. You can help me get our guest situated and then we have a wedding to plan. I'm getting tired of not having a wedding date marked on my calendar."

## 20

Ling Tseng poured another pot of steaming water into the bathtub that Wu-Pen reclined in. The room was dark, with multiple candles burning around him along with incense. The hot water felt good after getting a fair amount of sleep earlier in the afternoon. He smiled contently. All the planning, all the preparation, had paid off better than he anticipated.

The explosion at the mine wasn't such a mystery. It had been in the works for a while and, in Wu-Pen's inner circle of trust, it was known as the Dragon's Fire. Wu-Pen had men working in the mine on the graveyard shift scraping floors, laying track or whatever else they were instructed to do by Wy Gee. He was the only Chinese man employed by the mine who understood enough English to translate to the others. In truth, Wy Gee understood more English than he led on and listened to the men at the mine when they didn't think he could understand them. Wu-Pen had made it a rule that no other Chinese man who understood English could let any American know they understood it. If there were any communication with Americans, it would go through Wu-Pen and no one else. Those who did learn English had to pretend to limit their knowledge. The cost of breaking that rule was death by miserable means, which meant there would be a lot of pain involved. There was one exception to the law and that was Ah See. He had spoken English before Wu-Pen came to Chinatown and he was allowed to continue since he made decent money and caused no trouble. However, to control Ah See as a precaution, Wu-Pen had Ah See's little sister stolen from her home in China and shipped harmlessly to San Francisco and smuggled to Branson, where she remained entirely unharmed and hidden working in a kitchen of a restaurant in Chinatown. She lived with her brother and wrote home whenever she felt like it. It was expensive to kidnap and smuggle her unharmed to Branson but her value to Wu-Pen was having control over her brother. Wu-Pen had a kingdom to build and a loose tongue that could speak English to the law or anyone else was a risk that could bring his potential empire down. Wu-Pen could foresee trouble before it ever had an opportunity to happen, so like a chess game, he planned ahead for any advantages that benefitted him.

The Americans always said that all Chinese looked alike, so it was easy to replace two or three graveyard shift miners with men who knew geology and explosives. The geologist, who worked for the Chinese Benevolence Society in charge of the tunnels and basements being dug under Chinatown, told them where to drill holes in the ceiling's weakest points and the walls to create the most destruction. The holes were drilled over two nights in the fractured wall and ceiling far down in a winze where no one was at night. Finding an explosive that would be inconspicuous and keeping it dry in the wet mine was harder to do. It seemed impossible until Wu-Pen learned about gelignite. A nitroglycerine-based explosive made into a putty that was both pliable and waterproof. He learned about it from Hop Jim, who worked for a man that dug water wells. They used Gelignite to blow the holes deeper through the bedrock. Hop Jim took close to ten pounds of gelignite for Wu-Pen to use in the mine.

Five nights before, the geologist, Hop Jim and a man who specialized in making fireworks all posed as miners and worked their way down the winze. They set the gelignite, and blasting cap and built a customized delayed fuse with an unscented seven-hour joss stick concealed in a thin bamboo chute hidden on the timbering at the weakest point of the rock. The fuse of the blasting cap was tied to the joss stick. The Gelignite sat perfectly harmless for five days without a threat of it exploding until Wu-Pen commanded the day of the dragon's fire.

Wu-Pen was not a cruel man. He had given William Slater two chances to accept the Chinese Benevolence Society into the Branson Business Association and he refused. He was rude and treated Wu-Pen no better than a flea. The times had to change. William Slater needed to be humbled and lose favor while the Chinese Benevolence Society gained acceptance. The order to blow the gelignite came when all the preparations had been made among his people. The food supplies were collected, the seats were made, the tent was constructed, and every need was prepared according to plan. The dragon's fire trapped miners, killed miners, and closed production for two days. In the process, his people served the scared, hurting and hungry. It was not William Slater and his family that took care of the frightened families and exhausted employees. If Branson's population knew the good deeds done by the Chinese and took notice of the Slater family refusing to meet or comfort the families, it would cause hostility towards the Slaters and gratitude for the Chinese people. Gratitude is earned business and when the Chinese people prosper, Wu-Pen prospers. As he sat in his tub bathing, Wu-Pen thought of an evolving plan to help create more hostility towards the Slaters and their mine. He was committed to being a thorn in William Slater's side until William allowed him to join the Branson Business Association and be recognized as a respected businessman.

He had his locksmith make a key to get into the Engberg & Penn Assayers Office and, with a stethoscope, he opened the safe. It had been easy to steal the money and gold. His craftsmen had already melted the stolen gold into tea plates so they could never be identified. They would decorate

Wu-Pen's home until he sold them in San Francisco. There was no evidence to ever connect him to the robbery. In time, he would do it again. If there was one truth, it was the more money you had, the more power you owned. Wu-Pen had men working in every industry hiring cheap labor across the city and county. If he wanted more gelignite, he could get it. If he wanted to cause trouble in any business, he could. He learned more secrets about people every day from gardeners, house servants, or anyone who they wanted to know about. Those were the spies Wu-Pen used to gather information. Useful information concerning anyone or anything happening around town brought rewards and information that wasn't relevant was stored for use on another day.

The death of Oscar Belding had taken some time to get to. Personally, Wu-Pen didn't like taking his time to do a needed thing like that but Matt Bannister had suspected him of murdering Oscar's friends. That had been an unexpected setback. So, he waited for almost two months to kill Oscar. It had to seem natural and, in the chaos of the mine collapse, he knew extraordinarily little attention would be given to question a heart attack. Wu-Pen preferred a more personal touch to ending a man's life than poisoning but it was the best choice to remain Matt's friend and not a suspect in Oscar's untimely death.

The plant commonly known as Monkshood had delectable leaves for salads or other foods. It was common to use the plant's leaves in Chinese dishes but the leaves were toxic and needed to be boiled multiple times to draw the toxins out to make them safe to eat. A large pot of compressed leaves was boiled for a more extended period than usual to draw out as much poison as possible. Then several small vials were filled with highly toxic water. When Wu-Pen saw Oscar that morning and enticed him with American coffee, he told Bing to pour the water into Oscar's cup and fill it with coffee. It could not have been easier. Unlike common poisons used by Americans, the symptoms acted more like a heart attack with the faintness, difficulty in breathing, sweating, and chest pain. He would die and, in the chaos, no one would suspect poison because everyone was drinking the same coffee and no one else got sick. Everyone ate the same food and no one got sick. The only evidence of the poisoning disappeared in the flooding river. The death drink worked like a dream come true and no one knew any better. Aconite poisoning would never be discovered and even it was, there was no evidence it could be traced back to Wu-Pen or any of his men. The cup Oscar drank out of was also destroyed and thrown into the river. Every objective set by the dragon's fire had been successful. Now it was time to do more.

Ling came back into the dark room and poured another pot of hot water into the bathtub. "Is it warm enough?" she asked.

"Very nice. Join me."

She let her robe fall to the floor and sat in the tub across from Wu-Pen. He put his hands on her legs and smiled lovingly. "The Marshal is too strong in morals to be bought, too wise to be manipulated and too courageous to be threatened. How to get leverage over him without ruining the friendship we have? If I were to threaten harm to anyone he loves or to do so, it would bring harm to us. Any ideas?"

"What do you want from him? What good is he to you?" she asked in Chinese.

"Protection from other Americans. He is a good asset to have when I need him."

"And you like him?"

"I do. He is genuine and honest. And he treats our people well."

"Then you build that bridge and you strengthen it. The only thing over him you should have is a roof to keep the rain from weakening the bridge's strength. How can you help him?"

"I do not know yet."

Ling spoke, "Izu Chee has not paid all his dues. He is hoarding his pay and owes debts to other Chinese. Frame him and turn him in to prove your loyalty to American law and to Matt. You can translate for him and have him hung for the murders of the two white men. It is said Matt cannot solve those murders. Help him and yourself as well by being rid of Izu Chee. He is a bad example for the others."

Wu-Pen smiled slowly. "Yes. I will do that." he watched Ling affectionately. "You are my wise, shining star, my love."

"And you are my good master. The privilege is mine."

## 21

Lucille Barton had rested all night beside her boys in a soft, comfortable bed that felt like heaven compared to her uneven straw mattress. She had slept soundly and hadn't heard Mellissa put the two boys in bed with her sometime during the night. Her eyes opened to the sound of birds chirping and, for a moment, had to wonder where she was. The bedroom was nicely decorated and bigger than her whole cabin. She was warm, comfortable, and felt cleaner than she had in months after bathing in a real bathtub large enough to recline and soak in. The scented bar of soap Mellissa had given her to bathe with had made her feel like a lady for the first time since leaving Pennsylvania. Her memories were sweeter than the moment, though. She had been too exhausted to enjoy the bath or the clean borrowed nightdress she wore to bed. Hanging in an opened armoire was her dress that had been cleaned and pressed. Hanging on a hanger beside the dress was her newly whitened long johns. She was suddenly embarrassed to have had her underclothes cleaned by her hostess. She climbed out of bed, expecting to feel the cold air that she always felt in her cabin but was pleasantly surprised to feel warm and comfortable as she changed into her long johns and dress. A new pair of socks were provided, and she sighed with a bit of humiliation knowing how dirty her stockings with a hole in the toe and the heel must have appeared to Mellissa to give her a new pair of socks. Once dressed, she left the room and went downstairs, where the smell of fresh coffee was inviting. She felt refreshed by a long night of undisturbed sleep and owed her hostess a very appreciative thank you. She entered the dining room and found Mellissa sitting at the dining room table with her husband. Lucille was surprised to see a big man with bushy dark hair and a thick beard looking at her. He was dressed in casual clothing as he held a cup of coffee on the table. He appeared much meaner than she had imagined he would, being married to the kindhearted and gentle Mellissa.

"Good morning," Mellissa said enthusiastically. "This is my husband, Albert. This is our house guest, Lucille. The boys' mother."

Albert smiled kindly. "Good morning. I hope you slept well."

"I don't think I've ever slept better. Thank you for letting me stay the night and for watching my boys for as long as you have."

"You're very welcome. Would you like some coffee?" Mellissa asked.

"Please." She sat down at the table. "I am very embarrassed but thank you for washing my clothes and for the socks. I can never repay you enough for all your kindness. I know my clothes were filthy."

Mellissa snickered quietly. "I didn't wash them myself. I had Albert run them over to our laundress and had them cleaned, dried, and returned. Your socks I tossed away. You can have those."

Lucille lowered her reddening face. "Thank you."

"I heard about your husband," Albert said. "I'm sorry he lost his leg but at least he's alive."

Lucille exhaled heavily. "I am very thankful for that. He's my everything. He was going to take yesterday off work and talk to Billy Jo's father about a job at the quarry. We were going to try to rent her house and get away from the mine but he went to work instead. You know Billy Jo Fasana, right? Matt's cousin?" she asked Albert.

Albert lowered his brow and shook his head slowly. "No. Matt's my brother but we don't come from the same family."

"Oh," Lucille said a bit confused.

"Albert..." Mellissa warned as she poured a cup of coffee. "I apologize for my husband, Lucille. Sometimes he doesn't know when it's appropriate to tease or when it's inappropriate!" She slapped his shoulder as she set the cup of coffee down in front of Lucille.

Albert smiled. "Billy Jo is my cousin. In all seriousness, it's too bad he didn't talk to Uncle Luther.

Your husband probably would have been hired if Luther needed a good man. I don't know your husband but little Michael has been telling me about his Pa. You don't have to tell me that a man who spends that much time with his children is a good man. I already know it. Uncle Luther would have hired him in a minute if he knew that. I would too." He paused to look at Lucille sincerely. "With one leg, it is going to be hard for him to do much labor of any kind, isn't it?"

Lucille raised her eyebrows sadly. "Yes."

"Does he have any blacksmithing experience?"

She shook her head. "No. All he's done is farm work and the mine. We will most likely move back to Utah with his parents. They own a farm there."

"What brought you two over here?" Mellissa asked as she sat beside her husband across from Lucille.

"We didn't like living in Utah. I should say we didn't like living with his parents. We should have bought property there, in hindsight, but we heard Oregon had good soil and the land was cheap. We spent everything we had to get here and underestimated the cost by a lot. This is where we ended up. The mine provided housing and a job. It was never supposed to be permanent."

Mellissa asked, "Do you have any idea what's going to happen now? Has the mine reached out to you at all?"

She shook her head. "Not that I'm aware of. I was at the doctor's all day yesterday after Lawrence was carried out of the mine."

"Are they going to let you live there still if he can't work?"

She shook her head. "I can't imagine so."

"Do you have any money saved up?" Albert asked.

"About twelve dollars, maybe fifteen after this payday."

"That's not much," Albert said with an empathetic grimace.

"No. You don't make much out there. You make enough to survive and that's about it."

"You're going to see Lawrence today, right?" Mellissa asked.

"I'd like to but the doctor doesn't want any children coming to see him right away. He's going to be in a lot of pain and the risk of infection is still high."

Mellissa waved a hand towards her. "We'll gladly take care of them. Albert's taking today off work to spend the day with us. With your permission, we are going to take them out and have some fun with them."

"Of course. I appreciate you both so much for watching them for me. Thank you so much for that and for letting us stay the night here. You have no idea how much I appreciate it."

"It's our pleasure. Joshua will be here all day, so the door will be unlocked when you come back if we're not here. You are more than welcome to cook some food or whatever you want." She paused. "What are your plans when Lawrence is sent home?"

"I don't know. Take him home until we have to

leave, I guess," Lucille answered with a shrug of her shoulders.

Albert asked, "Isn't Slater's Mile kind of filthy? I can't imagine it's very clean."

"It is filthy and disgusting but I keep my house as clean as I can."

He leaned back in his chair. "I'll stop by the mining office and see what they're saying there. I know the owners. I'll try to get some answers for you."

"Thank you," Lucille said with a touch of relief. "My mind is going a thousand directions at once. I can't stay focused on any one thing without having some answers. Such as, do we have to move out of our house and if so, by when? We don't have much but we have some things there. My husband is injured now and we have no money to provide for any of us. Lawrence won't be able to work anymore and I know we'll have to go back to his parent's house." Her face went faint with a hopelessness that could not go unnoticed. "And we have two boys to raise."

Mellissa spoke softly, "Lucille, don't hurry to leave Lawrence today. Your boys will be well taken care of and, until Lawrence is sent home, you are more than welcome to stay here and come and go as you please. We would welcome you to stay, wouldn't we, Albert?"

He nodded. "Yeah, you're welcome to stay. We don't want anything in return. Just help your husband to adjust to losing his leg. I know that's tough and scary for you but it's going to be tougher and scarier for him. Not just pain wise but having to be on crutches for the rest of his life and not working to support his family as he could before. If he is anything like me, that's going to be one of the biggest trials he'll have to overcome, not being able to support his family anymore. I can't imagine how helpless I would feel."

Lucille's eyes filled with liquid.

Mellissa walked around the table and hugged her. "You'll be okay. Don't let the darkness of the moment override the brightness of your faith. Michael told me that you pray all the time and read the Bible with them, so I'm assuming you're Christians, right?"

Lucille wiped her eyes. "Yes."

"Then you'll be okay. I'm going to make breakfast while Albert wakes our kids up for school. By the way, I noticed your boots have a hole in the sole and tried to find a size on them but couldn't see one. Do you know what size you wear?"

"No. I've always just had them measure my feet and try on the sizes they brought out."

"Then will you do me a favor and come with us to the store before you go see Lawrence? I would like to buy you a new pair of boots."

Lucille grimaced. "No, really, it's okay. You've done too much as it is."

Albert reasoned with her, "You need to keep yourself well and your boots aren't doing you one bit of good. A pair of boots will not break us and you can't argue with Mellissa, trust me. Just say okay and go along with it."

Mellissa added, "Let me buy you some boots and

then we'll take you to see Lawrence. Okay? We can leave as soon as the store opens."

Lucille lowered her head not wanting to be a burden. "I already owe you for having my clothes washed."

Albert answered, "You don't owe us anything."

"I insist on the boots," Mellissa said with finality.

Albert took a deep breath. "I told you. You can't argue with her."

# 22

Matt walked into the W.R. Slater Mining Company office and was led upstairs into a large conference room with two large tables set together. Seven people were sitting at the tables with various papers and writing utensils set in front of them. On the walls were large pieces of paper with graphs, numbers and equations that Matt would never be able to figure out. A blackboard had drawings and arrows showing the collapse from different angles with chalk arrows pointing at various things with abbreviated gases and geologic terminology.

William R. Slater sat at the table's head in a plush leather back chair looking as stern as ever. Beside him to his right, Josh Slater sat with a glass of water in his hand. The company's Operations Manager, Howard Peterson, sat to William's left and beside him was the head geological engineer, Wally Gettman. Beside Wally sat the company accountant, Grant Rogers. Beside Josh on the right side of the table, the company secretary, the attractive Debra Slater, sat in the middle next to the mine operations manager, Ron Dalton. Matt was signaled to sit at the other end of the table with all their eyes on him.

"Thank you for coming so quickly, Marshal," William said respectfully. "Of course, you know that we've had a tragedy out at the mine. Thank you for your help out there. I hear you were there all night with the families and I appreciate that. I'm going to let these men tell you what we discovered." He waved toward his head engineer. "Wally..."

Wally stood up and walked to the blackboard and pointed at a drawing of the winze. "The area the explosion happened was just before the western drift of the south winze at about five hundred feet in depth. The rock is granite, a hard substance that is generally solid. However, this area had needed to be timbered heavily because of the pockets of softer minerals, namely Azurite and Pyrite Galena, close to it. The dynamite used to cut down in the exploratory winze and the cutting of a new drift under what we discovered to be a rich vein of quartz had fractured the ceiling. That fracturing had made the top of the winze weak, so it was timbered heavily, as I said. An explosion could drop the whole top-down and that's exactly what happened." He paused to look at Matt. "This was not accidental. We walked through the whole mine or as much as we could and, although there are quite a few areas with a weakened ceiling and walls, they are timbered very well. The most dangerous places with the weakest rock are indicated over here on this drawing; what you'll notice is most of them are in main drifts where men are frequently working and in the open if someone rounds the corner. The winze the explosion took place in is more isolated and at night there is no one down there unless they are building track, leveling the floor for track or timbering. None of those were happening down there for the night before the explosion. It left five-hundred-feet of empty and dark solitude. Someone went down there and set explosives and somehow lit a fuse without being seen. That explosion closed both the drift and the winze, trapping men inside. Marshal Bannister, this was done intentionally to kill as many men as possible. They could not pick a better location to cause the most damage. Whoever did this knows a bit about geology and explosives. And they accomplished what they set out to do." He looked at Ron Dalton. "Do you want to tell him about the explosives?"

Ron spoke, "There are different kinds of dynamite and each kind of dynamite creates a specific type of gas and smoke color. We exclusively use black powder explosives. We have a contract with the Tennison-Smith Black Powder Company and that is all they send us. It gives off a white smoke and leaves a lot of Sulfur Dioxide in the air, which smells like burnt sulfur. After each firing, we clear the area for half an hour to an hour to let that dissipate. We do it daily, so we know our dynamite. What happened yesterday was foreign to us. The explosion was much bigger, more powerful than anything we use. Ross Van Horn witnessed the smoke and dust come out of the winze right after the explosion and recognized the acrid smell and taste of Nitrogen Dioxide from his years in the Nevada mines. Ross sounded the alarm and got everyone out of there as fast as he could. We still sent several men to the doctor for breathing problems because of it. Nitrogen Dioxide is a very deadly gas caused by nitrous explosives. There was no trace of paper or sawdust in the winze. Not one flake of sawdust was found. If they used dynamite made with nitroglycerine, we should find at least a trace amount of something. We could not. A bottle of nitroglycerin isn't logical. The only other substance that could do that is gelignite. Do you know what that is?"

Matt shook his head.

"Gelignite is a relatively new nitroglycerine-based explosive made into a gelatin or putty. What makes it unique is that you can carry it, play with it, form it and do all kinds of things without it exploding. You can light it on fire and it will burn but not explode. The smoke will kill you, though, it's nitrous dioxide. Gelignite will only explode with a blasting cap but it is a stronger explosive than nitrous dynamite. It's been raining and it is very wet down in that winze. Gelignite is the only waterproof explosive; the water won't faze it all. Because of those reasons, we believe it was used. Someone could have placed the gelignite all around those timbers and rock and I doubt anyone would notice as dark as it is down there. I don't know how they lit the fuse and got out of there before it blew. But no one came choking out of that winze once it blew. Jim Longo sent a trammer named Lawrence Barton down there with water for the men to drink not long before it blew. If he had seen a lit fuse, he would have run and warned the others or yanked it loose of the blasting cap or something. I've not had the chance to talk to him yet."

"Did he survive?" William asked.

Debra answered, "He did. I gave you the list of survivors and deceased employees."

"Oh, that's right." He shuffled through his papers and pulled out the list of names. "Damn, we lost a mule." He smiled as he read the list of names. "Do we think Lawrence is responsible? He was the last known person to enter that tunnel."

"Winze," Ron corrected, sounding irritated. "No, we do not think he's responsible. You also lost five good men with families."

Josh scoffed at Ron with a smirk. "Don't get worked up, Ron. My father just made a little joke. But honestly, it does take time to train a mule in there and time is money."

William spoke, "It's a tragedy all across the board." He directed his attention to Matt, "We were sabotaged. Someone murdered these men in my mine and the person needs to be held accountable. I don't know if you're incompetent or taking your time to investigate the deaths of my two employees out at the mile but this takes priority. I want the person responsible for this standing in front of me in the court of law. Because I am having my company carpenters build a gallows behind the courthouse as we speak and whoever is responsible is going to hang. I want to pull the lever to release the trap door of the gallows myself and watch them hang. So, get to investigating and find out who's responsible!" William demanded. "I cannot afford for this to happen again. I need to know who it was and I need to know soon. I don't want my employees killed on the job. I need them to work." He smiled. "Do you think you could handle that or do I need to hire experts to investigate these crimes you can't solve? I could hire the Blackburn Marshals and they'd solve this crime within days."

Matt peered at William coldly. "Jeff Blackburn and his marshals are hired killers, not lawmen. If you bring them into our community, you are asking for trouble. More trouble than you want and a hell of lot more than you know," Matt said strenuously. He continued, "I'll do what I can with what you've given me to work with, which isn't much. Let me ask a very stupid question. William, do you know anyone who doesn't like you?"

William laughed lightly. "You should ask if I care. Many people don't like me but I can't think of one that would do this to get to me. They could blow my house up if they wanted to get to me. Blowing up the mine shaft doesn't affect me one way or the other." He chuckled.

"Winze," Ron corrected again.

Matt asked Ron, "Do you know of any grudges in the mine? Any fighting, threatening or anything like that involving any of the men? It could have been one of your miners with a grudge against another or a bitter ex-employee. There are all kinds of options and targets possible. Does anything stand out?"

Ron shook his head. "There's always petty arguments and sour tempers but they're handled then and there by the men themselves. Our employees are a rough bunch but I can't think of one that would do that. I would be shocked if it was one of our own."

Matt frowned. "Do you know of anyone who has access to the mine outside of your employees with the knowledge of where to set the explosives?"

Ron shook his head. "I don't know."

Matt asked Debra Slater, "How many Chinese do you have working in the mine?"

Her eyebrows raised. "Close to thirty, I believe."

William shouted, "Do you think it was the damn Chinamen?"

Matt shook his head. "No, I don't. I was just curious." He stood up. "I'll get started right now and go see who has bought or ordered Gelignite."

William clapped his hands sarcastically. "Whoa! You sound like a detective already. I figured if I mentioned hiring the Blackburn Marshals to do your job, it might motivate you. You do understand I could have that Marshal's badge stripped off your chest and put on Jeff Blackburn's and let him and his deputies run the county. Go find who did this and I want them alive." His hollow eyes glared at Matt with indignation.

Matt smirked slightly, keeping eye contact with William. "If you ever do hire the Blackburn Marshals, you better be prepared for the fallout. They are mere killers and take whatever they want." Matt pointed at Debra. "You better oversee your daughter carefully if you ever invite them around here because they won't ask your permission to court her. They'll just take her. You don't know them; I do. You better think twice before you ever send that wire."

"You sound afraid of them, Marshal," William said with a spiteful look in his eyes.

Matt shook his head. "No, I'm not. Generally speaking, sheep normally don't go looking for the wolf's den, William. I've already warned you what they'll do. Good day, gentlemen."

## 23

Matt walked to the W.R. Lenning Hardware Store on First Street and waited for Walter Lenning while he helped a young lady pick out wallpaper for her home. Walter was Kyle Lenning's father, Matt's former brother-in-law, who was married to Annie. Kyle died unexpectedly the past summer.

"Nice to see you, Matt. How are you?" Walter asked with a shake of Matt's hand.

"I'm all right. I have a question for you, Walter. Have you ever heard of, stock or order an explosive called gelignite?"

Walter nodded easily. "I have. I don't keep it in stock but I order it for Gary Lansky once in a while. Do you want to order some?"

"No. Who is Gary Lansky?" Matt asked with interest.

"Gary Lansky Well Digging? He has the only well-digging company in the county. And if you need a good well dug, he's the man for it."

"He uses gelignite?"

"Yep. He orders fifty-pound boxes of it, one or two sometimes three, at a time. He uses it to blow deeper into the bedrock. It's great stuff if you have wet ground like in a well."

"No one else around here uses it?" Matt asked.

"There were some miners up in Galt who inquired about it but it's expensive stuff, so they settled for dynamite. Other than Gary, no. It's the only explosive that works for him because of the groundwater."

"Where can I find him?"

"He lives down the road on Second Street right on the edge of town. He has a big sign in his yard that says Lansky Well Digging. Just go to his house and he'll either be there or his wife will tell you where he is."

"Thank you, Walter. How are you and the Misses doing?" he asked caringly. He knew losing their son seven months before was tough on them.

Walter inhaled deeply and let the difficulty of their loss show on his face. "It's been tough. I'm handling it better than my Misses but we'd like to see the grandchildren more. I think that would help. It would be nice if you could ask Annie to bring them over for a few days."

"I'll let her know. Thank you, Walter. I'll see you later."

Walter touched Matt's coat sleeve to stop him. "She's kind of rushing back into relationships, isn't she?" he asked, knowing Annie was courting Matt's deputy, Truet Davis. "It concerns us, you'll understand."

"I wouldn't say rushing, no. The fact is, Truet lost his wife about the same time Annie lost Kyle. They were both hurting with the same kind of ache and it is hard to find someone who understands what you're going through. They had their losses in common that they could share and it grew from there." He smiled. "Trust me, they didn't want to tell me. I was the last person to find out they were courting."

Walter asked sincerely, "Matt, is he a good man? He comes in here and purchases wood, and I've talked to him several times. But is he a good enough man to raise my grandchildren?"

Matt smiled slowly. "He wouldn't work for me if he wasn't a good man. You couldn't ask for a better man to raise Kyle's children. If they get married, those kids will be very blessed."

"Okay," Walter said sadly but with a bit of relief in his voice. "Will you tell Annie we'd love to spend some time with the children?"

"I will. Take care, Walter."

Matt went to the stable and got his horse so he could ride to the granite quarry outside of town after visiting with Gary Lansky. He found the Lansky residence on the eastern edge of town, hitched his horse to a granite hitching post with an engraved L on the sides of it. The homestead had been built long before and had multiple sheds and a large barn with a few horses in a pasture behind the house.

The entire property was fenced off and had No Trespassing signs wired onto the fence and gates. A large well digging sign posted in the yard stated he had the right place. Matt walked through a gate to the front porch and knocked on the door.

An old lady with gray hair and a kind face opened the door. "Hello. Can I help you?"

There was such a joyful spirit in the lady's eyes that Matt couldn't help but smile. "Yes, Ma'am, I was wondering if Gary Lansky is home?"

"Yes, he is. Can I get your name?"

"I'm Matt Bannister, the U.S. Marshal."

"Oh!" she exclaimed. "I've heard of you. Please, come in, and I'll get him."

"I'll wait outside, Ma'am; my boots are muddy."

A moment later, an old man with a stout round body dressed in overalls over a flannel shirt stepped to the door. He had a weathered face with gray hair. He appeared to be a hardened and demanding kind of man to work for. "Marshal, I'm Gary Lansky. Am I in some kind of trouble?"

"No," Matt said as he shook the man's hand. "I understand you're the only man in the county that Walter Lenning knows of anyway, that uses an explosive called gelignite. Is that right to your knowledge?"

Gary's brow lowered as he spoke, "To my knowledge, I'm the only one, yeah."

"Have you noticed any of it missing recently?"

Gary frowned. "I haven't looked in my shed but no. I use it every day once we hit the bedrock. Why do you ask?"

Matt hesitated. "Is it possible you can take a look at your gelignite and tell me if it's all there or if some is missing that you can tell?"

"Sure. I don't use a lot at any one given time. Let me slip my boots on and we'll go out to the shed and look."

They walked to a shed a reasonable distance from the house. "I used to work with your uncles at the granite quarry years ago," Gary explained as they walked.

"Oh yeah?"

"Yeah, I worked as the pit boss for thirteen or fourteen years before I decided to start my company. Now that your uncle Joel's retired, I've been thinking about doing the same. My son works with me and I'll sell the business to him. My lady and I were just discussing it when you knocked. Luther's never going to retire, is he? He won't," Gary answered the question himself. "Right in here is where I keep my explosives. I keep it far from the house in case the worst happens. Dynamite will explode if it catches fire but this stuff just burns. It creates a dangerous gas though. Let me look and see… One…Two… I'll be darned. This box has been opened and you can see where someone scooped out about ten pounds maybe, maybe more." He looked at Matt. "I hadn't opened these two boxes yet. My opened box of explosives is in my wagon locked in a strongbox. This is some powerful stuff and I'm always afraid of someone's kids getting a hold of it and playing with it. So, I keep it locked up and hidden if I can."

"So, you are missing some?" Matt asked, verifying what he had heard.

"There's no reason for this one to be open when I have an opened box in my wagon. Someone got into it, yeah. What's this all about Marshal?" Gary asked curiously.

Matt ignored his question. "Can you write down the names of the folks who work for you? And if you would, don't mention me inquiring about this to anyone, especially not to any of your employees."

"You're not suspecting my son, are you?" Gary asked with a hint of anxiety.

Matt shook his head. "No, I'm not. I would like to know who else works for you. So, if you would write the names down, I would appreciate it."

Matt rode to the Fasana Granite Works quarry and went into the office to talk to his cousin Robert and Uncle Luther. After some chatting about Billy Jo and the mine, Matt took a seat in Robert's office and waited for Luther to bring Ah See into the office. He was the only other Chinese man that Matt knew who spoke English in the Branson community. Ah See stepped into the office and was surprised to see Matt sitting there waiting for him. Luther stepped into the room after Ah See and closed the door. The two men sat down.

Robert Fasana spoke, "Ah See, you met my cousin Matt, the U.S. Marshal. He has some questions for you and I want you to answer them honestly. Okay?"

The small Chinese man nodded once agreeably.

Matt watched him carefully while keeping a friendly expression. "Ah See, I am glad to see recovered from your injuries and are back to work. I have not gotten to see you since that day. How are you?"

"I am well. And you?"

"I'm good. I need to ask you some questions. Do you have any idea who killed the men that attacked you and your friends that morning? I'm talking about Roger Lavigne and Leroy Haywood." Ah See kept his head downturned avoiding eye contact so Matt couldn't see any reaction to the question.

Ah See shook his head slowly. "I was kept in a room in bed for the first few weeks of my injuries. I have no idea who did those things to them."

"Are you sure?" Matt asked in a harder tone.

Ah See was a small man dressed in denim jeans and a black V neck loose-fitting shirt with long sleeves. His face was oblong with no sign of facial hair even though he was in his early thirties. His long black hair was in a queue and his dark narrow eyes avoided Matt as he answered, "Yes."

Matt lifted his brow questionably. "They were killed in retaliation for what happened to you and your friends. You don't know by who, though? Seriously? No one told you that they evened the score for you and your friends? I would find that odd if that were true."

Luther sat with his arms crossed over his chest. He spoke firmly, "Tell him the truth, Ah See."

Ah See answered Luther respectfully. "I do not

know."

Matt asked abruptly, "Who is Wu-Pen Tseng?"

Ah See looked surprised by the question. "Wu-Pen is the President of the Chinese Benevolence Society. He is helpful to the Chinese."

"How so?"

Ah See widened his eyes, uncomfortable with answering the question. "He controls the crime, feeds the hungry and helps with the poor families back home. If we need anything, he is who we go to."

"Like what kind of things might you need?" he asked with interest.

Ah See shrugged. "Chinese rice, rice paper, incense or anything from home. We Chinese have different customs than you and many things are not found here."

Matt leaned forward with his eyes on the small man. "Does Wu-Pen ever hurt anyone? Say someone steals some rice. Would the thief be hurt?"

Ah See smiled uneasily. "No, he does not hurt anyone. He fines them money and we work hard for our money."

"Could Wu-Pen order his guards Bing and Uang to hurt someone else? Have you ever heard of that happening?"

Ah See shook his head. "No. They have one job and that is to protect Wu-Pen from anyone who would try to take his place as President of the Chinese Benevolence Society."

Matt frowned and sat back in his chair. "Why is that important?"

Ah See shrugged. "He is the leader."

"Leader of what?"

"The Chinese Benevolence Society," Ah See answered simply.

Matt sat silent for a minute as he stared at Ah See trying to understand the significance, if any, in what Ah See was telling him. "Why is the Chinese Benevolence Society so important that someone would want to harm Wu-Pen to take his place?"

"To be the leader."

"So, he's the leader of the Chinese people?" Matt asked to get a simplified answer.

Ah See shook his head. "No. He's the leader of the Chinese Benevolence Society."

Matt narrowed his eyes questionably. "Okay. Is he a good leader?"

"Yes. Very good."

"So, you're telling me he's a good man and an honorable leader? He doesn't break the law or have anyone killed like the men that hurt you, for example?"

Ah See shook his head. "No. Wu-Pen is a good man."

"Okay. Do you know these two men?" He pulled the paper out of his pocket that Gary Lansky had written the six men's names that worked for his company. Two names were Chinese.

"Hop Jim and Sing Lim. Yes, I know them."

"Are they thieves?"

Ah See smiled. "No. Very honorable men."

Matt watched him carefully and noticed a slight nervousness under the relaxed composure. "If Wu-

Pen is the leader and let's just suppose he asked them to steal for him. Would they?"

Ah See answered quickly, "Wu-Pen would not ask them to. Stealing is a serious crime and Wu-Pen would not take part in a crime."

Matt exhaled with a bit of frustration. "What if he *did* ask them to? Would they do it?" Matt asked pointedly.

"No. Chinese are unliked by Americans and we know it. Stealing would make us guilty of a crime and possibly returned to China or killed by the Americans. No honorable Chinese will steal."

"What about a dishonorable Chinese?"

"Honor is all we have."

"That means, yes?"

"No," Ah See said with a touch of discomfort in his voice. "Chinese are honorable people. If there is a thief, I do not know one. And it would be a great dishonor for him who steals."

Matt hesitated. His growing frustration of talking in circles with Ah See came out in his voice, "If there is anything you want to tell me about Wu-Pen or anyone else, now is the time. I have two dead men and I'll bet my badge that Americans didn't kill them. And you're telling me you don't know anything about it?"

"I do not," he answered. His eyes once again avoided Matt's.

Matt stood up. "Ah See, I'm glad your injuries healed and you're back to work. It's good to see you again but I don't think you're telling me the truth. When you are ready to, come find me."

## 24

Matt was led into Wu-Pen's office by an old Chinese man wearing an orange robe who smiled kindly at him. Wu-Pen stood behind his desk with a welcoming grin and waved to the chairs in front of his desk. "Marshal, what a wonderful surprise. Please have a seat. I was just going to have some tea; would you like some tea?"

Matt walked in his socks to a chair and sat down. He casually slipped the thong off his revolver's hammer as he sat. "No, thank you." He nodded at the two guards, Bing Jue and Uang Yang. They nodded in return.

"So, what do I owe the pleasure of your company? Please say this is a non-business visit. I would like nothing more than to just talk as friends sometime." He spoke loudly in Chinese towards the door. His smile was warm and welcoming. "The tea is coming. I told Ling to bring two cups. We shall have tea together, like friends. Yes?"

"Sure. Unfortunately, this is not a friendly visit; it's business."

Wu-Pen frowned. "That is disappointing. I had hoped it was a friend visiting without business talk. So how can I help you today, my friend?"

Matt looked at him, suspiciously. "The collapse at the mine wasn't accidental. It was an explosion. It was sabotaged quite intentionally..."

"What? Why would someone do that?" Wu-Pen asked with surprise.

"I don't know. I know the person or persons used an incredibly unique kind of explosive called gelignite. There is only one person in this county that uses it and that's a well-digging company. Here is a list of their employees." He handed the paper to Wu-Pen. "You'll notice there are two Chinese names on there, Hop Jim and Sing Lim. Someone took about ten pounds of gelignite from an unopened box and the only ones who have access and knowledge of it are those two."

Wu-Pen's lips twitched with a surge of ferocity that quickly filled him. He had instructed Hop Jim to take the gelignite from an already opened and well-used box so it wouldn't be easily missed. His perfect plan was falling to pieces in front of his own eyes because of a fool. He would deal with Hop Jim later. He could hide his fury from the Marshal but he knew the Marshal was watching him for reactions. He would not hide all his fury, so he redirected the cause of it. "There are American names on this list too. Why do you assume it was Chinese and not American that took the...

what is it called?"

"Gelignite."

Wu-Pen shook his head and waved an arm unhappily. "You think the Chinese sabotaged the mine? We were helping the miners and the families of those dead and injured. Maybe it was Americans who committed such a horrific act. These men are honorable and would not risk their labors. Marshal, my people labor to feed their families back home in China; it's very poor there and to risk stealing and causing such trouble for the mine would end up in death. Not just their own but their families back in China too. It makes no sense. I must say, I am taken back by any allegation that we may have any part in this. Truly, the punishment is not worth the crime." He narrowed his eyes irritably at Matt. "Have you talked to the other three Americans on this list?"

"Not yet..."

"Then why are you assuming it is either of these two men that stoled the... explosives? What makes more sense? An American with a grudge against someone in the mine or a Chinese who has no English knowledge sabotaging something that has nothing to do with them? Were we not there helping? I must say, I am very taken back by this. If you do not trust me, Marshal, then do say so. But we seem to be your first...um, what is it called? Your first suspects every time someone does something out of the ordinary. First, it was those deaths and, now, this." He raised the fingers on his interlocked hands on the desktop questionably. "Is it because you don't like Chinese people?"

Matt didn't want his hand on the desktop if Wu-Pen ordered either of his guards to attack him, so he rubbed his beard thoughtfully so he could reach his gun quickly if needed. "No. I like Chinese people just fine. I'm asking because two of the employees are Chinese. I can't talk to them but you can. I did talk to Ah See, and he said they were honorable men and would not steal but someone did. I will question the three Americans but I know that the explosives came from Lansky's property. Someone took it and I'm going to find out who. I'll arrest all five of those men and question them day and night until I know they're not lying. I can't communicate with the two Chinese men myself but you can or I can have Ah See translate when I do question them. If I doubt either one of you are translating honestly, I'll find someone else from Portland if I have to and I'll bring them here to translate for me. By the way, someone is getting away with murdering Leroy Haywood and Roger Lavigne for now but I'm not giving up on that either. Just so happens, most curiously, now Oscar Belding is dead too."

Wu-Pen's hands remained clasped in front of him. "Very unfortunate. As I have said in the past… karma. His bad deeds have caught up with him. Our doctor got there too late to try to save him, unfortunately. I have no ill will towards anyone, Marshal. If Hop Jim or Sing Lim took the explosives, I will find out and let you know. I had no idea it was an explosion at the mine. I can understand why you want to find the killer or killers. If it was a Chinese man, I will find out," he said strenuously.

"I will start with these two names and get the truth out of them. I will not allow our people to become known as thieves or killers if, by chance, there is guilt in the Chinese community. You investigate your Americans and I will investigate the Chinese. I want you to know I have no part of anything you have come here to question me about. I only wish you would believe me."

Matt's eyes watched Wu-Pen carefully. "I go by the facts. No one had a reason to kill Leroy and Roger as cruelly as they did, except for the Chinese. As I said at the time, that's not how Americans kill someone. If he was shot, stabbed, or hacked to death with an ax, I might buy into it being another American. But Americans don't tie someone down, torture them with black widow bites or tie someone up to breathe in toxic smoke before pouring whiskey down their throat and burning them. There is only one possible shift that the gelignite could have been put into place without being seen in the mine and that is the graveyard shift when that tunnel was empty. Ironically, most of the Chinese employed there work on that shift. The gelignite was stolen and just so happens two Chinese men work there and have access to it. Do you see where I am going? It sounds a little suspicious, doesn't it? Oscar Belding has a heart attack and you're there. I'm going to have the doctor do an autopsy to make sure he died of a heart attack and not some kind of poisoning. And if it is poisoning, I will come back and arrest you with the charge of murder. There is just too much circumstantial evidence to not notice a Chinese connection to all of it. If I am wrong, forgive me, and I'll admit my error. I do not want to accuse anyone falsely but I will get to the bottom of it and that's a fact."

The door opened and a beautiful young Chinese lady in a long robe carried a tray with a pot of tea and two small cups. She smiled at Matt as she set the tray in front of Wu-Pen. He spoke in Chinese and she responded in a soft and lovely voice. He said in English, "This is Ling. She requests to know your name."

"Matt Bannister," he said with a slight smile.

"M...Matt," she repeated with a heavy Chinese accent. She bowed with a smile and spoke in Chinese. Wu-Pen translated in English, "She wishes to thank you for always being kind to us Chinese."

Matt forced a grin. "My pleasure."

She left as quickly as she had entered.

Wu-Pen said, "Back to what you were saying. You are forgiven because you are quite wrong and if you are not wrong, it happens without my knowledge. And nothing is supposed to happen without my knowledge. But I will, as you say, investigate right away. If I am being lied to by someone and I will find the truth."

"Wu-Pen, I hope you have nothing to do with any of this because I do like you and I would hate to have to arrest you or your men. I take friendship seriously. But I also take my job seriously and my job comes first if a friend breaks the law."

Wu-Pen's lips turned upwards in a fake half-smile. "I understand. Come, let's have some tea and discuss women. Ling is as beautiful as your fiancé, yes?"

"She's a lovely lady, yes. Is she your fiancé?"

Wu-Pen poured the tea. "You could call her my helper. But maybe in the future, yes. She means very much to me." He handed Matt a small cup of tea.

"Thank you. Well, maybe you will invite Christine and I to your wedding someday," he said as he drank the tea.

Wu-Pen drank his tea and smiled, pleased to see Matt drink the tea. If the Marshal suspected him of the crimes of murder, sabotage and poisoning, he would not have drunk any. They still had the fine strings of friendship despite the suspicions. Wu-Pen needed to move fast but the future was still bright. "Yes, I would be honored to have you and Christine at our wedding."

After Matt left the room, Wu-Pen turned to Bing Jue. "The Marshal has caught on to us. The fool Hop Jim opened an unopened box of explosives instead of getting it from the box they use, as I instructed."

"Do you want him dead?" Bing asked.

"No. Not now. But I want him here to answer to me. Ling told me Izu Chee has not paid his taxes or his debts. He is a bad example that we cannot tolerate in our community. Izu will be our sacrifice or his brother will die. We must give the Marshal what he wants, a pawn for the crimes." He glared at Bing with a cold and dangerous darkness in his eyes. "Late tonight, I want you to burn the doctor's office down or the mortuary, whichever one holds the body of Oscar Belding. Go tell Heop Lee tonight you and Uang must get into the doctor's office or the mortuary to know which one holds the body of Oscar Belding. I want it burnt to ashes but it must look accidental. Understood?"

"Yes, understood."

"Ashes, Bing!" Wu-Pen exclaimed loudly with a wild look in his dark eyes. He took a deep breath and exhaled. "Now, I must know what the Marshal and Ah See talked about. We have a very busy night ahead."

## 25

Matt entered the Branson Community Hall and walked upstairs where William Slater and his executives were meeting with the families of the employees killed and injured in the mine's collapse. Chairs had been set up in rows facing the stage and the floor was half full of weeping families waiting to talk to the company men and see what they had to say. Sheriff Tim Wright and his deputies stood in front of the stage like guardsmen over four empty chairs on the stage. Matt knew right then that any news from the Slater family probably wouldn't be good news. He spotted his brother Albert and his wife, Mellissa, sitting with Lucille Barton in the first row. Matt walked to the back of the room and leaned against the wall to wait and watch the families. There was no doubt hostilities could boil over and he wanted to be in a good position to see it coming and approach from behind if he needed to intervene.

William Slater, Josh Slater, Howard Peterson and Ron Dalton all walked on the stage and sat, except for William Slater. He waited until it was quiet before he spoke.

William spoke loudly, "Thank you for coming tonight. I know we had a horrible event and we lost some good men and others have been seriously injured. I'm going to tell you right now that what happened had nothing to do with how we do business or the mine itself. The mine is not liable for what happened to your loved ones."

Alan Rosso stood, inflamed. "What are you trying to pull, you son of a…"

"Not liable?" Betty Zuwalski cried out sharply.

"My husband died in your mine!" Wilma Jensen yelled.

"Listen!" William shouted over Alan and the numerous others who reacted angrily to his words. "Shut up and listen to me or we'll leave and you can just take your chances." He paused as the crowd settled down. "Like I was saying, the mine is not responsible, hold on!" he shouted at Alan Rosso, who was about to yell something. "But I know you folks are hurting. Let's talk about it and I'll tell you what we are prepared to do about it. But first, I want Ron Dalton to explain what caused the collapse. Ron."

Ron stood up to speak. He appeared to be heavily troubled. "It wasn't a collapse. The mine was sabotaged by dynamite."

William stepped forward and shouted to Matt in the back. "Marshal Bannister, have you made any progress on this investigation? Or is this one going to be pending forever too?" He addressed the families, "I want murder charges brought against whoever killed your family members. The investigation is in the Marshal's hands, so if you have questions, ask him. He's supposed to be the law, right? Well, Marshal, have you made an arrest yet?"

Matt could feel his cheeks turning red. It angered him to be called out like that in public. He nodded slightly. "You leave that up to me. The folks came here to hear what you're going to do for them."

"Am I going to lose my house?" one of the wives asked worriedly.

"What about housing? I have three children; what are we supposed to do now that Eunice is dead?"

William shouted, "Didn't you hear me? The mine was sabotaged!"

Joe Thorn stood up and yelled, "The people care about their lives, not your damn mine! It happened and the Marshal's on it like no one else's business, I'm sure. Now what? What are you going to do for Danny Rosso's family and Lawrence's? Lawrence lost his leg; it was not his fault! Danny's dead, that isn't his fault either. They worked for you! So, what are you going to do to help their families?" Many shouts of agreement followed.

William raised his hands and brought them down to lower the noise. "After careful examination of the laws and liability, it was an act of sabotage and all the injuries and deaths, as tragic as they are, are not the fault of the W.R. Slater Mining Works Company. We will not be accountable for any act of sabotage. Just as that man said about his friends not being at fault, the sabotaging of the mine is not my company's fault."

Alan Rosso stood up and pointed at William and yelled, "Are you not going to compensate my brother's wife and children for the loss of Danny? He was your best powder man and you are going to do this to his family? Why are any of us working for you, you son of a…"

Joe Thorn's voice carried over Alan's, "We already know you don't give a damn about us workers but what about the women who lost their husbands? Are you going to kick them out on the streets?"

Alan's younger brother, Tony Rosso, stood and glared at William. "Did you call us here to tell us it's not your fault and that's it? If you don't compensate the families and men, we'll bury your whole damn mine ourselves! Enough is enough! If you can't care about how my brother's family will survive without him and the other families here too, we aren't going to care about yours either. You can go into the poor house and we'll destroy everything you have to get you there!"

William waved Matt forward. "I want this man arrested! Marshal, arrest him! That was a confession if I've ever heard one."

Tony Rosso laughed bitterly and sat down with a shake of his head.

"Marshal Bannister, did you hear me?"

Matt shook his head. "He didn't blow up your mine."

"How do you know? That sounded like a confession to me!"

"I know because his brother was killed in the mine," Matt answered irritably.

William glared at Matt, angered to have his authority questioned. "He threatened me. I want him arrested!"

Matt shouted just loud enough to be heard, "No, he made a conditional threat against your property. And in the heat of the moment, I don't blame him. These folks are worried about their future and all you've told them is it's not your fault. They get it! But that doesn't answer their questions."

"Right," Henrietta Hendricks agreed. "My husband has worked for the silver mine for years and now has a bad hip. He can't work anymore. Are we going to lose our home at Slater's Mile and if so, how can we afford to live anywhere else? We have a young daughter that we are still raising."

William kept his furious glare on Matt for a moment and then turned to Ron Dalton. "Ron, tell them what the company is offering." He turned back to the audience. "The Miners Law states that the company is not liable for injuries or death because the employee agrees to work in the mine, knowing the risks and dangers. We are not legally obligated to give you a dime! But..." he yelled above the angry shouts of many of the men. "We have decided to compensate you. Now shut up and listen or I'll take my money and go home! Ron, tell them what I am prepared to do." He walked to his seat and sat down, obviously upset.

Ron pointed at Henrietta Hendricks. "Henrietta,

I pray Walter recovers and can walk again without difficulty. He is a good man. So was Danny Rosso, Lloyd Jensen, Eunice Zuwalski, Fred Longley, and young Jason Collins. Our sincere condolences to the families of those five men. Walter has a fractured hip, Bobby Alper broke his arm, and Lawrence Barton lost his leg. Joe Thorn was the only one to come out of this uninjured. Although those four men survived, they endured being trapped in a narrow, dark winze that was filling up with water and lived with the fear of wondering if they'd make it out alive or not for just about twenty-four hours. My condolences to all of you who are here tonight for your losses and suffering. Let's talk about what you came to hear. The point Mister Slater was trying to get to is, legally, the mine is not liable for injuries since it was not an actual fault of the mine or our practices. It was an act of murder. The Marshal is investigating that, so our focus is on you folks and what we can do to make this right."

"It's about time someone mentions us!" Wilma Jensen shouted as she wiped her eyes.

Ron continued, "The Slater Mining Works Company has agreed to compensate you for your losses and for being dislodged if you must leave the company housing complex. To answer that question, if your husband passed away and no other family member living in the house works for the company, then you must look elsewhere for housing. They have decided two weeks should be enough time to relocate off company property. I'll add that if you need help finding a place to move, you can go to the

Branson Home and Land Broker's Office for help. Lee Bannister is well informed of what's going on and is willing to work with each family. I suggest talking with Lee to ease your worries about that. Now let's talk finances." He paused.

"That bad, huh?" Joe Thorn yelled out.

Ron continued, "For the families that lost a loved one, the company is willing to offer a thousand dollars and pay the funeral expenses for your loved one. For injured employees, the company is willing to pay your medical expenses and one month of your wages while you recover. That is conditional with a promissory note that you return to work when you are healed. If it takes longer to recover, then a second month's wages will be paid, but nothing after that. For those injured so severely that they'll never be able come back to work, primarily, I'm talking about Lawrence Barton. The company is giving five hundred dollars. And that's what we're going to do."

"A thousand dollars for the life of my husband? It should be five thousand, at least!" Wilma Jensen cried out. "He choked to death on poisonous gas!" she said and broke down emotionally into tears.

Alan Rosso seethed in anger. "Are you so greedy that you can't provide more for my brother's family? He has children and so does most of the others!"

Henrietta Hendricks asked with concern, "Ron, Walter may never be able to work again. We don't know, so what about him?"

Ron ignored the other questions and pointed at Henrietta. "Walter is right on the border. We're going to give him some time and see what the doctor says. We'll talk when this is over, okay?"

Joe Thorn stood up. "What about me? I wasn't hurt, but I was stuck in the mine for a day! Am I not being compensated?"

Ron sighed. "That was brought up, Joe. The company decided that you were not injured, so there is no compensation. However, as the mine superintendent, I am giving you two paid days off to recover. And all four of you will be paid for the time you were in there. That's what I can do for you."

William Slater's head turned towards Ron with a disapproving glare.

"Thank you for thinking of me, at least," Joe said sincerely. He looked around at the others around him, "We all know if it weren't for Ron, none of you would be getting anything."

Alan Rosso stood up, "That's a fact! Ron, Jim Longo, even Matt Bannister never left the mine until those men were brought out. Hell, even the Chinese were there for us, feeding us free food, coffee or anything else we needed to get these men out alive but not once did we see you there, William!"

William stood and walked to the edge of the stage. "Enough! You heard our offer, take it or leave it. But it's all you'll get and if you try to start a lawsuit, fine, you'll lose and I'll spend twice the total amount to make sure you get nothing! Absolutely nothing! Goodnight."

"We'll strike! You won't pull anything out of the mountain," Joe Thorn shouted. "You need to pay these people more money and an extra two hundred dollars for spending a day buried in the mine for those of us who did."

"We could strike," Alan Rosso agreed.

William Slater smirked slowly and peered over his glasses at them. "I could live in comfort for far longer than you can. If you want to threaten to strike, go ahead. I have a smaller mine in Aurora County and we're opening a copper mine in Loveland and have plans of opening a new mine outside of Galt. Your strike won't hurt me. I can hire the Chinese to do your jobs at half price. But do keep in mind, we'll have many openings for better positions and better pay in the future. Here's my promise, anyone who strikes will either be fired outright or will never be promoted above where you are. I won't be blackmailed by laborers. Think of your futures, gentlemen, and your families. If you strike, I'll have you thrown out of our company housing the first day you strike. Goodnight." He walked off the stage, followed by his son and Howard Peterson, escorted out by the Sheriff and his deputies. A few of the men in the crowd cursed at them as they left.

Matt watched the crowd stand to leave. The large Rosso family was leaving when Tony spoke loudly, "Are you going to arrest me, Matt?"

Matt answered, "I'm sure I will eventually for something but not today, Tony."

Tony laughed as he stepped down the stairs.

Before long, Lucille Barton approached Matt. "Thank you. Mellissa and Albert have been a Godsend."

Matt smiled sadly. "You're welcome. How is Lawrence?"

"I don't know. The doctor has him on morphine and all he does is sleep for now."

"They did the same thing to Christine when she was shot. He'll be okay. How are you?"

She shook her head with her eyes filling with water. "I don't know what we're going to do. I guess I will go see your brother Lee tomorrow since we must leave our home. Lawrence can't travel to Utah for a while, so we'll have to survive on the money they're giving us until then."

Matt frowned empathetically. "You know sometimes the Lord has a plan and he'll use the absolute worst circumstances as the catalyst where you look back and say, 'thank you for that, Lord.' This just may be the point that changes everything for the better."

Her frown deepened as she sniffled. "Matt, you seem to have a habit of trying to make a person feel better. But unfortunately, it doesn't work like that. I don't think I'll ever look back and be thankful for Lawrence losing his leg or us losing our home. I think we never should've come to Oregon." She sighed hopelessly. "No, we never should've left Pennsylvania. Anyway, you have a good night."

Matt believed in a Holy God who cared for and loved His people. What he had told her was the truth, God often uses the worst circumstances to lead to new and exciting directions in life. However, what Lucille said was true as well. Better times don't always come quickly and it could be just the beginning of a long and severe season of drought in their lives. Even so, the Lord is able to bring about a springtime of beauty and freshness and that's something to always hope for. It does not matter how cold, bitter or long winter may last; spring, eventually, comes.

Albert put his arm around Matt's shoulder and spoke lightly, "Ron had to threaten to quit his job to get these folks any money at all."

Matt shook his head with disgust. "That does not surprise me."

## 26

Izu Chee was thirty-two years old and had been in America for four years. He and his younger brother, Wang Chee, left their small village and came to America to make a fortune in gold like so many other men dreamed of doing. Like most of the dreamers, they had struck out in finding gold and found jobs instead. Izu and Wang worked for the Chinese Benevolence Society digging tunnels underground between the buildings in Chinatown. They were often out of sight and unknown by any Americans. Izu was a hardworking man but he had a gambling problem with fan-tan and wasn't paying his debts around Chinatown. Wu-Pen paid the workers a fair amount to dig the tunnels and, although he could withhold their dues, he preferred to pay what was earned and leave everyone to pay their dues on their own accord. Izu had not been paying his tax to the Chinese Benevolence Society and had been warned and still, his debts were more than he was paid. He was a pestilence that could corrupt others as he continued to work and live without paying his tax.

Now with his hands tied behind his back, sitting uncomfortably in a chair nervously staring at Wu-Pen, Izu's fearful eyes revealed his desire to pay what he owed and never be late with his tax again. Izu could not say so due to the cloth shoved in his mouth. In the chair beside him, tied and gagged as well, Izu's younger brother Wang, sat with the same terror in his eyes.

Wu-Pen sat behind his desk, calmly with a scowl on his face. He slid a scroll of paper across his desk for Izu to look at. It was written in English and could not be read or understood by Izu. Wu-Pen spoke in Chinese, "You might think you know why you are here. You haven't paid your taxes to us in three months. You owe the restaurant, you owe for fan-tan, you owe for laundry and you owe me. Those debts would bring you here and maybe leave you with some wounds but I will overlook them. Instead, I have a mission for you. A favor that only you can accomplish, but you may not like it. I have taken the liberty of writing a confession. I will have you sign your name to show your willingly making a commitment to make it legal. Let me tell you what you are confessing to the American's of doing. You confessed to threatening Hop Jim's life to tell you where the gelignite explosives were stored on the well-digging property. You took the explosives and walked into the mine posing as a miner during the night and set the explosives in cracks where you knew it would cost the most American lives by trapping and killing them. You set the explosive cap and lit a seven-hour long unscented joss stick tied to the fuse of the blasting cap on top of the timbering, which burned slowly until it lit the fuse. The explosion was timed to explode during working hours to murder Americans. You committed this crime for what American miners did to your friends Ah See, Chee Yik, and Kot-Kho-Not. As for the two men that harmed your friends, you murdered Leroy Haywood and Roger Lavigne as cruelly as you could imagine. This scroll is a confession for all the crimes you have committed to avenge your friends. Do you agree?" Wu-Pen asked pointedly.

Izu shook his head vigorously and tried to speak through the gag shoved in his mouth.

Wu-Pen shook a finger at him and frowned. "Let me answer for you. Yes, you agree, because if you refuse, your brother will pay for the consequences and take your place. Your brother is a good young man but if he must take your place, your family back at home will also pay the consequences and I will send you immediately back to China to witness what happens to them." He ordered Bing Jue. "Remove his queue."

Bing grabbed Izu's long braided queue tightly, while Izu's eyes widened in horror and tried to plead for mercy. Bing pulled a knife from his waistline and cut through the thick hair like a knife through soft butter. Bing dropped the braided queue in Izu's lap. He would not be able to return to China without his queue or it was certain death by the Qing Dynasty laws.

Wu-Pen asked, "I will ask you again. You are guilty of these crimes, yes?"

Izu's tears rolled down his cheeks as he looked at his frightened younger brother. He nodded painfully.

"Yes, I thought so. Sign your name." Wu-Pen asked Bing Jue to untie Izu's hands but keep a hold of his left hand in case Izu tried to attack him while he signed the document. Reluctantly and emotionally, Izu signed his name where he was directed. Wu-Pen continued as Bing tied Izu's hands together again, "Izu, do know, your sacrifice will be rewarded by me personally supporting your family back home. I will not allow the Americans to sacrifice an innocent Chinese man without taking care of your family. Your sacrifice will benefit our people and your brother too. You are a hero and will be remembered as such." He instructed his guards, "Take them both to the hiding room until morning. Let them have one last night to say goodbye. And Wang," he spoke pointedly to Izu's brother. "No words to anyone else in our community about this or you will suffer greater than your brother."

Bing and Uang took them by the arms and led them out of Wu-Pen's office. Wu-Pen reread the confession. He had summarized quickly to Izu what it said but had neglected to share a few things such as Izu had an accomplice, his brother, Wang Chee. Wu-Pen could not afford to have an angry brother seeking revenge against him in the community. For now, Izu didn't need to know that they both were being turned over to the American judicial system for murder.

Ling Sheng entered the office through a hidden door in Wu-Pen's home and guided a young, fourteen-year-old girl into the office. The young girl was scared and held her arms close to her shirt. She stood straight and still while Ling opened the main office door and called Ah See into the office. He stepped into the office timidly.

"Ah See, my friend, come have a seat. You too, Meili. Sit please," Wu-Pen invited them both to sit in the two chairs in front of his desk with a smile. They seated themselves nervously.

Wu-Pen spoke in English, "I know you talked with the Marshal today. What was said?"

Ah See answered in English, "He asked questions about you. I told him you were a good man. You did not hurt anyone and only wanted to help all Chinese. He asked if I knew who killed those men; I said I did not. I don't think he believed me but I said no more," Ah See's voice shook nervously.

Wu-Pen smiled. "Do you know why we are speaking English?"

"So no one understands?"

"Yes. Do you know why?"

Ah See shook his head. "No."

"Why do you think Meili is here?"

"I do not know," he answered, growing more anxious. Meili was his youngest sister that Wu-Pen had kidnapped from China and sailed to America under guard to keep her safe from the sailors and

215

anyone else who would take advantage of the young lady. She was smuggled into Portland and brought to Branson. Meili lived with Ah See and worked at a Chinese restaurant in Chinatown.

Wu-Pen answered, "Your sister is beautiful. I have no intention of hurting her or allowing anyone else to. But..." he paused to glare warningly at Ah See. "I will be forced to if you ever turn against me. You are a danger to me and what I want this community to be. The danger is you speak English and the Americans know it. You could speak to anyone and say too much about me and what I do here. Unlike you, I'm not here to get rich and go home but I could make you rich enough, so you never have to work again and send you and Meili both back home. I like you, so I will give you a choice, either commit your loyalty to me and the vision of the Chinese Benevolence Society or lose your queue and be shipped back to China immediately while Meili stays here with me." He glanced at Meili and smiled appreciatively.

Ah See narrowed his brow sincerely. "I am loyal to you and the society. I have not betrayed you and pay my share of taxes. I have done nothing wrong." His sincerity showed in his expression.

"Not yet. The Marshal may ask you to translate for him when he talks to Izu Chee or his brother. If that happens, you are to make sure the Chee brothers are guilty and are proud of their deeds. I will read to you the confession and the story we tell must be the same. We will meet daily to make sure we know all that was said. I want no errors

216

or a reason for the Marshal to doubt me. So, we must communicate and if you do translate for the Marshal, I want to know every word that was said, as I will tell you when I translate. The Marshal will compare our words and if he outsmarts you and finds a lie in our story, your sister will pay the price. Are we clear?"

"Yes," Ah See said anxiously.

"Good. Meili may leave," he said with a smile as she smiled awkwardly. When she left, Wu-Pen continued, "Meili needs not to know what we are talking about. Tell her we are discussing her wages in the restaurant because she is working hard to receive a raise. Now, let's discuss what the confession says and what you are to say if Matt ever asks you to translate."

## 27

The flames rose high above the two-story house that had been the Fasana Furniture & Undertaking Parlor. The entire structure was engulfed in flames and the roof had already collapsed into the fire that raged uncontrollably. The top floor was full of furniture for sale of all types and price ranges that had been profitable for Solomon and Deloris Fasana. The ground floor had the office, a good-sized chapel for funerals, and an area of more furniture displayed that was for sale. The basement was the undertaker's embalming room and storage area, where he kept the deceased bodies that needed to be cared for along with some extra furniture to replace what was sold. There was a lot of material for the fire to consume, including the rope and pulley elevator lift they had installed that traveled between the three floors. It made the furniture moving and body lowering into the basement much more manageable than carrying heavy items up or down the stairs. It had been a wise and expensive investment that made the business much easier now that Solomon was in his fifties. He had put everything he had into his business and, now, he stood a half block away in a slight mist watching it all burn to the ground. One of the sheriff's deputies woke him up, informing Solomon that his business was fully engulfed in fire. A crowd had gathered on the streets surrounding the burning house and the Branson Fire Brigade couldn't get close enough to try to put the blaze out. Instead, they focused on keeping neighboring houses from catching fire.

Matt could see the sorrow on his uncle's face as he neared him. "Uncle Solomon, I'm sorry about your business. Any idea what caused the fire?" He had been woken up by the commotion outside as the news of the fire spread through the sleeping community. It was almost five in the morning and still dark out.

Solomon shook his head sadly with the reflection of the flames glowing off his damp face. "No." He scoffed with disgust. "I might've forgotten to turn off one of my camphene lamps in the embalming room. If I did, that might've caused it. I always turn them off, though. I was down there all day preparing for tomorrow's funerals and maybe I didn't turn them off. I don't know, Matt. Maybe some coal fell out of the fire and smoldered, I don't know. It could've started anywhere."

"I was going to have Doctor Ryland do an autopsy of Oscar tomorrow to verify he died of heart failure. Do you think this could have been arson?"

Solomon shook his head, doubtfully. "There's no reason for someone to burn me out of business. The more I think about it, the more I think I might have forgotten to turn off my camphene lamps. If they get hot enough, and certainly they would've by now, they can ignite the camphene reserve and explode. At least that's what they used to say when everyone went to kerosene. Of course, I've never had a problem with my lamps until now, maybe."

Matt frowned curiously, "You use kerosene in them, don't you?"

Solomon shook his head. "No, I use camphene. It's hard to find nowadays but Albert Jackson worked back east years ago in the manufacturer where they made the stuff and mixes me up a gallon at a time. I imagine his homemade stuff burns a little hotter than what was sold to the public. I told him I needed brighter light and I had brighter light with two of those lamps burning." Solomon paused in thought. "If I forgot to turn one of those off, the lamps going to get really hot by now and if what they say about those old lamps is true, it might have caused the fire. And if the keg of homemade camphene caught fire, which it obviously has…there's no stopping it."

Matt's first thoughts had been Wu-Pen had sabotaged the building to hide any evidence of poisoning Oscar Belding but, now, there was reason to doubt Wu-Pen had anything to do with the fire. Camphene lamps were popular in the past but as the Civil War started, a two-dollar tax was placed on alcohol to help fund the war. Alcohol was one of the main ingredients of camphene and the tax drove the burning oil price up and camphene was soon replaced with the cheaper and safer burning oil called kerosene. Camphene was highly volatile and there were many reports of fires caused by the camphene lamps combusting when they got too hot, dropped or the flame got too close to the reserve. Kerosene burnt well and wasn't as volatile but lacked the brightness of a camphene lamp. The camphene product that Albert Jackson made for Solomon was apparently hotter than the original and put off a brighter light than kerosene could. As people age, their eyes become weaker and brighter light is needed sometimes to see more clearly. Matt had no doubt his uncle needed bright light in the dark basement of the mortuary but he doubted the wisdom of burning a substance that was homemade by an old man in town without knowing precisely what it was and how volatile it was. Solomon may never have had a problem with his old camphene lamps but his need for brighter light quite possibly cost him his business. It was sad to see all Solomon had worked for burn to the ground. "Uncle Solomon, do you think it's accidental?" Matt asked.

"If I forgot to shut off one of those lamps? Sure. They get hot, especially if they have been burning for this long. That's my guess to what happened."

"So, what are you going to do now? Rebuild?"

Solomon looked at his nephew and gave a disheartened smile. "Yeah, with brick and mortar. But for right now, I might as well watch the fire. It's not every day we get to watch a fire like this one.

That smoke rising in the sky is probably the most expensive smoke Branson's ever seen and it's just dark enough that no one can see it. Don't get too attached to your stuff, Matt. All that you own can go up in smoke in a matter of hours. But as long as we're still breathing, we can start over and rebuild."

Wu-Pen stood on the temple roof, staring at the fire's orange glow in the sky across town. A small, wicked smirk of pleasure was on his face as he stared at the beautiful light. There would be no autopsy on Oscar and the secrets of his death would be preserved to use again when needed. He had avoided being discovered and there was no evidence left to find. Like he had done to the Engberg & Penn Assayers Office, his locksmith opened the mortuary door and allowed Bing and Uang inside the building to pour kerosene in the basement and across the two upper floors before lighting the place on fire and locking the door on their way out.

In a day or two, Wu-Pen would approach Solomon Fasana and offer some Chinese men to clean up the rubble and construct a new building for a fair price. During a time of devastation, a helping hand was very much appreciated and the Chinese Benevolence Society was all about helping hands for anyone in need. Today, however, he would deliver Izu Chee to Matt Bannister along with the confession. If it was always himself translating for Izu, Wu-Pen knew Matt might be skeptical and send for a Chinese interpreter from out of town. There was little doubt that Matt would ask Ah See to translate to verify the story. It was best to cover all angles and be prepared for the worst and the least unlikely turn of events. Ah See knew what would happen if he messed up or he could be rewarded for his cooperation. Like any man would, Ah See agreed to becoming a rich man as long as he was loyal to Wu-Pen. Of course, that was not entirely true either. A man cannot let a threat to his livelihood remain. Ah See would have an accident someday soon after Izu and Wang Chee were prosecuted for their crimes. For now, Wu-Pen needed to free his name from any suspicion before he could move forward.

## 28

Billy Jo was happy in her Slater's Mile home. Joe Thorn had changed since being trapped in the mine. He was more sensitive, more caring and more appreciative of her and the boys. He had been given two paid days off to recover from the trauma of being trapped in the mine. He took the two boys for walks and took them to town to buy candy and spend time with them. He had laid with Billy Jo one night and spoke of admiring Lawrence Barton for being the kind of husband and father he was. The time Lawrence spent with Lucille playfully chasing their boys around the community was something Joe had wished he could do as freely and easily as Lawrence did. Lawrence didn't care what anyone else thought; he just enjoyed playing with his boys. Joe had realized he never played with his boys and was ashamed of that. He wanted to change his life. He was a lighter-hearted man with an interest in his boys and Billy Jo. It was nice to have a home filled with laughter and joyful boys instead of all the anger they had known in the past. It was what she always wanted and Billy Jo prayed it would last. However, Billy Jo had foolishly started a relationship with Wes Wasson. Her feelings for Joe were far more substantial than her feelings for Wes but she felt an obligation to explain to Wes that she was going to stay with Joe. It was only right and he deserved to be told by her rather than Wes finding out from Bruce Ellison. The problem was, she had no one to watch her boys. Lucille Barton had not been home since Lawrence was hurt and no one knew what was happening with them.

It was Joe's first day back to work and she took advantage of his absence to walk to town with her boys. It was a muddy walk, but the rain had ceased, and light gray clouds filled the sky. She anxiously tried to think of a way to break free of her boys to go see Wes. The last she heard, Lucille's children were at Albert and Mellissa's and on that thought, she walked to their house, curious if they knew where Lucille had been staying. She knocked on the door and Mellissa opened it.

"Oh, hi, Billy Jo. What a surprise, come in and take off your boots, please," she invited, noticing the muddy boots on her and the boys.

"Thank you, but I'm wondering if you have seen Lucille?"

Mellissa pointed with her thumb behind her towards the inside of her house. "Oh yes, she's been staying here with us. We're watching the boys while she goes to see Lawrence. The boys

225

aren't allowed to visit yet. That's where she is now. The boys are in the back room drawing. Would you like to come inside?"

Billy Jo shook her head slightly as an idea came to her. "No, but could I ask a huge favor? I need to go to the store and want to stop by and see Lawrence too. Would it be too much trouble to ask you to watch my boys for an hour or so?"

Mellissa looked at the two boys and made a crooked funny face to make them laugh. "I'm sure I can handle two more boys for a while." She bent over and asked the boys, "Wyatt, how would you and Brice like to draw some pictures with Michael and Ray?"

Wyatt smiled, as did Brice. "We would."

She swung her arm around her body to wave them inside rather dramatically. "Then get in here and get your boots off." The two boys hurried inside and sat on the rug laid out on the clean wood flooring and began untying their boots in a hurry. "Have they eaten, Billy Jo?"

Billy Jo answered, "No. I'm sorry, I should have fed them."

"No worries, I'll feed them. I'll see you when you come back."

Billy Jo did need to go to the butcher shop and store but she walked quickly, not to waste a moment, towards the Ellison's home. Her stomach was filled with nervous butterflies and her throat was dry as she knocked on the door and opened it up. "Hello?"

"Oh, Billy Jo, come in," Florence Ellison said invitingly. "Wes was just wondering where you have been."

"Hey!" Wes shouted excitedly with a wide grin as he sat on the davenport with his foot resting on a stool. "It's about time you showed up. I didn't know if you were okay or not. Get over here, Sweetheart." He held out his arms for a hug.

Billy Jo giggled. She leaned over to hug him and he tried to kiss her but she sat down beside him, avoiding the kiss and smiled awkwardly. "So, how are you?"

"I'm doing better every day. It won't be long and I'll be up on my feet dancing again. Frank says when I'm ready if I promise to behave, he'll get me a job at the sawmill. So, it won't be long until I can support you and the boys. Are you all moved into your house now?"

Wes's older sister Florence sat in her rocking chair listening. "Yes, what is happening with that? Have you left that beast, Joe Thorn?"

Billy Jo bit her bottom lip hesitantly as Wes took hold of her hand affectionately. "No, I haven't," she said sadly.

"Did he threaten you again?" Wes asked with hardening eyes.

She turned her body to face Wes and Florence. "No. I was going to move back into my house but Joe was trapped in the mine. I couldn't leave him after he came out of the mine. He's changed for the better and I'm giving him another chance."

Wes tilted his head and glared at her, not understanding precisely what he was hearing. She had climbed on his lap to kiss him a few days before and now she was forgetting about him and staying with Joe. "No, he hasn't changed. He'll go back to being himself in a week or two; just wait and see."

Her face reddened. "I have to give Joe one last chance. That's why I'm here. I need to let you know that."

"Well," Florence said, "I think I'll go upstairs and mend some of Frank's shirts. It was nice seeing you again, Billy Jo."

"You, too." She could tell Wes was frustrated. "I'm sorry, Wes."

"Sorry?" he asked dumbfounded. "Billy Jo, I'm not a bit sorry for what we have. What I am sorry for is you and your boys. He was trapped in a mine shaft; I get it. It was scary. He appreciates what he has for a minute until it gets old again and then he'll go back to being the Joe Thorn the town knows. And you'll have another split lip and bruised ribs. If that is what you want, good for you, you'll have it! A dream come true, huh?" he asked, irritated.

Her head lowered. "It's not like that," she said softly. "He's changed."

Wes scowled. "How many times have you said those same words over the years?"

Her eyes grew moist. "A lot. But this time is different. He wants to change for the boys and me."

Wes turned his head away from her. "Well, I hope he does because you're giving up a great thing with me." He turned his head to look into her eyes. "Is it over between us?"

She smiled sadly. "I have to give Joe another chance."

"And what if he blows it like usual? Am I supposed to sit here and wait like a fence post? You already know I'm hooked on you. You are the light in my life and the daisy of my soul. What am I supposed to say? I'm healing and I might meet one of the dancers at the dance hall and fall in love or some crazy thing like that. I could be hooked up with someone else when you realize you've been fooled like so many times before. What then, Billy Jo? But you know, I don't want one of the ladies at the dance hall, I want you. I was hooked from the first time I saw you and still am. We had a plan, I thought and that is all I could think about as I sit here waiting. I don't want it to be over between us, Billy Jo. I will not hound you like a fly or chase after you like a dog in heat, either, but I don't want to lose what I have with you. You mean a lot to me," he said softly.

"Wes..." she said with a single teardrop balancing in the corner of her eye. "I never meant to hurt you."

"Shh...you're so beautiful," he whispered and moved his lips closer to kiss her.

She turned her head and gasped. "Wes, please... let me try to explain."

He jerked his hand out of hers harshly. "I can't stop you! But damn it, once I'm healed, the wait's over. I'll turn my back and never look at you again, so make up your mind soon," his voice had a sharp edge. "I'm not a wall to bounce your mixed emotions off. You either stick with me or not."

She grasped his hand affectionately. "I think you're a wonderful man, Wes. And maybe I am a fool but I need to give him one last chance for me."

He grinned slowly and then laughed. "You'll find out for yourself. Go on and get out of here."

## 29

Lawrence Barton opened his eyes slowly and turned his head to his left, where his beautiful bride was sitting beside him with a tightly squeezed, sad smile. The world's weight appeared to be on her slumped shoulders and her usually bright eyes revealed the worry that she carried. He spoke to her a few times over the past couple of days but he had been heavily sedated with morphine and barely remembered what they had said.

"Good afternoon," she said kindly.

He didn't care what time it was. "I'm thirsty," he said dryly.

She helped him to sit up where he could get a drink. He drank from a glass of water and wiped his mouth. "How are the boys?" he asked. Lucille told him where they had been staying and that the boys missed their father and were praying for him.

"How are you?" he asked dryly. Since the morning of the explosion, he had not smiled and there was no trace of one now.

Her eyes slowly grew moist. "I'm hanging in there." She squeezed her lips together as her emotions took over her facial features.

Lawrence's brow lowered with concern. "What is it?"

"We have to move. We have two weeks to be out of our home. They are giving us five hundred dollars for your injuries. I don't know what we're going to do," she began to weep.

Lawrence sighed hopelessly and a rare angry reflection overcame his eyes. He spoke bitterly, "There's not much I can do about that, Lucille! I can't just get up and go to work. I don't have a leg anymore! There's nothing I can do about that." Tears streaked down his cheeks as he sucked on his cheek and breathed in deeply. His angry eyes burned straight ahead, refusing to look at his bride.

Lucille wiped the tears from her face. She spoke through a strained and broken voice, "I know that, Lawrence. Maybe I was hoping one of us could be strong enough for the other. I have no strength left. I've been so worried about you and thank heavens, Mellissa is helping with the boys…"

His snarl was ugly when he turned his head and glared at her impatiently. For the first time in their marriage, he shouted at her, "Lucille, I lost my leg! I'm trying to deal with that. I stare at it all the time and it's gone! I can't walk, I can't run, I can't take the boys fishing, I can't work! Do you understand that? I'm no good anymore. I'm no good for anything. What can I do to help you? I can't go anywhere;

I can't hop over to the mine's office and ask them for more time. I can't hop along the mine shafts leading a mule. I can't work!" he screamed loudly. "I can't even carry a bucket of water." He threw the glass of water across the room, shattering the glass. He buried his face in his hands and wept.

Lucille was shocked by his display of anger. "I'll have to get a job," she said softly.

He looked at her hopelessly. "That's supposed to be my job. I'm the one that's supposed to work."

"I know." She put her hand on his. "Lawrence, I don't know how but we'll get through this. The Slater's had a meeting and said Lee Bannister would try to help those of us who are being displaced. I'll talk to him tomorrow morning. I stopped by his office a few times but he was with another family from the mine. Maybe I'm just feeling overwhelmed and I shouldn't be. I'm sure we can rent something small and I can find work to pay the rent when the five hundred dollars runs out or we can just stay here long enough for you to heal and move back into your parents' home."

He groaned with frustration. "Why? So I can listen to my father tell me what a worthless man I am during planting season and again during harvest? No. If I have to lay around and be crippled, at least let me do it in peace. I'm going to be sick of being worthless on my own. I don't need my father and brothers reminding me of it."

"What's that supposed to mean?"

"It means exactly what I said. I know we have to move; I can't help. We need to find a place to live; I can't help. We might have to live in a tent, we don't have one, but if we did, I couldn't help put it up! If one of the boys falls in the river, I can't help save him! Lucille, I'm worthless as a man. I'm worthless as a husband and a father too." The agony in his face appeared more excruciating than the pain of the tons of rock that crushed his foot.

She bit her bottom lip tightly as she breathed in deeply. "Lawrence, you're not worthless. You'll have to learn to walk with one crutch, not two. So, you can carry a bucket of water and you can fish. Once you get used to it, you could save your son if he fell in the river too. You'll be able to do a lot of things, even work in an office or something not so physical. No one ever said you had to lay in bed for the rest of your life."

He closed his eyes as another tear slipped out and rolled down the side of his face. "If you went to work somewhere, you'll probably meet someone some successful man who is a whole man and leave me..."

"Shut your mouth!" she snapped with her eyes burning into him. "I have committed my life to you and our family for better or worse. Right now, it is worse, but it could have been a lot worse. You could have been killed. And then where the boys and I be?"

Lawrence turned his head to face her. He spoke weakly, "Better off than with me."

Her beautiful brown eyes narrowed in on him angrily. "Lawrence, you lost part of your leg, not your mind or your health. You are still the man I love and our boys adore. Our home's a little shaky right now but we will get through it! We won't get through your self-pity if you can't look in the mirror and be the man you've always been. Nothing has changed, except part of your leg. You're alive and your two boys and I are so thankful for that. I wish you would be too. Then we could be happy again. I love you, Lawrence. Maybe you don't know it but you're a whole a lot more than part of your leg!"

He licked his dry lips and tried to speak, but his eyes filled with emotion. "I'm scared. I'm afraid I won't be the man I've always been. I'm afraid we'll be on the streets and I have to watch my family suffer because I can't labor to support you." Tears silently slipped down his cheeks.

Lucille ran her teeth over her bottom lip as she wiped her eyes. "God didn't provide for you in the mine for nothing, did he? I'm scared too and I don't know what's going to happen but I do believe, a year from now, we'll look back and be able to say, 'the Lord took care of us.' I do believe that but until then, yeah, it is scary."

"I don't want to sit around and not be productive. What can I do to support my family?" he asked, staring upwards towards the ceiling.

"You could work in a store or a bank, anywhere where it's not too physical. You'd make money and it's safer than the mine. It's not a hopeless future Lawrence, just a change."

He gazed appreciatively at his wife and wiped his face clear of his tears. "I love you, Lucille. All I could think of in the mine was how I didn't want to leave you and the boys."

She smiled emotionally. "Then don't. We have boys to raise and a family still to make. This is a big bump in our path but we will get past it. Don't give up on the boys and me. Please."

He frowned. "I never would."

"When you give up on yourself, you're giving up on us. We need you. I'll spend tomorrow looking for a place to live and hopefully find a place before you get out of here. I was very flustered when I came in here and I apologize. You have your own fears. You don't need mine added to you. But we're going to be okay."

He spoke softly, "It helps to face those fears when we're together. I miss seeing you when I wake up. And I can't tell you how much I miss my boys."

She kissed his cheek. "And I miss having you beside me when I'm sleeping. This is just temporary."

He smiled for the first time. "Pray with me?"

"Always."

## 30

Wu-Pen entered the Marshal's Office, followed by his two guards, Bing Jue and Uang Yang, who guided the third man with his hands tied in front of him into the office. Wu-Pen appeared agitated. "Is the Marshal here?" he asked.

Truet yelled, "Matt."

Matt came out of his private office with a yawn. He glanced at the man with his hands tied curiously. "Who's this?"

Wu-Pen glanced at Izu and then back at Matt. "To our shame, this man might be of interest to you." He held out a rolled-up scroll. "It is his confession. You'll find it interesting."

Matt unrolled the scroll and began reading it quietly. He glanced up from the paper. "Did you write this?"

Wu-Pen nodded.

"Does he speak English?"

"No."

Matt handed the paper to Truet to read and opened the gate to the partition. "Bring him back to the table. How did you come to find him so quickly after our discussion yesterday?"

Wu-Pen explained, "Your information. Hop Jim, who is an honest employee of the well-digging company, confided that Izu and his brother, Wang, threatened his life if he didn't tell them where the explosives were kept. That led me to Izu and with some, shall we say, more severe pressure than you can apply, he confessed. His brother, Wang, ran away but we will find him. All my people are looking for him." He paused and lowered his head in shame. "My apologies. I thought you were a fool for thinking a Chinese man would or could do these things. I was wrong. It is to our shame."

Matt's suspicions had been on Wu-Pen for the crimes but now he was relieved to know Wu-Pen had been telling him the truth. "Can you stay here and translate for me? I have many questions for him. What's his name?"

"His name is Izu Chee. I am more than willing to translate."

For the next hour, Matt spoke to Izu while Wu-Pen translated. Truet wrote the questions and answers on a tablet as they were being asked. Phillip copied the confession onto another piece of paper to keep in their files. The original would be delivered to the District Attorney's Office with an arrest report.

Izu Chee did not appear menacing or dangerous in the slightest. His dark eyes seemed to be frightened and helpless but appeared hostile when they gazed at Wu-Pen. Izu, like many of the Chinese men, wasn't too tall. He stood five foot seven inches tall and weighed a hundred and forty pounds. He had an oblong hairless face with soft features with a small scar on his upper lip. His hands were small but calloused from hard work. There was nothing about his appearance that would cause any alarm or hint to being capable of doing such awful crimes as he had confessed to. He appeared harmless and that was far different than the hardened criminals Matt had dealt with over the years. It was abnormally strange for Matt to hear the soft-spoken Izu explain his reasoning of why he committed some of the most heinous and cruel crime scenes Matt had ever witnessed before.

Matt would ask a question and Wu-Pen translated the question into Chinese. Izu answered in Chinese and then Wu-Pen would translate the answer into English. Perhaps it was his suspicious nature that made Matt wonder if Wu-Pen was repeating the questions precisely or giving Matt accurately translated answers in return. Matt had an underlining sense of doubt the more he watched Izu's body language. Indeed, the Chinese may have been a different society with different customs but human beings were not that different, no matter where they were from. Matt observed Wu-Pen and Izu carefully and it was striking how Izu's facial expressions and body language didn't line up with his answers the way Matt thought they should. His shoulders were tight with his arms crossed at his chest. Every few minutes, he lowered his hands to wipe the sweat off his palms on his pants. He blinked frequently and the tendons stood out in his neck and his leg shook uncontrollably under the table. Those signs of a frightened man were not in alignment with the answers Wu-Pen was giving. The answers were too forthcoming, up-front and eager to give a full confession of guilt. There was no attempt to lie, hold back the truth or deflect his guilt elsewhere. Izu didn't try to justify his actions nor, according to his answers, did he have a conscience. In Matt's experience, most of the time criminals who were scared tried to lie and deny their crimes and those who knew they were caught and wanted to confess were more relaxed and relieved to tell their story. Izu's body language said he was scared but his words came across as relaxed and calm. It made Matt suspicious if Wu-Pen was telling him the truth. Matt decided to use some trickery himself. "Ask Izu, what color was the candle he used when he killed Leroy, red or yellow? What color wax did I find?"

Wu-Pen spoke in Chinese and Izu answered shortly. "He says, white."

The answer was white. It proved one of two things either Izu did as he supposedly claimed or Wu-Pen was the one that did it. "Does Izu know how to physically control someone like your guards, Bing and Uang do? Does he know how to fight as they can?"

Wu-Pen asked Izu. He answered after Izu spoke shortly, "No."

Matt furrowed his brow curiously. "Then how did he get Leroy to sit down in a chair?"

Wu-Pen asked and then explained after Izu answered bitterly. "The man was sleeping when they put a cloth of chloroform over his face. Then they moved him."

"Where did he get the chloroform?" Matt watched Izu answer Wu-Pen with cold eyes.

"From our doctor in Chinatown. They stole it."

Matt had noticed that Izu had cut his queue off which he had never seen a Chinese man do before. He pointed at Izu and asked Wu-Pen, "Why did he cut his braid off?"

Wu-Pen's lips turned upwards. "I had Bing Jue cut it off to shame Izu when he told me what he had done. It would assure if he escaped that he could not go back to China and he would be easily identified without his queue."

Matt paused for a moment to let Truet get caught up with writing the questions and answers down. "Ask him if there is anything he would like to say before I put him in jail?"

A moment later, Wu-Pen answered hesitantly in English. "Izu says he is sorry he was caught before he could kill the third man, Oscar. He hoped he was in the tunnel."

"Does he know Oscar died?" Matt asked curiously.

"I will ask him." He spoke to Izu in Chinese, "Look at the marshal and smile slowly with a nod and speak one word. You know what will happen to Wang if you do not."

241

Izu turned to face Matt with a sneer and quivering bottom lip. He said one word with his eyes pleading like a frightened child's.

Wu-Pen answered Matt in English. "I told him Oscar died of a heart attack. He said, 'good.'"

Matt could not help but question Wu-Pen's translations. The answers and word phrases didn't match up to the body language. He spoke to Wu-Pen, "Tell Izu he is under arrest for seven counts of murder." He addressed his deputy Nate Robertson. "Nate take our guests and lock him up, please."

When Izu was secured in a jail cell and Wu-Pen and his men had left, Matt asked Truet, "What do you think?"

Truet was rereading through the questions and answers he had written on the tablet. "I think every question was answered and he's guilty."

Matt spoke thoughtfully, "I want to question him again tomorrow with the same questions and have Ah See translate and see how different the answers are. If he is guilty, the answers will be the same. If not, then we know Wu-Pen is."

Truet grinned. "Good idea."

Matt walked back into the jail and saw Izu on his knees beside the bottom bunk with his hands pressed together at his chest with his head bowed. He had his eyes closed and praying with foreign words in a near whisper. Matt sat on a bench facing the jail cell and watched.

After a few moments, Izu lowered his hands and

faced Matt. He spoke in Chinese but Matt could not understand his words. Yet, the sincerity in the man's eyes spoke of his innocence.

Matt shook his head, trying to communicate. "Izu, I have no idea what you are saying. Tomorrow we'll talk through Ah See without Wu-Pen here." It was frustrating not to be able to communicate with an accused man.

Izu started speaking his native language and raised his hands questionably. Matt could almost swear Izu was asking if Matt understood him.

"I don't speak Chinese. I wish I did. Tomorrow, we'll talk. Phillip will get you some supper soon, Izu." Matt said softly.

Wu-Pen was concerned. He had not considered Matt having his questions and the answers written down as he asked them. Smart man, Matt was. Chess was a game of strategy and mind against mind in a head to head competition. Matt had him in check and it was time to move Ah See. If Ah See were to die, it would be too suspicious, and a translator from Portland would be brought into town. Sacrificing a pawn is to be expected when maneuvering against an opponent. But to sacrifice a knight and its unique ability to move is a more carefully thought out decision to make. Ah See was a step above a pawn, more valuable to Wu-Pen than Izu or Wang Chee. There was only one thing to do and that was to sneak into the Marshal's Office late at night and steal the notebook Truet wrote in and copy it while Ah See studied it. A good chess player knows future moves depend upon foresight and planning. Wu-Pen had offered to repair the Marshal's Office when it was destroyed by angry miners for Matt arresting Leroy Haywood and his two friends. Those repairs costed some money but Wu-Pen had his locksmith press all of Matt's keys into clay blocks and then had keys made. He could enter Matt's office, jail or even his home without Matt ever knowing at any time he wanted to. Tonight, he would and if he was right, Ah See would memorize the questions and would give the same answers Wu-Pen did tomorrow when Matt asked Izu the same questions again. It was not hard to guess a man's actions when he trusted you, nor was it hard to foresee a man's actions when the man didn't trust you. Matt was too smart to trust Wu-Pen too quickly. He would second guess him. If all went well with Ah See, then Matt would trust him, and that friendship could be secured.

He glanced at his guard. "Uang, I need Ah See in my office as soon as his workday is done. We have much to do and discuss."

## 31

Joe Thorn walked into the house after his first day back to work and smiled at his two boys who were wrestling on the floor. "Hey boys," he said with a joyful tone. Joe noticed Billy Jo wearing a pair of his denim jeans and his grin expanded. Billy Jo was not afraid to put on some of his jeans and she was too cute in them for him to complain. "Dinner smells fantastic. And lunch was great too. Thank you."

She walked over to him and kissed him. "You're welcome." She held him in a warm embrace. "You see, if you're nice to me, I'll be extra nice to you."

"I'm a slow learner but I'm learning that."

"I got hot water on the stove for you to clean up with. How was your first day back to work?"

"Ugh. They're checking everyone's pockets on the way in and out of the mine for dynamite. I could not sneak a pebble of ore out of there right now." He sat and began untying his boots. "I had to go back down the south winze and into the drift to drill into that ore vein. It was strange to be down there and walk back to where Danny was killed and where I had to take Lawrence's leg off. It was strange without my crew with me. Now I have Bruce Ellison on my new crew and he's no Walter, that's for sure. It was haunting to work where four of my friends died in that drift."

Billy Jo's heart began to race, hearing that Bruce Ellison was working with Joe. Bruce had caught her kissing Wes just a few days before. "I bet. You know, maybe you could think about working for my father. The job is much safer and you'd learn the business. We could live in my house and get out of here."

He scoffed lightly. "Your father hates me with a passion."

She stepped forward and knelt to look into his eyes. "Not if we talked to him honestly. Joe, I don't want to lose you in a collapse or any other way. It's not worth it."

"I'll think about it. Your father and cousin, Robert, aren't as bad as the Slaters. Let me wash up and play with the boys for a while. We'll talk more about that tonight after dinner. What are you making, steak?"

"Yes. I went to town and got some steak and vegetables. We're having a good dinner tonight."

"Pa, we got to play with Michael and Ray today. Look at what I drew!" Wyatt said and grabbed some papers off a table to show his father what he had drawn at Mellissa's.

He looked at the pictures and rewarded him with some praise. "Where did you make these at?" he asked.

Billy Jo cringed, "I wanted to go see Lucille and Lawrence at the doctor's office. Lucille and the boys have been staying at Albert's and Mellissa's. No children are allowed in to see Lawrence yet, so Mellissa watched the boys while I went to see them."

"Oh. How is Lawrence?" Joe asked with concern.

Billy Jo repeated what Mellissa had told her. "He's recovering. They had to cut his leg off up higher than it was. But he's recovering. They should be home in a few days."

"Did they find a place to live yet?"

"It...it didn't come up. I don't know," she shrugged.

"Well, if we have Sunday off, I'll go see him and find out. I never realized how much I like him until now. I feel bad for them."

Billy Jo was filling with anxiety. Why she lied rather than saying she went to the store, she didn't know. It wasn't smart of her but it was too late now. She had to find a way to keep Joe away from the Barton's for a while. Lies...so many lies. It occurred to her that if she did take Joe to talk to her father about a job, Joe might ask if he was feeling better or her father might ask her why she was telling people he was sick. Either way, it would come out that her father was never ill and she was making up an excuse to go to town for something. She would be caught in her lies and have to come up with another lie to cover for the truth. Her world was just coming together and now her past was filled with lies that might creep out of the soil like a gopher's head pushing up fresh dirt. It could come from Bruce Ellison if he told Joe what he knew about her and Wes. She took a deep breath and said a quick little prayer to keep the lies buried underground where they needed to stay.

Later that night, Joe had laid the boys down in their bed, which was compressed in the same small room as their parent's bed. He told them a funny story to make them laugh before going to sleep, unafraid and in good spirits. He had never made up a bedtime story before but had heard Lawrence talking about the stories he'd tell his boys before bed. A relationship like Lawrence had with his sons is what Joe wanted with his boys. A bedtime story was something he started doing and found it fun and enjoyable for himself too. He hugged his two sons and kissed them goodnight.

Wyatt hugged him and said, "I love you, Pa."

Joe smiled. "I love you too, Wyatt. You know, I'm trying to start a new life with you and Brice and your Mama. I want to be the kind of father that you love and like being with. You let me know if I start failing, okay?"

Wyatt grinned. "I will."

"Goodnight, boys." He left the room and closed the door. He wiped his eyes and sat beside Billy Jo on their ripped davenport. He took a deep breath. "When we were trapped in the mine, Walter said his biggest regret was not taking the time to play with his children. That was one of mine too. The last thing I remembered Wyatt saying to me was he hated me. It's the last thing I heard from my family was no one loved me. In the dark space of that winze, we had hours to do nothing but think and it's all I could think about. If I died, my family wouldn't care. And it hurt. If a man's family doesn't love him, then who can? And it is my fault. So, I decided if I lived, I would do all I could to change that. I wanted to play with my boys and start over trying to be a good father." He nodded towards the bedroom. "Wyatt just hugged me and told me that he loves me." He gazed at Billy Jo with a layer of water in his eyes. "I don't remember the last time I heard the boys say that."

Billy Jo smiled warmly. "It's about time."

He smiled lightly. "I know. I've also treated you bad over the years. I've made a lot of mistakes, Billy Jo. I promised myself that I would treat you better. It doesn't take any more than facing the end of your life to realize who you love. And I love you. I want to apologize for all the times I have mistreated you and I know there have been many. I cannot make up for the past but I can start over. I was going to wait until I have the money to buy you what you deserve but I want to marry you. Will you marry me?"

Her mouth dropped open. "Are you serious?"

He chuckled. "I am. Walter told me to make it solid, so I'm trying to. Will you marry me? I don't have a ring but I will get you one when we can afford it."

She had been waiting for ten years to hear those

words. "Yes. Oh, my word, yes!"

He kissed her. "I never thought I would say it but if it weren't for that collapse, I wouldn't know how good of a life I really have. I like it. I love you, Billy Jo."

She wiped her eyes and hugged him. "I love you."

## 32

Ah See sat on one side of the table facing Izu Chee. Truet sat at one end of the table and read the questions one at a time that he had copied in his notebook the day before and waited for Ah See to question Izu. Ah See then translated what Izu said in answer. Truet marked in the notebook with a check if the answer was the same for the most part and if the answer was different, he had a piece of paper to write the new answer on. So far, the answers had been too close to mark a difference.

Matt sat at the other end of the table, watching the two men's facial expressions and body language carefully. The one thing he could not overlook was the tension between the two Chinese men. For being friends like Ah See had stated they were, it seemed odd. Izu no longer acted afraid as he had the day before, he was more agitated with Ah See. Matt remained quiet and let Truet continue without interrupting.

Truet asked, "Who showed you where to put the gelignite in the mine?"

Ah See repeated the question in Chinese.

Izu glared at Ah See with a repulsed expression. Izu answered in Chinese, "You are a puppet for the devil's hands. Cut the strings and tell them the truth, you spineless coward!"

Ah See spoke to Truet in English, "No one. The tunnel was the only one empty and Izu knows about rock. He could see the weakness in the rock himself." When Ah See had come home from work the day before, he was met by Wu-Pen and was given a drink by the Chinese doctor that put him to sleep. At midnight, he was woken and summoned by Wu-Pen to memorize the questions and answers in Truet's notebook. He studied them over and over and was quizzed by Wu-Pen until he had them all memorized. Ah See was motivated to memorize them by two factors, one was keeping his younger sister safe, so she would not have to pay for his failure, and the other motivation was the promise of going home a rich man if he was successful.

Truet checked the answer. It was, basically, the same as the day before. He asked, "How did you know about Gelignite and how it works?"

Ah See asked the question in Chinese.

Izu sneered. "You know I didn't do this. Tell them the truth!"

Ah See responded to Izu in Chinese, "I cannot, or my sister will be fed to the beasts. You know I have no choice, just like you."

"You do! Tell them the truth," Izu shouted angrily.

The intensity on Izu's face forced Matt to ask quickly, "What did he say?"

Ah See looked at Matt with irritation showing on his face. "He asked why you are asking the same questions as before. He told you the truth and has nothing more to say. I told him just to answer the questions. He asked why he should. It is pointless."

Matt sighed heavily with discouragement. "How are we doing, Truet?"

Truet gave an exaggerated shrug. "Every answer is the same. We haven't learned anything new."

"All right, ask him one last question. What color candle wax did I find in Leroy Haywood's cabin, red or yellow?"

Ah See spoke in Chinese and Izu answered while glaring at Ah See.

Ah See answered, "White."

"Okay, we're done. Phillip put him back in jail. I'll send the arrest report to the District Attorney right now. Let him know I just wanted to make sure Wu-Pen wasn't lying about the answers." Matt stared at Ah See with a hard and serious expression. "You are translating correctly, right? Because right now they are building a gallows in the park to hang him and his brother on. This man's life is on the line."

Ah See nodded. "Yes. I am aware and I have spoken honestly."

"Let our guest know I was just trying to look out for him. That is why I asked the same questions, to root out the possibility of a bad interpreter."

Ah See spoke to Izu in Chinese, "I have done as

you have asked. As you can see, he looks disappointed and will make an investigation into Wu-Pen. He
wants you to know he is keeping you here for your
own safety for now. Give him a few days before you
are freed. For my safety and my sisters, say nothing
to anyone and do not smile. You know Wu-Pen has
spies everywhere, maybe watching now. Be patient
and wait. Understand?"

A ray of light broke through the darkness that
had been clouding Izu's soul. The sense of relief
brought a bright smile. "Yes! Thank you, Ah See.
I will say nothing. But the American knows the
truth now? Yes?" Izu questioned with growing
satisfaction.

Ah See answered in Chinese, "Oh yes. My life
and Meili's are on the line, too, Izu. No words about
this to anyone else even if they speak Chinese. Also,
they have your brother in a locked room. They plan
on bringing him here on Sunday. Let them do as
they plan; they will get caught in a trap set by the
Marshal when the time is right. No harm will come
to you or your brother. The Marshal knows the
truth, I told him."

Izu licked his dry lips through a pleased grin.
"Thank you, my friend."

Ah See smiled at Izu and then turned to Matt. "I
have told Izu all you said."

Matt glanced across the room. "Phillip, take
Izu back to his cell." Izu stood and bowed towards
Matt multiple times in appreciation. Phillip took
him back into the jail.

He pointed at Izu with his thumb and questioned Ah See, "Why is he bowing to me like that? Is there anything you want to tell me? Anything at all? Now is your chance."

"You treat him fair and well. He is thankful for you as an American to care about the interpreter but he is honored to have killed those American men. No one knew he had done this and it is the gossip in Chinatown now. If I had known it was him, I would have told you the other day."

Matt stared at Ah See as he rubbed his beard thoughtfully. He had expected the answers to be different than the day before to prove Wu-Pen was the killer. He would have bet his badge on it and there was still a part of him that doubted Izu had done the crimes he was accused of. He spoke Ah See harshly, "You do know your friend and his brother are going to hang, right?"

Ah See exhaled in shame. The pressure built in his chest, knowing two innocent men would die because of him and his lies. He also knew his sister would become everyman's woman for her lifetime if he failed or told Matt the truth. He nodded with his eyes downcast. "Yes. It is unfortunate what they did. But I will not lie to save my friends. It would be dishonorable."

Matt spoke sincerely, "You're telling me the truth? Ah See, I don't want to hang an innocent man. I know hardened men; I know killers and Izu does not fit the character. I watched him talking to you and he acted like anyone being falsely accused would. Yesterday, he sat right there acting scared to death of Wu-Pen and today he's forceful with you.

It raises some red flags with me, so how about you tell me the truth."

Ah See took a deep breath and exhaled. "I was not here yesterday but Izu answered the questions the same, yes?" He knew Wu-Pen had returned the notebook to Truet's desk while it was still dark that morning.

Whatever encouraged the wind that pushed the sails of Matt's quest for the truth was just wiped away. His intuition may have told him one thing but the fact was the answers were the same. He lowered his head and exhaled in defeat. "Yes, they were."

"Then, the only explanation is the interpreters told you the truth. I know I did."

"Good point."

Ah See added, "Why he is scared of Wu-Pen one day and not me the next is because Wu-Pen has authority and I am his friend."

"All right. I'll take the arrest report to the District Attorney." The facts didn't lie but he couldn't shake the feeling that something wasn't right. It may have been that he couldn't talk to Izu himself and relied on others to tell him the truth. Trust was something that needed to be earned and not taken for granted when a man's life was on the line. Matt folded his hands thoughtfully under his chin. "I'm telling you though, he doesn't act like I would expect. None of this makes sense to me, Ah See. I am wanting to tell you that if you're lying in any way, this man and his brother's blood, when he is found, will be on your hands." Matt said warningly.

Shame filled Ah See's soul like a wine barrel to be corked and capped and never be emptied of the sorrow within. He faced Matt squarely. "My words are true. Men do not always act the same. May I go?"

"One last question, does Wu-Pen know we talked the other day?" It was a trick question because Matt told Wu-Pen so himself. He was curious if Wu-Pen had spoken to Ah See since then and coached him on what to say. Trust had to be earned but that didn't mean it was earned easily. Matt trusted very few people.

Ah See shrugged his shoulders. "I don't know. I haven't seen him." The wisdom of Wu-Pen knew no limits. He had warned him that Matt might ask a question along those lines. Ah See had completed his duty and left the office and walked to the nearest alley and entered it. He had not only lied to the Marshal. He had betrayed his friend Izu and gave him false hope. Izu would be content believing a lie until he had a noose around his neck and then realize his friend had betrayed him. Ah See knelt in the soft mud hidden between the buildings and wept. There was nothing else he could have done. The protection of his sister was his priority.

Two hours later, towards the end of the day, the door to the Marshal's Office opened and William Slater stepped in with a grin that only a pleased rat could have. "Where's our good Marshal?"

"Hi, Mister Slater, I'll get him," Phillip said,

standing from his desk.

William walked through the partition gate uninvited. "Never mind, I'll get him. He's in his office, yes?"

"Yeah," Phillip said, watching him walk past.

William knocked once and opened Matt's private office door. "Matt, you did it! You finally caught the men who sabotaged my mine. Chinese, I understand. I knew we never should've allowed those folks here. Well, good job!"

Matt slid his chair back from his desk and stood. "It wasn't *those* people who did it. Two brothers took it upon themselves to take matters into their own hands in the act of vengeance for what your men did to three falsely accused Chinese men by the Sheriff. It was *those* people who fed and sheltered the families at the mine. It was *those* people who fed *your* employees to keep their energy up. Don't judge *those* people by two killers that happen to be Chinese."

William's eyes hardened as he handed Matt an envelope. "*Those* Chinese people are going to hang. I've already got my carpenters working through the weekend to make some gallows behind the courthouse. It will be ready by Tuesday. This summons is from the District Attorney, have those heathens in the courthouse by 10:00 a.m. on Monday. I expect to hang them on Tuesday at noon. I'm giving all of my employees the day off to come watch, get drunk and celebrate."

Matt was appalled. "Yeah, you told me about your gallows being built before there was even an arrest. Let me ask, does Judge Jacoby have a say in this or are you running the court of law now?"

William chuckled. "I'm preparing for the inevitable. Jackson Weathers said they confessed and your questions prove their guilt. They are, without a doubt, going to hang. And I will pull the lever to drop the gallows. I gave you the court notice, so I am done here. Can I see the killers?"

Matt shook his head with disgust. "I don't see any reason why. You don't speak Chinese and they don't speak English."

"I want to see what they look like."

"I only have one of them. The other one will be arrested when he's found. Hopefully, soon."

William's anger slowly came over his face. "The court document said you had them both."

"It does not. Read it again. Why are you allowed to read my reports anyway? You're not affiliated with the law in any way, shape or form. Jackson should never have shared any of that with you."

William smiled. "They killed my employees and sabotaged my mine. That makes it personal. I have the right to know; that's why. I'll see you on Monday." He tossed a silver dollar on Matt's desk. "A tip for your good work."

Matt tossed it back. "Give it to one of those employee families you care so much about but who can't afford to eat."

William grinned while putting the dollar back in his pocket. "I'll do that." He whistled joyfully as he left.

## 33

It was Saturday evening and the man hired to light the ten-foot-tall ornamental light posts illuminating Main and Rose Streets set his ladder up to reach the post across the street from where Lucille Barton stepped outside of the Doctor's Office. She watched the man's legs as they climbed up the ladder. It wasn't a grueling job or physically demanding, but it was one Lawrence would never be able to do. Even such a simple task as climbing onto a wagon would now become a challenge for him. Lawrence was a bit more hopeful today than he was the day before but the need to work was essential to surviving. They were young and once dreamed of owning a farm and striving year by year to create a good life for themselves and their children. Those dreams were no longer possible now that Lawrence couldn't do such a simple job as lighting the streetlights or walking a mule in and out of the mine. It would be difficult for him even to clean a horse stall.

There are moments in a person's life when hopelessness comes like the fading sunlight on a cold winter's day. Circumstances remain and the hope fades away. The outside forces of pressure were constricting her chest and draining her spirit to the point of desperation. She leaned against the building and wept softly. Every door she knocked on to find a place to live ended a day late or with no availability. She had very high hopes when Albert offered to go to the Branson Home and Land Brokers Office with her and talk with Lee Bannister about finding a home. She had stopped by his office a few times during the week but Lee had been with other families or out of his office. With Albert with her, she hoped Lee would make the time to help her. Unfortunately, Lee informed her that he had just rented his last cottage out to the Jensen family. If Lucille had come to Lee earlier in the week, he could have helped her, but now he had nothing left to rent and he couldn't finance the sale of any property without them having a reliable income. She could buy a parcel of land with the money she was getting from the silver mine but buying an acre or two would do them no good for now without the means of building a home on it. Lee apologized for not being able to help her and recommended she talk with Big John Pederson to see if he had an empty apartment in the Dogwood Shacks. Lucille spoke to Big John and again, there was nothing available. One other man in town owned multiple places he rented, but upon query, he simply told her she was out of luck. Between the placer miners wintering in town and new folks moving into the community, there was a shortage of empty apartments and houses to rent. Some rentals would open up in the spring as the placer miners went back up into the goldfields but, for now, there was nothing available. Her last hope was that Billy Jo would rent her house to them but Lawrence had just told her that Joe had mentioned that she was leaving him and moving back into her home.

It was frustrating and made worse by the pressure of Doctor Ambrose telling her moments before that they were releasing Lawrence on Sunday because they needed the bed space. She had no choice but to take him back to Slater's Mile, where he'd lay on the uncomfortable and filthy straw mattress for a week or two before they were forced out. They had time to find somewhere to live before that day came but now she was faced with the more immediate priority of finding a way to get Lawrence and her boys back home. She and the boys could walk, they'd done it many times before but Lawrence couldn't walk. Once she got him home, it would become her responsibility to care for him. Lucille would have to do what she always did, cook and clean, supervise and teach her children while adding the changing of the bandages on his leg, cleaning him and making sure his leg didn't get infected and all of the things his healing would need. It would all fall upon her as she took the responsibilities head-on, including finding a home to live in and a job soon after to support her family. It was overwhelming and becoming too much to bear.

She prayed to the Lord in a quiet desperation to help her meet the needs of her family while she made the long walk back to the large and beautiful home of Albert and Mellissa Bannister. She was very thankful for them allowing her and the boys to stay there and for watching the boys so she could spend more time with Lawrence. She had explained to Michael and Ray that their father was injured and missing half of his leg. The boys had yet to see him and although they missed him greatly, she doubted that they genuinely understood the gravity of his condition. It was going to be a shock to them to see Lawrence for the first time. She already knew the boys would want Lawrence to get down on the floor and play with them or take them outside to run and chase them around as he had always done. Unfortunately, her family was going to change and she feared Lawrence would lose his playful spirit now that he couldn't play with his sons the way he always had. The thought of it made her sad.

She entered Albert and Mellissa's house with the weight of the world on her shoulders. She found Albert sitting in his overstuffed chair with his feet on a padded footrest reading the newspaper. Mellissa was likewise sitting in her overstuffed chair, reading the Bible. She smiled as Lucille entered the family room. "How is Lawrence?"

She sat on the comfortable davenport facing them. "He's not as negative as yesterday. They're sending him home tomorrow. Albert, I hate to ask, but if I rented a wagon, could you drive him home for me tomorrow?"

Albert lowered the newspaper. "I suppose so. What time is he being released?"

"Whenever I can get the wagon." She had not gotten any money from the silver mine yet and only had twelve dollars or so in a can in her cabin. She didn't know how much a wagon and a horse would cost but she'd go to the cabin in the morning and get her money. The thought occurred to her that she'd probably be renting the same wagon and mule team they had sold to the livery stable. The idea of it left her feeling sick to her stomach.

Albert asked, "How about after church? You and the boys come to church with us and then we'll go get him. I know the stable owner pretty well and can probably get a lower rate for you."

"No. I have to go back to my place and get my money before I can do anything. After church, I can meet you at the livery stable, though."

"Lucille," Albert said seriously and paused. He could see the burden weighing on her and felt guilty for trying to tease her. "I own a carriage with seats. You don't need to rent a wagon."

Her eyes grew moist. She could feel the weight of that burden being lifted off her shoulders. However, she was beginning to feel like a burden on their family. "You and Mellissa have done so much for me. I don't even know how to thank you."

He yawned tiredly. "As I've said the new boots for you and the boys weren't going to break us. Using my carriage to give your husband a ride home in a bit more comfort won't break us either."

Lucille spoke softly, "No, I mean just letting us stay here with you and watching the boys for me every day. I know it's a big inconvenience having us here and feeding us and all you've done to help us. You two have been amazing and I'll never be able to pay you both back for what you've done for me. I really appreciate you both. You have no idea how much."

Mellissa's lips tightened into a small emotional smile. "It's just a spare bedroom we weren't using anyway and your boys are very well behaved. It's been our pleasure. But we'll get you all home tomorrow and then don't become a stranger."

Mellissa's words were nice but her final sentence about not becoming strangers had hurt her feelings. Lucille thought they had become friends on a personal level that would last and not be strangers who just helped another stranger. It didn't sound like Mellissa shared that same view. Why would she, though? Lucille and Lawrence were low society poverty-stricken folks about to become homeless and Mellissa and Albert were at the top level of Branson's social circle. Lucille could feel her spirit fall further down a dark well knowing she still had not made a good friend after all.

"How's the house-hunting going?" Albert asked. "Did you talk to Big John?"

She pulled her attention out of the mire she felt herself sinking in. "I did talk to Jon Pederson about his places. He doesn't have any vacant places either.

He recommended we stay at a place called Lucky Man's Bunkhouse. I've never heard of it."

Albert chuckled. "What an ass. That's no place for a family, especially a young lady. How long until you have to leave Slater's Mile, two weeks?"

"At most. I don't know," she said falling deeper into a dark pit of despair. "If the train was here, I'd just purchase train tickets back to Utah and make the best of it."

Albert yawned tiredly. "The train's getting closer. They say by summer it will be here. But that doesn't help today. At least you have two weeks and who knows, something might open up by then."

Maybe they were worn out watching her children or perhaps felt like she had taken advantage of them. Either way, they had been an enormous blessing and she was grateful. Something had changed, though, and she could feel it. Lawrence was being released to come home and maybe they were regretting helping her so much and feared she'd ask if Lawrence could stay there until they found a place of their own. Lucille would never ask for such a thing, but maybe they feared she would. It hurt her deeply and it nearly brought tears to her eyes to realize the great couple wouldn't be the friends Lucille thought she had made. The sadness in her heart probably couldn't go unnoticed, but she wasn't going to ask why they seemed so anxious for her to leave. The answer was probably as simple as having their home and life going back to normal. Lucille could understand that and would take her family back at home tomorrow. She spoke halfheartedly to end the conversation and go up-stairs to leave Mellissa and Albert to have some time alone. "The Lord will help us find something."

"How is Lawrence taking this whole transition of going home?" Mellissa asked.

"He's trying not to worry but he's scared. He has to learn how to use the crutch and I'm afraid he will be struggling for a while. I'm afraid of him falling and breaking his sutures open. He is the one who normally takes care of these kinds of things that I'm trying to do and I am letting him down. I haven't accomplished anything. I promised him I would take care of everything and I haven't been able to do a single thing." A tear slipped out of her eyes and rolled quietly down her cheek. If there was ever a sense of betraying her husband, it was failing to meet their needs during his most helpless time. "It is so frustrating."

"I'm sure he understands," Mellissa said gently as she reached over to grab Lucille's hand. "You're trying and that's all you can do sometimes."

Lucille's voice became high pitched as her emotions took over, "Every door I knock on is closed. I'll talk to Billy Jo when I see her and ask if we can move into her place with her if we have to. If not, then I don't know."

Albert spoke softly, "There's not much we can do, unfortunately. I've spoken to everyone I can think of and there's just nothing available right now. But if we can help somehow, don't hesitate to ask."

Lucille shook her head not wanting to be any more of a burden. "You both have already done enough. Giving Lawrence a ride home tomorrow is all I can ask for and I'll never ask for anything again. You've done so much already," she heard herself say.

"Well, not quite," Mellissa offered with a more positive tone, "since this is your last night with us and I made a cake today. How about something to eat? A piece of cake before dinner, perhaps?"

Lucille smirked sadly. "That sounds good." The sadness in her voice couldn't go unnoticed.

"It does," Mellissa stated optimistically. "Albert and I are not chubby for nothing. We like our desserts."

"Yes, we do," Albert agreed.

## 34

Matt had reserved a buggy like he did every Sunday to take Christine to church. They had sat behind Albert's family who brought Lucille Barton and her boys. It was the second time Matt had seen Lucille since the morning at the mine. After church, the Reverend Eli Painter stood by the door as the congregation left. He was introduced to Lucille and said, "Lucille, it's nice to meet you. I want you to know our church has been praying for your husband and all the families. Mellissa has informed us that your husband is coming home today and you need to find a place to live. Let me ask around and Lord willing, maybe we can find you a place. Thank you for coming today, and may the Lord put his blessing upon you and your family."

"Thank you," she said kindly. "It feels so good to be back in church."

Reverend Painter smiled. "You're welcome anytime. Come back next week. We'll be having our monthly potluck in the community center. There will be lots of good food, I promise."

"I'll try to come."

Albert's sixteen-year-old son, Joshua, stepped inside the church and said, "Uncle Matt, someone named Wu-Pen, is looking for you outside."

Matt frowned as he shook the Reverend's hand and went outside. Wu-Pen was talking to Lee and Albert Bannister.

Wu-Pen's attention went to Matt as he approached. "We have found Wang Chee and have him tied up and waiting to bring him to the jail. Can we meet you there?" His eyes went to Christine when she ended her conversation with the Reverend's wife and joined Matt. "Christine, so nice to see you again."

She smiled kindly. "Hello."

Matt spoke to Christine regretfully, "I need to go to work."

"You're not going to have lunch with your family?" she asked, sounding disappointed.

Wu-Pen waved his hands innocently. "Please, go to lunch. We can hold him for an hour or two. We will bring him at two o'clock. Would that be okay?" he asked Matt.

"Yes, it would," Christine answered quickly. She glanced at Matt with her big brown eyes and a wonderful energetic smile. "Everyone's looking forward to having lunch together and I'm hungry."

Matt grinned. "I'll see you then, Wu-Pen."

Albert spoke, "I have to pick up Lucille's husband and take them back home after lunch. Have you met the new doctor yet?" he asked Matt.

Matt held eye contact with Albert and nodded his head slowly. "Yes, I have. He's a very nice and understanding man. Tell him hello for me when you see him today."

Lee used his thumb to point down the street. "Let's get going."

After eating lunch in the Monarch Restaurant, Matt gave Christine a ride back home and hurried to his office. He waited inside for Wu-Pen to bring the second accused man to the jail.

Before too long, Wu-Pen stepped through the door, followed by his two guards holding Wang Chee with his hands tied in front of him. Wang Chee was younger than Izu and appeared to be in his mid-twenties, frightened and exhausted from running as well. His queue was cut off short like Izu's had been. Matt had seen the same anxiousness on many faces over the years. There was a specific fear-filled expression that most young men have when they are arrested for the first time and Wang Chee had that expression. Matt stood by the large table and scrutinized the young man from head to toe, deciding if he wanted to question him or not. It was Sunday and the arrest report had already been turned over to the court. His brother Izu had implicated Wang and they had court in the morning. Although Matt would have liked to have done something else on his day off, he had Wu-Pen sit across the table from Wang. Matt asked Bing Jue and Uang Yang to sit at the desks across the office, out of sight and mind of Wang. Matt sat with his back against the wall at the end of the table to watch them all.

Matt opened the notebook Truet had copied the questions and answers in and took a drink of coffee. He noticed the tiny beads of sweat on Wang's upper lip and nose. His quivering bottom lip and white knuckles as he clenched his hands. The young man was scared but his dark eyes avoided Wu-Pen and kept glancing at Matt like a frightened child.

Matt spoke calmly, "I'm Matt Bannister, the United States Marshal. Wang Chee, you have been accused of murder and other things that won't matter if you're convicted of murdering seven men. We've asked your brother many questions and I'm going to ask you some of them. Translate that," he said to Wu-Pen.

Wu-Pen spoke in Chinese to Wang, "Wang, listen closely. I'm going to speak, and you're going to speak in a calm voice without getting angry. You should know when Heop Lee and the others fixed this building for the marshal, I had Heop test the locks and he took pressings of the keys and then made me a key to every lock in here and the Marshal's house too. If you do not do as I say, I will come here tonight, and you will watch your brother suffer for hours. You will disappear from here and spend your life lying in a room, without the use of your arms and legs. You will crawl like a maggot across the room to eat and drink like one too. Are we in agreement? You'll do as I instruct?"

Wang Chee stared at Wu-Pen with a loose jaw and horror locked in his eyes. "Yes." Wang knew how brutal Wu-Pen could be to make a small point clear. There was no conscience within him, just wickedness and evil that had no limits that he would not go to. He did not doubt that what Wu-Pen said was true. The weight of what Wu-Pen could do was as heavy as a millstone.

Wu-Pen answered Matt in English, "He is fine with questions."

Matt asked only five of the original questions he had asked Izu and watched Wang answer. Wu-Pen translated the answers and all were about the same as Izu had given. It was hard for Matt to pick up the tone changes without knowing what the words were that the changes took place on. Like a puzzle piece that didn't quite fit, the facial expressions and body language didn't quite match up to the answers given. Like his brother Izu, Wang's answers were upfront, concise and a confession without the expected denials, deflecting the blame or offering an excuse for their actions. Matt had known other men who confessed to their crimes and some showed no emotion; others showed remorse when they confessed. Wang Chee, like his brother, appeared to be more fearful of Wu-Pen than he was of Matt. Maybe that was because Wu-Pen was the only one Wang could communicate with and the questions were from him and not Matt.

Matt closed the notebook and stood. "I've heard enough. Your timing couldn't be any better, Wu-Pen. Let him know they will face the judge tomorrow. Let's go put him in with his brother."

Izu Chee stood in his jail cell when they entered and questioned Wu-Pen in Chinese, "What's this? You promised Wang would be fine."

Wu-Pen answered, "He is fine. I kept my word. I'll see you both in the American courthouse tomorrow. The Marshal will take good care of you."

Wang Chee spoke as he was pushed into the jail cell, "I'll draw pictures to speak with the Americans! They'll know we're innocent of your crimes."

Wu-Pen frowned noticeably for Matt's sake since he was watching. "I thought we already talked about this. Write him a letter and see what happens to Izu. Wang, I promise, you will wish you were dead for many years to come if I must correct your loyalty to the Chinese Benevolence Society. Your sacrifice will be long remembered and your family back in China well compensated."

"The Marshal doesn't speak Chinese. How can we say a thing?" Izu asked, trying to deflect the question from his brother.

"I know." Wu-Pen kept his saddened expression, although he wanted to grin. "He only knows what I tell him."

Matt asked, "What are they saying?" He had noticed a flash of anger in Wang's eyes for a moment.

Wu-Pen answered Matt in English. "Wang is mad for giving him and Izu to the Americans to punish. He didn't want to be caught."

"None of them ever do," Matt said simply before locking the cell door and leading the others out of the jail cell.

Wu-Pen glanced back at the two brothers with a hideous smirk that was hidden from Matt. "I'll be talking for you both tomorrow in the American court."

Matt waited for Wu-Pen to walk out of the jail cell and then he closed and locked the steel door.

Wang Chee turned to his brother. "Are we going to die? What can we do to make the lawman understand we did nothing wrong? Wu-Pen is lying!"

Izu put a finger to his lips. "Shh. The Marshal knows Wu-Pen is lying. He knows we are innocent. Ah See told him so. I was there when he told him and saw the Marshal's face. I trust Ah See. We can say nothing until the Marshal finishes his investigation in Chinatown. Ah See is helping us get Wu-Pen arrested and then we will be free. We are here to be kept safe from Wu-Pen until then. Relax, my brother. We will be okay."

"Tomorrow they will face justice," Wu-Pen said as he reached for the office door to leave. "I will meet you at the courthouse just before ten in the morning. Have a good evening, Marshal."

"Wait a minute," Matt said with a troubled expression on his face. "I am afraid I'm at a disadvantage when it comes to those two brothers. I do not know their language, so I have no idea what they or you are saying. By watching them both answer questions, they don't act like I would expect someone to act who was in their shoes. Do they understand the kind of trouble they are in?

Did you explain to them that murder is a capital offense and they will probably be hung? By their answers to my questions, it seems to me like they want to be caught and hung or don't understand the trouble they are in. Not once did either one try to deflect or deny their guilt. I find that odd. Yet, by their body language and expressions, they appear more afraid of you and innocent of any crimes to me. Can you explain that?"

Wu-Pen lifted his brow for a moment before answering. It was a chess game but, occasionally, one had to put on a poker face and raise the pot on a bluff. "I will try. We Chinese do not wear our emotions on our sleeves as the American saying goes. To deceive, to lie, to hide are all dishonorable. There is what is right and what is wrong. The difference between an American criminal and a Chinese criminal is the Chinese criminal will not blame another for his actions. He will admit it because it was a choice. He decided to commit a crime knowing the consequences. Those two brothers made choices to take revenge, knowing they could be caught. They never spoke of it to anyone until now. They are caught. They will admit it and die like men without lying about it. As for your conflict of why they speak one way and act another, our custom is to speak the truth no matter how afraid we are. You have two interpreters. I have not spoken to Ah See, did Izu's confession change?"

Matt answered thoughtfully, "No."

Wu-Pen stated simply, "Maybe our customs and mannerisms are what you are conflicted with

276

because it is different than you expect from your American customs. Perhaps, yes?"

"Perhaps so." Matt's eyes and instincts said the men were innocent of such horrible crimes but there was no other explanation of how two interpreters gave the same answers to every question if it wasn't the truth. Even Wang Chee's answers were in line with what Izu had stated.

Wu-Pen smiled. "Our people and customs are very different than yours, Marshal."

Matt put his hand out towards Wu-Pen. "I think I owe you an apology, Wu-Pen. I'll admit that I thought you, Bing and Uang were the ones responsible for the crimes these men have committed. I apologize for not believing you. I was wrong."

Wu-Pen grinned slowly. He shook Matt's hand. "I understand. I never thought it would be Chinese, myself. Now, we can be friends, yes?"

"Yes. Let these two gentlemen know I apologize to them as well."

Bing Jue and Uang Yang nodded when Wu-Pen translated and both shook Matt's hand before they left.

## 35

Doctor Mitchell Ryland shook Albert Bannister's hand heartedly. "I know your brother, Matt. He's quite a man. We've become pretty good friends in the short time I've been here. Mellissa, nice to meet you as well. Lucille has told me how gracious you both have been to her and the family."

"It's been our pleasure," Mellissa replied.

Doctor Ryland asked Albert, "Are you the hunter? Matt was telling me one of his brothers does a lot of hunting."

"Some. But more than likely, he's talking about Adam. He's the mountain man in the family. I don't get out hunting too often anymore," Albert said.

"Well, it's been nice meeting you folks but, unfortunately, I can't let you take Lawrence home today. It's nothing too serious yet," he added quickly to keep Lucille calm. "But Lawrence's leg may be infected, so I need to keep him here where I can stay on top of it. I want to make sure it doesn't become gangrene."

"How serious is it?" Lucille asked with alarm. She knew gangrene could be as dangerous as a bullet to the heart if it was not caught early.

The doctor put a palm up to calm any fear. "It's just precautionary, Lucille. Right now, he is fine, but I'm not willing to risk him going home yet until I know for sure he'll be okay. We've come this far; a few more days won't hurt, right?" he asked in his usual upbeat manner.

Lucille said, "He sounded excited to come home yesterday. Is he feverish?"

"No, he's fine. It's not even been a week and the wound is still very fresh. A few more days to heal and rest can only help him. I don't want to send him home too early. I know Doctor Ambrose mentioned needing the bed space but Lawrence is my patient and I'm not willing to release him at this time. Okay?"

Lucille frowned helplessly. "Okay. Whatever is best for him. Do you know when he can come home?"

"Soon...a few days. I'll let you know. Anyway, go see your husband. He's awake and in a fair mood anyway."

Lawrence sat against the wall at the head of his bed with his amputated leg wrapped heavily in gauze reddened slightly by the leakage of blood. He raised his hands for a hug with a loving smile when Lucille stepped into his small room and hugged him tightly. "The Doctor's not letting me go home today."

"I know. How are you?" she asked.

"Still in pain but that's expected." His eyes went to Albert and Mellissa, who followed Lucille into the room. Lucille introduced them.

Lawrence spoke, "Oh! Thank you for taking care of my family. It's nice of you."

Mellissa put a hand on Lucille's back. "You're very welcome. We were going to take you home today but it looks like Lucille and the boys will be staying a few more days with us."

Lucille questioned her, sounding surprised, "You're not taking us home?"

"Not now. Unless you want us to?"

"No, if we could stay a few more days, that would be great."

Albert stepped forward. "It won't hurt to have you stay until Lawrence is released. We would invite you to stay longer but we don't have a bedroom on the ground floor. It would be too hard for Lawrence to go up and down the stairs. We would never forgive ourselves if he fell down the stairs. So, unfortunately, when you are released, Lawrence, we will have to take you back home. Lord willing, between now and then maybe you can find someplace to live. It gives you a few more days anyway. But until then, Lucille knows she is free to come and go as she pleases. And that's been working out just fine. Except for that one fellow who came over the other night to see her kind of late. I didn't like him too much...but the other men she meets up with are okay."

Mellissa slapped his arm with a loud whack.

She scolded him harshly, "Albert, knock it off! It's not a good time to tease!" She looked at Lawrence, irritated and shook her head. "Forgive my husband for a bad attempt at a terrible joke. He's not funny!"

Albert snickered with a broad grin. "I was just teasing."

Lucille glanced at Albert and then back at Lawrence. "Albert…Never mind. I promise you; no one has come over."

"I would hope not," Lawrence said with a bit of an irritated glance at Albert.

Mellissa glared at Albert disappointedly. "That was terrible."

"I couldn't help it." He tightened his lips to keep his mouth shut and then chuckled. "You should've seen Lucille's face, though." He laughed.

Mellissa's face reddened as she glared at him. "You are making light of their situation and it's not appreciated, Albert Bannister. Not by them or me." She looked back at Lawrence sincerely. "Please forgive him. He was kicked in the head by a horse, I think, when he was little or something. Anyway, he's a good man and you'll like him when you get to know him, I hope. Until then, I will get him out of here before he tries to apologize and makes it worse. Lucille, don't worry about the boys. I'll just unpack their clothes and count on you staying longer."

"Thank you so much." She hugged Mellissa.

Albert shook Lawrence's hand. "I was just making a little joke. I hope you don't take it personally. It was nice to meet you. We'll get out of here and let you two visit. I'll see in a few days, Lawrence."

## 36

Monday at 10:22 a.m. Izu and Wang Chee were both convicted of seven counts of First-Degree Murder and sentenced to be hung the following day at noon. It was the shortest Capital Punishment trial that Matt had ever heard of. The Chee brothers had given a very clear confession and pleaded guilty to the charges. There was very little more to decide upon and after reading the confession, Judge Meryle Jacoby sentenced the two men to death. Matt took them back to the jail and Ah See came to visit with the brothers for a while.

It wasn't the first hanging Matt had been to or the first criminals he had watched over before they were executed. However, the two brothers were the first two prisoners he'd ever watched talk back in forth, laugh and smile with a relaxed countenance hours before being put to death. Their actions went against every experience Matt had known in the past. They appeared to have either no fear or no knowledge of what would happen to them. It was bizarre how they smiled at Matt and seemed almost appreciative to be where they were. It made no sense at all.

Now, the time was at hand and Matt stood in a slight drizzle on the twelve-foot high gallows William Slater had his carpenters build over the weekend. It was built against the backside of the courthouse in the city park. The park was full of spectators who had come to watch. Many of them were employed by the silver mine since William Slater had shut the mine down to allow his employees to enjoy the hanging. To make it more of a carnival atmosphere, William had beer kegs and a bar set up where the men could get drinks. Matt had suggested to the court to delay the execution just long enough to make it a private hanging in a fenced-off area. William Slater argued; he had already invested money and promised his employees that they could witness the execution of those responsible for the deaths of their fellow miners and Judge Jacoby agreed to keep it public. William had stood on the gallows moments before and spoke to the crowd like a proud host, welcoming them to a carnival show. Then he went below the platform to wait for the signal to pull the lever that sprung the two trapdoors.

Izu and Wang Chee had their wrists shackled behind their backs and stood on the platform trap doors that would be sprung and lead them to their death. Both men appeared nervous but not readily as scared as Matt had seen other men in the past.

They kept looking nervously towards Matt while Judge Jacoby read the death warrant to the crowd.

Matt did not enjoy hangings but it was justice for the crimes committed and part of his job. He was not the hangman but he suspected if William Slater had his way, he'd want the nooses set wrong to allow the two men to strangle slowly to death for a touch more torture and entertainment. Matt had firmly warned the hangman, a local man with the last name of Clemmons, to make sure the nooses were set right or he'd pay the consequences when it was all over. Clemmons swore to his ability and promised to set the nooses correctly to break both men's necks at the rope length's end. Matt may have stood on the platform as the law representative, but he did not want to be there.

Reverend Eli Painter approached the two Chinese prisoners and told them the Gospel while Wu-Pen translated. The two brothers spoke to one another through it all, except Wang prayed between talking to his brother. When Reverend Painter finished, he walked past Matt with a sad smile and descended the stairs.

Judge Meryle Jacoby asked the two men, "Do you have any last words?"

Wu-Pen translated in Chinese, "The man wants to know if you have any last words?"

Izu spoke calmly to Wu-Pen, "Only that we are not guilty, you are."

Wang spoke nervously, "Where's Ah See? Ah See should be here to tell the Marshal."

Wu-Pen smiled coldly and turned to face the

crowd. He shouted in English, "They say they would do it again if they could!"

The men and women in the crowd became enraged and began cursing and demanding that the brothers hang. An apple flew past Wu-Pen and hit Izu in the stomach. The apple was followed by rocks and a bottle that barely missed Wang.

Matt walked next to Wu-Pen and yelled loudly, "Knock it off! No more!"

"Shut up, Marshal!" one of the miners yelled.

Matt pointed at him. "When this is over, how about I give the chance to make me? Settle down!" he demanded loudly. He glared at Wu-Pen angrily. "Don't get them worked up again!" He glanced at the two brothers who seemed to be waiting for him to do something. Matt walked back over to the side of the platform.

Wang asked, "Where's he going? He should be arresting, Wu-Pen." Ah See had told them the night before that Matt would arrest Wu-Pen at the last minute while the brothers were about to be hung. It was all part of the Marshal's plan to arrest Wu-Pen in front of everyone who would be there. Ah See had told them they could relax because nothing was going to happen to them.

Wu-Pen turned back around to face the two brothers and laughed lightly. "Ah See lied to you to keep you quiet. He is my puppet now. The Marshal knows nothing but I know all." He winked at them and then nodded to Judge Jacoby and walked over beside Matt.

Judge Jacoby waved for Matt and Truet to step

forward to help the hangman. They stood behind the brothers and held them in place while Clemmons pulled white cloth hoods over the two brother's heads. The two brothers spoke hurriedly and frantically while Clemmons put the nooses around their necks, adjusted and cinched them tight. Matt and Truet left the two shaking and begging men and went back to stand next to Wu-Pen. "What are they saying?" Matt asked as the two men spoke frantically in Chinese.

Wu-Pen answered smoothly, "They are praying and cursing."

Judge Jacoby walked to one side of the platform and waved a hand for William to pull the lever that sprung the trap doors open.

Izu, enraged by the deceit, screamed, "Ah See!" as the trap door opened. Both brothers fell quickly and with a loud thud of the rope reaching its end, the rope snapped both men's neck upon impact. A momentary silence was followed by loud applause and cheers by the miners. Matt closed his eyes, hating the sound and moment of a hanging.

"Justice is done," Wu-Pen said sadly.

"What was Izu yelling when the door opened?" Matt asked tensely with his head still down. He was angered by what Wu-pen had told the crowd and he was afraid he had made a mistake. Those brothers acted like they had no idea they were going to be executed and Matt wanted to know why.

"In essence," Wu-Pen answered, "see you in hell. He was a bad man." Wu-Pen turned around and walked down the stairs and walked away with his two guards away from the crowd to go back to Chinatown.

Matt hesitated. The more he thought about the way the brothers were acting before the execution and then the panic that followed when the hoods and ropes were being applied, the more it troubled him.

Truet stood beside him waiting. "Should we cut the bodies down before the crowd begins dragging them through town?"

Matt stared at him irately.

"What?" Truet asked alarmed by the fire burning in Matt's eyes.

Matt bit his lip thoughtfully. "I don't think those men knew they were going to die." He walked quickly down the stairs leaving Truet standing on the platform alone. Matt was sickened to see the two bodies being pelted by rocks and bottles as they hung there by drunk miners and their wives and kids as well.

Matt pulled his revolver and fired a shot into the air. He shouted loudly, "The next person that throws anything is going to get shot! I'll consider it as an attack on my deputies and myself. You saw what you came here to see, now go home!" It was Matt's responsibility to take the bodies down and dispose of them. He waved for his three deputy marshals forward to cut the two brothers down to put them in cedar caskets and load them on a wagon to be returned to Chinatown for burial.

"What are you a Chinaman lover?" a red-headed miner yelled at Matt.

Matt glared at him dangerously and the man lost his nerve and stepped back. "There's nothing left to see. Go home," he shouted to the crowd.

Matt walked back to Marshal's Office and entered his private office and closed the door to be alone. Sadness had crept into his heart and he couldn't quite shake it as easily as he usually could. Law and Order were a good thing and Justice was only right; however, this time it didn't feel right. Matt had always been one to seek the truth and talk to the men he arrested to learn about them and to treat them like human beings if nothing else. Matt was always interested in why the individual committed whatever crime they did. Over the years, he learned to read people and trust his instincts.

He could not communicate with Izu or Wang and that created a barrier that couldn't be crossed. He could look in their eyes and see something wasn't right because neither one had the hardened eyes of a killer or a life filled with anger. If he was to judge just on body language and facial expressions, he would have bet his badge that they were innocent. However, there was no way for Wu-Pen and Ah See to translate the same story when the questions were asked on two separate days. The evidence lined up to prove they were guilty and deserved to be hung but it kept nagging at him. One of the great fears of being a lawman was making a mistake and arresting the wrong man, or worse, putting an innocent man to death. To Matt's knowledge and conscience, he had never done so. Matt hoped he had not made a mistake now. The evidence said no but the evidence was not in direct communication and that left a bit of room for doubt and that haunted him. He wanted to trust Wu-Pen but his instincts just wouldn't let him. And Ah See, Matt knew he was hiding something. Matt would wait a week or so to let things settle down and perhaps be forgotten before he questioned Wu-Pen and Ah See again. He wanted to know why it appeared like the two brothers didn't know they were going to hang. It troubled him. One thing was for sure, he needed to find a new interpreter if he ever had to deal with any Chinese criminals again.

## 37

Matt smiled when he watched two black coaches stop at a single-story wood-built building two blocks up from his office on Main Street. Lee Bannister stepped out of his coach and helped his wife Regina and Christine Knapp step down on the boardwalk without getting their feet muddy. Behind Lee's coach, Albert stepped out of his coach and helped his wife, Mellissa, and Lucille Barton out onto the boardwalk and then assisted Lawrence Barton down from the coach. Lucille handed Lawrence his crutch to walk with.

Matt met Christine with a warm embrace. "What are you all doing here?" he asked curiously.

Lee answered, "I don't have any houses available right now but I figured this might be suitable for the Barton family to live in. We're going to take a look and see. Do you want to join us?"

"I have a few minutes, sure." Matt replied.

Matt grinned when he saw Lawrence step towards him awkwardly using the crutch in place of his right leg. "Lawrence, how are you doing?"

Lawrence's right pant leg was tied off where his knee should have been. He was still in pain. "It's nice to be out of bed anyway. I'm not used to walking this way."

After some brief talking between them on the boardwalk, Lee pulled a key out of his pocket and said, "Well, shall we go inside and see what you think?" He unlocked the door that had a large glass window on the top half. Inside, it was an open square space with wood flooring, three walls of empty shelves and a store counter three feet from the right-side wall. It had once been a general goods store but the owners had moved out of town and the building had been empty for three months.

Lucille and Lawrence stepped inside and inspected the open area of the room. They didn't appear to be too excited about living in an old store on Main Street. It was the only space Lee had available to rent and asked them to consider it for a temporary home. They had less than two weeks to move out of Slater's Mile and every avenue of housing had closed on them tighter than the bolts that held the machinery together at the stamp mill.

Albert directed their attention towards the front of the building with a wave of his arm to where two large bay windows exposed a close view of Main Street. Two curious kids about twelve years old walked by looking at them through the windows. Albert said, "Not everyone has the opportunity to put their beds next to windows like this. You could make that window the boys' room, and this window your room. No one's going to stand outside there and stare once you're in bed. This isn't Rose Street, after all. So, you'll have to make a decision between putting some curtains up or cutting a coin slot in your door for the peep show."

"Albert!" Mellissa exclaimed. She turned to Lucille and Lawrence. "Of course, we'd put curtains up."

Albert glanced at Matt with a wry smile. "It was just a business suggestion. One thing is for sure, they'll have more shelf space than any other house in Branson."

Matt laughed lightly. "They could rent some of that shelf space out, probably."

Lawrence gave Matt an unappreciative smirk. "Maybe we'll do that because we haven't got a lot to store and need the money."

"We don't have any furniture," Lucille stated as she looked around at the open space and then pointed at the long horizontal round woodstove with concern. "I don't think I can cook on that stove. So maybe this place won't work for us, Lee. I do appreciate you showing us, though."

Lee peered at the round woodstove thoughtfully. "Well, dang. I was really hoping I could help you two. You know, Albert's a blacksmith. Do you think you can jerry-rig something out of this, so she can cook?"

Albert lowered his brow and took a deep breath. "Yeah, I can bolt a metal plate on top. It might look funny and the bolts might get hotter than the metal plate, but eventually, you know, the heat will transfer. It'll be fine."

Lee shrugged. "Albert can bolt an iron plate on top and it will be fine. What do you think? I'll only charge you fifty dollars a month."

Lucille's eyes widened. "We can't afford that."

Lee leaned against the store counter. "I really was trying to help you two. I mean, it's unfortunate that you don't want to live here. I can't lower the rent, though, because it's a business space and it wouldn't be fair to the other people that rent business spaces from me. I think Albert had a good idea and I am willing to cut a coin slot in the door if that would help?"

Lucille stared at Lee, wondering if he was making a bad joke. He seemed to be quite serious though, with no hint of humor on his lips.

"The place is better than nothing," Albert stated simply.

Lucille glanced at Albert and then back at Lee. "It *is* better than nothing but not at that price." she said slowly.

"I'm trying to make you a deal. I'm willing to have Truet cut a coin slot in the door for a peep show business. That will help cover the cost," Lee offered.

"No," Lucille said with a horrified grimace on her face.

Albert scratched his beard while looking at the door. "Actually, it's not a bad idea. You have to use what you're given in life and you have a big window on a busy street. You could get all kinds of fellas dropping nickels, dimes and silver dollars through a coin slot for a peep. It could add up."

Lawrence glared at Albert losing his patience. "No one's going to be looking at my wife! And I don't appreciate the suggestions of it from either of you," he barked with a nasty scowl.

Lucille added, "Maybe this isn't such a good idea after all." She was far more disappointed in Albert for suggesting she put on a sideshow for nickels and dimes than she was offended or mad. She expected more integrity and moral judgment coming from a Christian man like Albert.

Lee raised his hands, defensively. "This is a business rental. I thought you understood you must have a business or you can't stay here. I'm trying to help you. So, we can put a coin slot in the door and..."

Lawrence had enough. "I think we'll just take our chances out at Slater's Mile." He spoke to Lucille, "Let's go over to the Slater's Mining Office and talk to them and see what work they have available that I can do."

Lee grinned. "Before you go, take a look behind you."

Lucille and Lawrence turned around to see Mellissa and Regina had unrolled a paper banner. The banner read, Barton's Pottery Shop.

Lucille lowered her brow curiously. "What's that? What's going on?" she asked, looking at Christine and Matt. They stood together watching her with wide, expectant grins.

Mellissa answered with a joyful glow radiating on her face, "This isn't your home, Lucille. This is your pottery shop!" She laughed. "You told me it was a dream of yours to own a pottery shop like your parents did. Well, here it is."

Albert explained, "We all pitched in and bought a kiln and ordered it along with the spinning foot pedal wheel thing. We got all off the hardware for the kiln and will install it when it arrives. We'll start laying bricks in a few days to put the kiln on. In a month, you'll be making pottery again and running your own business." He hesitated. "I apologize for the coin slot comment. We were just teasing." He laughed lightly.

"And," Mellissa added while shaking her head disappointedly at Albert, "It's something Lawrence can help do as well. You're going to be business owners but none of us know anything about pottery. Aside from the kiln and throwing wheel, everything else you need, you will have to order yourself. The good news is you have approximately six hundred dollars left on your spending account to start this business with."

"What?" Lucille asked astonished. "No. It's too much. We could never pay you back."

Albert smiled softly as Mellissa stepped into his arms. "We don't want to be paid back, Lucille. Many families lost loved ones and their homes this past week. We donated to them too, but we got to know you. Lee is helping the other families get into homes but you and your family found your way into our hearts. You and Lawrence needed a new career and our city doesn't have a pottery shop. We thought we'd help you get one started. We don't want to be paid back but I do want a pencil holder, though. That would be a fair trade."

"No, it wouldn't," her voice was high pitched and breaking. Lucille covered her face with both of her hands and began to weep. "Thank you," she said in a high-pitched voice through her hands. "I don't know how to thank you."

"Now you both have a job. Unfortunately, it's kind of a long walk from Slater's Mile," Albert said with a shrug.

Mellissa laughed and slapped his arm. "Are you going to tell them or am I?"

"You go ahead," Albert stated.

"Tell us what?" Lawrence asked.

Mellissa continued sincerely, "Lucille, you know how you haven't been able to find a place to live?"

She removed her hands from her face. Her cheeks were wet from smearing her tears. "Yeah," she said with a sniffle.

Mellissa squeezed her lips together and raised her eyebrows, hesitating to ask. "Do you remember I told you Albert likes to tease at the wrong times?"

"Yeah," she whimpered.

"Yeah, he does," Lawrence agreed without much humor.

"Well," Mellissa hesitated to continue. "Albert, Lee and Matt went all over town and made sure everyone with rentals told you they didn't have anything available."

"What? Why?"

Mellissa bit her bottom lip nervously. "I think I'll let Lee tell you in case you get mad."

Lee chuckled. "I might have lied to you a little bit. I may have had some places left. I still do. But one place came to mind and I was having it cleaned and painted and some repairs made to make it easier for Lawrence, the day you came to my office." He smiled. "You were already being taken care of before you met me. Don't be mad, Lawrence, when you hear this but the place wasn't quite ready on Sunday, so Matt talked to Doctor Ryland about keeping you there for a few more days."

"What?" Lawrence asked. "I thought I was going to die of gangrene."

Lucille stared at Matt, bewildered.

Lee continued quickly, "The place is ready now, though. Would you like to see it? It's not far from here, so the walk will be easy."

Lucille turned to Albert and Mellissa. "You knew about this?"

Mellissa laughed and nodded. Her eyes filled with thick tears. "Of course. And I can't wait for you and Lawrence to see your home!"

"Where?"

"Are you ready for this?" Mellissa asked with an excitement.

"What?"

"Your house is right next door. You do not even have to go outside. This building is a shop and a house in one. That door leads to your house. Go on in."

"No!" Lucille exclaimed in disbelief.

Lee grinned. "Go check out your new home. I think you might like it."

"Lawrence, let's go see."

Lawrence was awestruck. He had just met Albert and Lee's families, along with Christine and could not believe they had done so much for his family. The outpouring of love and caring by strangers was incredible and Lawrence wasn't sure how to react to it. He hopped forward awkwardly on his single crutch past a door, through a short storage area and opened another door. They were, suddenly, in a dining room with a table and chairs, and saw a kitchen with pots and pans, and a dish on the counter. He could smell the delicious aroma of good food that sat on the counter. They turned a corner and heard a chorus of, "Surprise!" The family room was full of more strangers that Lawrence had never met.

Lucille's mouth dropped open while her face contorted in unexpected emotion. She covered her face with her hands overwhelmed. Reverend Painter, Doctor's Ryland and Ambrose were there along with several people they've never met before from the church and other places from town. Bella from the dance hall was there with her husband, Dave, and a few of the ladies were there. Henry Redlin was there with a large pan of his famous meatballs. Beside him was Sylvia Ballenger and her daughter Barbra as well. Quite a few others also waited to introduce themselves to the young couple.

"Daddy!" came the excited voices of Michael and Ray Barton. They had been in their new bedroom playing with Albert's younger children. Lawrence heard them and was immediately overwhelmed with emotion when his two sons ran to him. Lawrence tried to bend over to hug them but was quickly guided to an overstuffed chair by Doctor Ryland. Lawrence closed his eyes tightly and wept uncontrollably while he hugged his sons. He held them close and refused to let them go when both, Doctor Ryland and Mellissa reminded the boys to be careful of his amputated leg.

Lucille stood in the family room repeatedly saying, "Thank you! Thank you!" to everyone there. She hugged Mellissa tightly and cried on her shoulder, overwhelmed.

Regina Bannister put her arm around Lucille. "You have three bedrooms and they're fully furnished. Well, two of them. The third we made into an office where you can keep your books. You have everything you need here, including a cord of wood and a bathtub on the back porch."

Lucille wiped her eyes. "How did you do this?"

Mellissa wiped her eyes pleased to see her young friend's reaction. "Albert and I knew we wanted to help you and Lawrence and the boys, so we asked Lee and Regina, Matt and Christine, and Reverend Painter if they'd like to help. And they did. So did many others in our church congregation and some other folks around town. Christine got a good collection from the ladies at the dance hall. Those ladies wanted to help a lot. When Matt spoke to Doctor Ryland, he and Doctor Ambrose also wanted to help. All this furniture was donated or bought but you liked our bed so much, we put it in your master bedroom. Now you and Lawrence don't have to sleep on a lumpy straw-filled mattress. This is your home and it's ready for you to move into right now. Lawrence doesn't have to go out to Slater's Mile ever again. Albert and the boys can bring whatever you need back here for you."

Reverend Painter stood with his arm around his wife. "As I said in church on Sunday, we'll try to help. We have ladies making you dinner all week and willing to help in any way they can until you're all settled in. Henry and Sylvia brought your supper tonight, though. You're going to love it! Shall we eat?"

"Thank you," she said weakly as her tears fell once again. "Thank you, all." She wept as her son, Ray, came to her.

"It's okay, Mama."

She dropped to her knees to hug him. "I know it, Baby. I know."

Matt knelt before her and looked into her teary eyes. He spoke gently, "Lucille, do you remember that night at the mine when you told me that you were alone and didn't have anyone here? I told you, 'maybe not, but the Lord does.' Do you remember that?"

"I do," she answered softly.

"Well, my friend, He does. And if you give them a chance, they'll be there for you. We are your church family and from all of us, I just want to say... welcome home."

# A Look at Just John by Reg Quist

FROM SLAVE TO RANCHMAN – A HISTORICAL WESTERN BASED ON TRUE EVENTS.

In return for his freedom, a slave is tasked with the job of delivering a valuable stallion to a horse farm in Tennessee. The Civil War is dying down and the roads are dangerous but with some help the horse is delivered and the slave sees freedom.

Wishing to be freed from any remembrance of the slave farm, John has a last name that he refuses to use. John's skill with horses opens doors for him which eventually take him to Fort Worth, Texas. More open doors, over a period of years, find him on a cattle drive to Montana, followed by a second drive into Alberta, Canada. From there, he chooses the name Ware. John Ware stays in Alberta, where he becomes a much loved and respected Alberta rancher.

The John Ware story is well known, however since he never learned to read or write he left no historic record of his background.

AVAILABLE APRIL 2021

# About the Author

Ken Pratt and his wife, Cathy, have been married for 22 years and are blessed with five children and six grandchildren. They live on the Oregon Coast where they are raising the youngest of their children. Ken Pratt grew up in the small farming community of Dayton, Oregon.

Ken worked to make a living, but his passion has always been writing. Having a busy family, the only "free" time he had to write was late at night getting no more than five hours of sleep a night. He has penned several novels that are being published along with several children stories as well.